A Murderous Innocence

Other Five Star Titles
by Susan Oleksiw:

Friends and Enemies

A Murderous Innocence

Susan Oleksiw

Five Star • Waterville, Maine

First Edition
First Printing: April 2006

Published in 2006 in conjunction with Tekno Books and Ed Gorman.

Set in 11 pt. Plantin by Christina S. Huff.

Printed in the United States on permanent paper.

Library of Congress Cataloging-in-Publication Data

Oleksiw, Susan.
    A murderous innocence / by Susan Oleksiw.—1st ed.
      p. cm.
    ISBN 1-59414-375-7 (hc : alk. paper)
    1. Police—Massachusetts—Fiction. 2. Police chiefs—Fiction. 3. Drug addicts—Fiction. I. Title.
PS3565.L42M87 2006
   813'.54—dc22   2005030202

To
Charlie Van Buren
And in loving memory of
Michael Osborn Ryan
1942–1995

Cast of Characters

Ann Rose—community activist and volunteer
George Faroli—owner of Faroli's Provisions
Paula Faroli—his wife, and friend of Ann Rose
Edna Stine—mother of Miles and Chandra
Denny Clark—director of the Mellingham Community Center
Tiny Morley—homeless former addict
Steve Dolanetti—newcomer to Mellingham
Chief of Police Joe Silva, Sergeant Ken Dupoulis, and the men and women of the town of Mellingham

Chapter 1

A Tuesday Evening in November

Ann Rose never missed a funeral. She wasn't sure how she had come to know so many people in Mellingham, but she had, and they or their relatives had a habit of dying. The optometrist's daughter, for example, a cranky, dissatisfied girl if there ever was one, turned her life around in a matter of weeks, and then she died in a car accident. Her funeral was one of three that summer. Ann Rose didn't like funerals, even hated them in fact, but she had a resolve that subdued all dissent. She went to funerals.

She had taught herself to make a game out of it, gaining a certain emotional distance by rating funerals and memorial services according to whether or not they were designed to please the minister leading the service, make a good impression on the mourners, or satisfy those closest and dearest to the deceased. The last type rated the highest, and these were definitely the quirkiest, with as much glorious bad taste as tears. Such funerals restored Ann's faith in the deceased's authenticity as a human being by freeing those closest to him or her to be a little crazy too. All these thoughts shaped into anticipations made the distasteful duty palatable for Ann.

But deciding to attend Ron Faroli's funeral had been easy, requiring no fortitude, no hour-long silent arguments about how glad she'd be when it was over, no offering herself bribes to get through the evening, no days of testy replies to her husband until he practically begged her to go and get it over with. No drowning in fantasies of what it might be like. None of that. Not this time.

Ann Rose had grown up with Ron Faroli's mother, Paula Benoit Faroli. They had passed each other in the halls between classes, watched older brothers play on the same teams, and once they even spent an enjoyable afternoon in the Benoits' back yard while the brothers negotiated the sale and purchase of a second-hand car. Ann's father was letting his son sell it to Paula's brother. The two girls had chatted contentedly on the back steps of the Benoit house for more than an hour. It was the only time they had enjoyed an entirely natural rapport and empathy. The next time they met, when Ann was home from college, their lives had already diverged onto different paths. Paula was dating George and finishing up a secretarial course at a nearby college. She planned to marry in a matter of months. As it turned out, she married in a matter of weeks, and Ron arrived in a matter of months.

As though she knew someone was thinking about her apart from the present sad circumstances, Paula Faroli turned in her seat in the front row to look over her shoulder. She turned her head and gave the kind of vacant look people in the front row give to the crowded seats behind them—not a look in search of any particular person, just a glance to take in the number of people facing her and who they might be. Ann caught her eye and smiled in the way friends do when one wants to be sure the other knows she is sympathizing with her. Paula blinked and began to smile in recognition when her husband leaned closer to her and whispered something. She nodded, murmured something, and turned back to face the collapsible altar covered in linen and decorated with flowers.

The Sara Meya Funeral Parlor was located on Main

Street, in Mellingham, a sad business discreetly concealed in a two-family home. It gave Ann the shivers to think that the owner's wife might be washing up after lunch on the other side of the wall. She kept waiting to hear the dishwasher kick on.

By the side of the door through which the Faroli family had just entered, walking awkwardly to their seats in the front row as though Paula had forgotten how to manage two feet and George wasn't sure what the trouble was, the pastor was conferring with the organist and a few more guests slipped into seats along the side. Funerals almost always started on time, unless the pastor forgot to tell all the family she had changed the time or the funeral director forgot to write it down before the phone rang for the twentieth time that morning, or the family kept telling the minister to wait just a little bit longer for the guests who had a long drive from Boston. Ann suspected the last reason was in play here—the Farolis had a lot of friends. She listened for the sounds of a restless congregation—coughs not squelched, shuffling feet, chairs being repositioned as a man moved closer to his wife or child, a few murmured conversations, coat pockets being searched. The polite silence was being replaced by that distinctly American weakness, boredom.

"It's a lot of people." A tall man whispered to her as he folded himself into the next chair.

"Hello, Denny. George and Paula have a lot of friends in town," Ann said.

"So did Ron." He nodded to a cluster of men and women on the opposite side of the room. They were dressed in jeans and leather jackets or lumberjack shirts, to ward off the November chill.

"Tiny looks so uncomfortable," Ann said. "Why do you think they always give large men such a ridiculous nickname?" The large man in question perched himself on the last chair at the end of the row and hunched over, his hands resting on his thighs as though trying to shrink himself down to average size. His hair was almost short enough to be called a buzz cut and he was clean shaven, but he glanced around at the people in front of him as though fearful someone would notice him and find him unacceptable.

"He came by the Community Center earlier today." The man paused. Ann turned to him, waiting. Denny Clark was executive director of the Mellingham Community Center and, though no one questioned his competence at keeping the disparate groups in town satisfied, Ann thought him a bit vague, a bit prone to lose himself in his own thoughts at inappropriate times. Like now. She nudged him.

"You were saying, Denny?"

"What? Oh. Tiny wanted to know what to wear," he said. "Do you think if I told him he had to wear a suit he would have bought one?" He turned to Ann and smiled down at her, sitting bolt upright in his folding chair. "Or would he have stayed home?"

Ann shrugged. Poor Tiny, she thought. He's completely out of his depth, but he's a loyal friend. He broke his own code to attend his friend's funeral. She wondered how he coped with life in Mellingham; it wasn't as though it was a city where young men having difficulties could find others in similar predicaments and lean on them, or could find a place to hang out. Wherever he went in the town, Tiny faced the curious looks, and sometimes even disparaging comments, of the residents who thought the town was all gracious old homes and lanes leading down to private docks on the harbor. Even a smaller home in town cost three times its equivalent in the next town over. Tiny's was a parallel world, she thought, populated for the most part by sons and daughters who had fallen out of the other, safe worlds, tucked away in quaint Mellingham.

Her eyes strayed back to his heavy form rocking forward to listen to his friends' conversation, his fingers gripping his thighs. He was wearing a red and black wool lumberman's jacket and jeans and heavy work boots. Except for the coat, she'd never seen him in anything else, even in summer. He had drifted into town in his teens, with a single mother and no other known relatives. As soon as he was able, he was on his own, living in rented rooms that seemed to change with the season, taking any job he could get. He seemed to have no ambition, no drive; he just got through the day and drank his way through the nights.

"He looks well," Ann said, somewhat surprised. "He doesn't look as flushed."

"He's been out of detox about two weeks. Looks pretty good. He only looks fifty, not bad for someone who's been drinking pretty much non-stop since he was fifteen," Denny said.

"How old is he now?"

"Maybe thirty. Younger than Ron by a year or so. Maybe a couple of years."

Ann shook her head. She wasn't one for platitudes but she knew all the ones that had popped into people's minds when they'd heard Ron was dead:

"He's so young."

"What a waste."

"And from such a good family too."

"I feel sorry for his parents. He put them through hell."

"It's for the best."

"He lasted a long time, considering."

"He was really trying to change."

How many times had she heard that last one? That

painful defiance of reality and the need to hold onto hope, the hope that he might live long enough to change, get clean, start a new life. And the disappointment. That was painful too. And the anger just hid the pain of hopelessness and the slide into despair. For some like Ron, it seemed inevitable. Something seemed to happen to them; a switch was thrown; a clock ticked; something triggered a turning, and they were gone. She never knew which ones would make it back and which ones would disappear into their own private hell, but she too held onto hope for every person like Ron or Tiny she met.

"He was never around the Barrow Building very much, was he?" Ann asked.

"Who? Tiny?"

"Ron."

"Were you volunteering when he was a teenager?" Denny Clark shifted in his chair to get a better look at Ann. "That'd be fifteen years—at least." He waited. Ann frowned, trying to think back to the day when she had read an article about children living in cars with their parents, or in one room in a motel on a highway miles from a town center, with no sidewalk to the nearest fast-food restaurant. About latchkey kids and cuts in school lunches and no breakfasts. And all the rest of it—all those little Republican changes that had turned the war on poverty into a war on children.

When she had first approached two or three friends about offering an after-school program at the Community Center, she had been dismayed by their reactions:

"Ann, you don't have any children."

"It's not for me."

"Well, who, then? Irma is always at the house in the after-noon."

"It's not for you either. It's for the children whose parents work and can't be home after school."

"Who's that?"

"Well, I don't know their names. I was thinking about something I read in the paper."

"You read too much."

Rallying the troops had required a certain amount of remedial education on her part, after a tennis match or on the drive into Boston for lunch and shopping, or over drinks on a terrace while the husbands gawked at each other's boats bobbing in the harbor. But she had rallied them, and they had followed her into battle.

"Ron might have been too old even then," Ann said, secretly counting back on her fingers to those early years. It was annoying to have gone to the best schools in the East and not be able to do basic arithmetic in her head. She was secretly in awe of any student who passed the MCAS test. She stopped counting at the index finger of her left hand. "I think I started in the late nineteen-eighties. But I was just taking a few—displaced—kids out to the park or the playground or over to the Y for an afternoon. It wasn't nearly as elaborate as it is now."

"With thirty-seven volunteers, eight after-school programs, housing and medical—"

"Shhh," Ann said, hissing at him and pointing to the minister, who was just then approaching the center of the room. She hated it when people looked at her like she had two heads and started talking about her as though she had to be told who she was. But Denny Clark turned to look in the direction she indicated, paused, saw nothing that interested him, and passed on to survey the crowd on the other side. She relaxed in the shadows that concealed her, and allowed herself to feel some of the surprise that these days accompanied her review of all the programs that had sprouted up around her. And pride too. After all, some of these projects had turned out to be pretty darned good.

"Children have to play," she muttered. "It's a natural thing."

The grayness of November seeped into every crevice of the evening—the parking lot, the sky tinged with black, the cars lining the dusty street; even the water lying still in the harbor, glimpsed between the houses across the street, was a dark steel gray. Everything was a colorless drab. November gray.

Tiny Morley stood erect with his hands in his pockets watching the other mourners eddy past him to their cars. He stood stock still, moving his eyes left to right, right to left; his neck moving only an inch or so if absolutely necessary. Sometimes his eyes unfocused, and that's when he was listening for those coming up behind him. His stillness was a habit developed early in life and perfected in adulthood, when he spent eight months in prison for assault and learned about personal territory—his and that of the other felons around him. He never threw out his arms, made sudden moves, took up elbow space; his life was precious to him.

He stood this evening as a sentinel, watching those weighed down by grief drift past, oblivious to his inchoate need to be swept up and included by them in the warmth of their communal grieving. The small parking lot was emptying in a decorous manner and Tiny was poised as a protector of safe departure, but he was of course nothing of the sort. He only had a vague idea of what was happening now; he was still stunned by the loss of his friend, Ron, his pal, his best buddy. He felt a light touch on his arm and looked down.

"Evening, Tiny." Ann Rose smiled up at him. Tiny stood a little straighter and felt a broad smile take over his face. He liked Ann. That was the only word for it; he genuinely liked her. He was wary of his mother, he trusted his boss at the lumberyard where he worked occasionally; he was mildly fond of his neighbor's dog; and once he'd been so hung up on a woman he met in New Hampshire he couldn't remember to eat or shit regularly. But he'd never actually liked anyone, just Mrs. Rose. He liked her. It felt kind of funny.

"Hello," he said.

"I'm awfully sorry about Ron."

He listened to her say a few things about how she was sorry he'd died and how she knew how hard it was for him, and he believed her. He could tell when he was getting a lot of bull from someone—that was easy. Most people were phonies anyway, always trying to trick you into believing things about them that weren't true. You had to watch them all the time. They'd pick you clean, Tiny thought, his mind drifting to the groundskeeper who'd been "testing" Tiny on gardening skills for a whole week before deciding not to pay him; telling him that he wasn't quite right. He'd wanted that job, really wanted it. Just goes to show you, he'd said to anyone who would listen; if you really want something, you were sure not to get it. That's just the way things worked.

"I'll miss him," Ann said.

"Yeah." He wished he could say more and he was sure someone else would know the words and he'd recognize them if he heard them, but he just couldn't seem to find them inside his own head.

"I know you do too. You were a good friend to him."

Yeah, thought Tiny. That's right. We were pals, him and me. Hearing Ann Rose's words reverberating through his heart left him feeling that yes, indeed, as he watched her push a button on her key to open her car door, he had indeed said all those right and gracious things. I was a good friend of

Ron's, he thought. We had good times together, him and me. The minister asked people to remember Ron if they wanted to and Tiny thought of the time him and Ron went up to Lake Winnepesaukee and broke into a cabin and—Jees, he was afraid he'd start laughing right then, with all the others sniffing into Kleenex and remembering when Ron was in the three-legged race as a kid or taking his cousin to her prom. So he hadn't said anything about New Hampshire.

Then there was the time he and Ron had—but no, he couldn't tell them that either. That was too raunchy. Even Tiny was embarrassed by that one. Another group of mourners drove out of the parking lot, all quiet and subdued, promising to meet each other in a few minutes and later go on to someplace else. They made their plans in a calm deliberate manner. He wondered how they managed to be so together all the time. Just the few hours this evening had been a strain for him.

He wondered about that sometimes.

Sitting around with people could be overwhelming, and often, when he found himself in a circle of men and women, he started to feel a panic rising in him and he wanted to bolt from the room. He wanted to run and run and run until he got so far away there were no people around him; no one with eyes to bore into him, to expect him to look back; no one to take a bit of himself with their hungry, curious eyes and seductive smiles. He kept himself to himself, as he had heard his mother say, quoting her own mother. It seemed her one bit of useful advice. But then, all alone, he had no fun and got edgy and was afraid his head would blow off. So he pulled out a bottle and tried not to think about it. But that didn't seem to help anymore, and now he was trying life sober. All his good times had turned into a haze. Ron said as much; said he was getting scared; said he might get off alcohol. And then try something else, Tiny had said. He had no illusions. He knew what he was.

"I had to talk to them." A man a few years older than Tiny leaned close to him. "I knew Ron awfully well, you know."

"You didn't tell them that, did you, Steve?" Tiny frowned. Steve Dolanetti was pulling down his Irish sweater so it fell smoothly and evenly across his corduroy slacks. He cast a wary eye at the puddles still polka-dotted across the parking lot. His brown loafers were shiny with a new polish.

"Tiny, really." Steve twitched a shoulder toward Tiny. "What do you take me for?"

Tiny knew what his reply was supposed to be, but he just didn't have the heart for it tonight.

"But I did know him, you know." Steve sighed and looked around. "I ran into him that day. Did I tell you? He told me to drop by."

Tiny's head began to droop until he was staring down at the ground.

"I didn't. He was with Miles, you know." Steve buttoned his jacket and dusted it down. "But I wonder if I had, if he might—"

"There's no percentage in talking like that." Tiny swung his big head back and forth. "Miles is lucky to be alive."

"He wasn't here tonight."

Tiny looked at Steve. "Would you come if it'd almost been you?"

"I suppose not."

"Besides, he probably hasn't even come down yet," Tiny muttered.

Steve reached out and squeezed Tiny's arm. "Let's wait for Missi and go someplace."

Tiny nodded. "Yeah, yeah." The idea seemed to relieve him of some worry.

"And to think he was just getting clean. Ron, I mean." Steve's last words came out into the dark silence and hung there. Only one car remained in the parking lot; only Tiny and Steve standing near the handicap ramp leading up to the back door, which served as the entrance for the funeral parlor.

"So's he could try something else," Tiny said.

"He and Miles weren't—"

"Shhh." Tiny shook his head and barely more than a hiss escaped his lips, but Steve's face went blank and a moment later he heard a pair of sharp-heeled shoes sound on the ramp.

"I was looking for you." The short woman in the black coat and black heels kept her eyes on her shoes as she made her precarious way down the ramp. Her heels were tall and spindly, and wobbled beneath her thick legs. Her blonde hair fell over her face but didn't impair her view of her shoes. When she reached the bottom of the ramp, she tossed her head, flinging her curls away from her face.

"Missi! Those shoes." Steve squealed, trying not to make too much noise.

"I was just saying good-bye to Ron's parents," Missi said, trying to head off any more comments on her wardrobe. "You okay, Tiny?"

"Yeah, I guess." He moved away from the ramp.

"Are we going to the reception?" Missi asked, looking around at the near-empty parking lot.

"Huh?" Tiny said. A look of terror flashed across his face. "You guys go."

"You don't wanna go? I do." Missi shoved her hands into her pockets.

"No, you don't." Steve wrapped his arm around her shoulders and leaned close to her, drawing Tiny over to them by putting an arm through his. "I came across that new perfume display at the drugstore. It's spectacular," he whispered.

"Really?" she said.

"Really."

"Wow. Okay. Let's go. I wanna get down there before it closes."

"Oh, good, let's walk," Steve said.

"You're just a streetwalker at heart," Missi said.

"You got that right," Steve said.

"You shameless whore," Missi added gleefully.

"You better believe it." Steve winked at Tiny and dragged him along.

"Don't do that, Steve, you're embarrassing him," Missi said. Steve grinned and trotted along next to Missi. Tiny hunched over even more, but followed along behind them.

The Jeep Cherokee turned into the parking lot, descended the hill, and pulled into a space at the foot of the building. The rest of the lot was empty, and no lights shone from inside Faroli's Provisions—Since 1864.

When George Faroli's great grandfather had founded the store, the word *Provisions* appeared on half a dozen shops in Mellingham, but by the time his grandfather retired, the original competition had been replaced by markets of all kinds, and the Faroli sign was an anachronism. And then came the '60s and the '70s, and the sign was quaint. In the '80s, the store was all the rage as newcomers thought the name Faroli's Provisions exotic. Then George's father retired and George became the fourth generation to ignore comments about the store name and concentrate on inventory.

The small grocery, one step up from a convenience store, was still in its original location on the corner of Trask Street.

The Farolis added three tables about forty years ago, for customers to enjoy their sandwiches, but otherwise things were much as they'd always been—canned goods, Italian breads fresh from the North End, a tiny meat counter rented by Lenny Stillman from Saugus, rows of Italian cookies, soft drinks, packaged foods, and the like—more interesting than an ordinary grocery store but not very different in the important things. It was a comfortable living, and now Paula, George's wife, didn't have to help out. But she never lost her sense of responsibility for the place. At least that's what George was telling himself as he shut off the headlights and the ignition and climbed out of the car.

"I know you think I'm foolish," Paula said, searching in her purse for a set of keys, "but I just want to be sure I didn't forget something." George didn't bother arguing. He rubbed his large hand across the small of her back, then took the keys from her and pulled open the back door to the store.

"I'll just have a smoke," he said.

"Sure." She spoke without looking at him, her eyes on the ground, stepping carefully in the dark.

Not until last weekend—had it only been last weekend?—had Paula seemed older than when he married her. He'd heard his father tease his mother about never changing—and his Ma always blushed—but he, George, had always thought it was just his parents' way of joking around. And then he found himself saying the same thing to Paula—and meaning it.

She was as beautiful today as when he first knew he wanted to marry her—the same clear brown eyes, the same fine brown hair brushing against her neck, the same small fingers with perfect fingernails, the same round figure, the same walk with her head erect and her hands held in front of her waist, and the same habit of starting off with a kick of her right foot, recalling her childhood training to break the habit of an inturned foot. Not until this last weekend did he ever see a sign of age in her. Her hair seemed lank and dirty, full of dandruff, and her toe dragged across the bedroom carpet as she crossed the room to hang up her colorless slacks and sweater. She didn't seem to inhabit her own body.

Had it only been Saturday?

George turned away from the Jeep and lit a cigarette. A telephone rang in the distance. He looked up at the back of the store, where he could see Paula standing at the window on the floor above him holding a telephone to her ear with one hand, the other one resting on the glass. She listened, nodded, then opened the window and leaned out.

"It's Marjorie. She saw a light on and wanted to make sure everything was okay." Paula withdrew and pulled the sash down with one hand, still talking to her friend.

George turned to look across the stream at a number of houses, not sure which one was Marjorie's. She and Paula had been friends for years. He supposed it was natural for Marjorie to keep an eye on the place, but from so far away—well, they were friends. He took another pull on his cigarette and approached the old revetment backing the parking lot: a wall of huge granite blocks between which weeds persisted, giving the impression of a tired giant ready to let go, no longer able to keep the whole thing—store, parking lot, street—from sliding into the stream.

The damp ground sparkled beneath a barely visible waning moon. He usually sent someone out to sweep the place down once a week, but he'd forgotten on Saturday. The call from the hospital had driven everything else from his head. He flicked the cigarette butt over the revetment into the sluggish water. Sometimes, during a heavy rain, he looked out from his desk, drawn by the noise of water rushing and churning to get through the narrow channel, and felt for a split second that he was on the verge of a different world; something challenging, different from anything else he had known, bringing out something inside him he didn't know was there. But then the water coursed on, and he went back to work, the rain subsided, the stream drained; life went back to its predictable ways.

He strolled along the revetment, stopping to kick another butt and some debris over the side. The tarmac was starting to crumble here; little bits of macadam breaking apart, like the edges of an ice floe. If left untended, the whole parking lot would disintegrate over time. He looked across the black ground, trying to imagine weeds growing through the macadam, litter piling up along the building, a general air of neglect and carelessness taking over. It wasn't hard.

The light was still on in the office, and George didn't want to hurry Paula. He knew she was putting off going home, because when she went home this time there would be no more Ron, not even the lingering role of planning for his funeral. Nothing. George didn't blame her. He didn't much want to go home either. He shrugged and drew his coat collar up around his neck; he began another turn around the parking lot. The office light caught a bit of glass in the weeds along the edge of the revetment; it glistened.

His sister and her family had tried to get him and Paula to stay with them at least one or two nights, but Paula would have none of it. She would force herself to face it all the way she felt she was supposed to. She was a stoic; claimed she wouldn't run away from the hard stuff; would face it head on. Life goes on, and so shall we, she said with a toughness she had to squeeze out of herself. That image she had of herself frightened him, a belief that she could drive through grief and pain as though it were a snowdrift, vulnerable to the repeated onslaughts of a four-wheel drive truck. Sorrow was like a soaking rain, the beginning pellets pricking him everywhere, before turning into a silky massage; and when it was over, the sky was clear. The heart was pure.

It surprised George how angry it all made him—not his wife's stoic behavior, but the damage this kind of death could do to a family. He'd seen a show once, a television documentary, about parents of teens who had died drug-related or violent deaths. The survival rate was not good—and that little tidbit of information, gleaned from a television show over a decade ago, had become an obsession with him, waking him up in the middle of the night, driving him to think up ways to persuade Paula that Ron's death had really been something else: a bad heart, an aneurysm, something, anything, else.

George turned to the water, stopped, then abruptly turned and began pacing again. Whenever he stopped moving, he could hear the voice in the night. Of course, it wasn't that late, but no one expected to get a call from a doctor friend at that hour.

"He's in the ICU, George. I'll meet you there."

But they were too late. George knew they would be as he and Paula hurried down the nearly empty corridors. It was almost midnight, and Paula's sharp heels echoed off the walls. The nurses let them stand there by Ron's bed, holding his cooling hand. When George couldn't stand it any longer, he coughed and drifted out to the nurses' station. The only thing he remembered from the doctor's conversation was a question he couldn't answer; a question that left him feeling doubly estranged from his son.

"Was he on any prescription medication, do you know?"

George shook his head.

"No pain medications, not being treated for anything?"

George couldn't find the words to tell his friend how little he knew his own son. Facing the truth when Ron's drinking catapulted out of control had been hard; getting the boy to face it had been even harder. Keeping his mother from running to him and bailing him out had been the toughest part. And they had made it. Well, as good as.

And now this.

He didn't know how to feel any more. His alienation grew and settled beneath his everyday veneer like decay.

Tyrone Lane was pretty much what it sounded like: a street developed in the 1930s that had been neglected ever since. Defined by a row of two-family houses on one side, which would now be called duplexes, and were then called semi-detached homes, and small ranch houses from the 1950s on the other side, Tyrone Lane was a quiet street whose residents struggled with their ambivalence. On the one hand, the real estate development in Mellingham was making the most unexpected people well-to-do, or so it seemed when their house values were published in the local paper after every mandated reevaluation. But on the other hand, the residents of Tyrone Lane could still afford to live there because their homes, for the most part, had remained unpretentious. No one had a swimming pool—in-ground or above—and no one had a two-car garage, or even two cars.

From her front window Edna Stine could look across at a tidy white ranch, and then through its back yard to the rear of Basker Court. The houses there were starting to undergo renovation—one had been sold recently when it became clear that the owner—Vic Rabelard—was never going to be able to live in it again. Edna sighed. Sad, that. He had nice girls too. Teenagers.

Her own boys had been nice too.

Edna pulled a throw blanket off the back of the sofa and

began to refold it, shaking it out as it hung well above the floor, then threw it onto the sofa. She had thought as a girl she might grow to six feet, but she had stopped abruptly, three inches shy of her goal. Still, she was a good height for her generation, sprouting up in the 1950s like a lava lamp. Only Chandra had taken after her. Jacko and Miles had been shortish, like their dad.

Edna looked around for the dust cloth she'd been using earlier in the day, polishing the small table in a frenetic attempt to push away morbid thoughts. They came upon her when she was desperate to know her son was safe. Son. Singular. One son. Only son. One and only. Only. Just two letters away from lonely. One and lonely. Only lonely. Just one.

It wasn't fair. She began to slip into self-pity. Just Miles. Jack gone. How can a person disappear like that? Just evaporate? She had to train herself every day to think about what was real. Jack had been real. And then one day he wasn't real. He was gone. He evaporated. But sometimes she thought she could turn and there he'd be, coming in the back door. For months she'd seen something, heard something, and thought, I must tell the boys. That was normal. She knew that. But Jack didn't fade away the way others had said he would. They'd been wrong.

Edna worked the afternoon and evening shift on Wednesdays, when the small clinic on Main Street stayed open until eight. It meant that she spent all Wednesday morning restless and uneasy until she could lose herself in her work. It was her drug.

Jack had first told her that.

"You hide from life in your job. Did you know that, Ma?"

Edna spun around, looking for the body that carried the voice. An old sofa was shoved against the wall. In the center of the room was a braided rug Miles had found in a pile of trash and lugged home when he was ten. He had looped a piece of string through the braids and tied the string to his bicycle seat, like a cowboy capturing a steer and tying it to the pommel of his saddle. He was very proud of that achievement and after depositing the rug on the front stoop he had raced his bicycle up and down Tyrone Lane in a frenzy of painful exhilaration. Edna washed and washed and washed the rug until it was tolerable, then rolled it out onto the floor. She knew what the neighbors were thinking, but to hell with them. It was hers now, and she didn't care what they said. She hurried across it and slammed the door into the front hall. Jack might have come in that way.

But he couldn't have. He was gone.

Edna made her way across the room, passed through the small dining room, and went into the kitchen. She threw the dust rag into the sink and braced her hands against the counter. Her dark brown hair flopped over her face, split ends of long-neglected bangs brushing against her eyelashes.

Her mother was right. She was weak. She needed reassurance, calming, promises that everything would be all right. Was that such a bad thing? Yes, her mother had said. It was.

"It makes you dependent on others," the old woman had said. "And that's bad. You keep yourself to yourself."

"I try," Edna said to the empty kitchen. "I try. I really do. Give me credit for it. I really, really try. But I just need to know that everything's all right. That's not bad, not really. That's why I worry about my children. It's normal for a mother to worry—that's the sign she's a good mother, isn't it? What would people think of me if I didn't worry?"

Edna sighed and slid her arms onto the counter and rested her head on them. A puddle covered the counter where she had been washing the dishes; her sweater sleeves soaked up the water. She didn't notice.

It's because of Miles. She knew it was. The way I'm feeling now. It's not me. I'm just upset because of him.

He doesn't answer the phone sometimes because I bother him. My worrying over him is oppressive, I know.

She tried not to think about the last time she called him; about his anger that was more than irritation. Two days ago he'd been enraged when she'd called, leaving her standing in the kitchen with the phone next to her ear too stunned to speak. And when she'd seen him downtown yesterday, he'd glared at her. Just glared.

All right, she thought. I won't call him. I'll take him something.

Edna turned her head to the refrigerator, walked over and pulled open the door. Except for a few jars of condiments, it was a shiny, stark white. She closed the door and opened the freezer compartment above.

"I know," she muttered, pulling out a thick package wrapped in aluminum foil. She lifted one edge of the wrapping and peered in. "Lasagna, I'll bet." She began to smile.

Twenty minutes later Edna Stine drove to the end of Tyrone Lane, turned right onto Trask Street. She drove on and turned left onto Main Street, followed it through the center of town, and over the train tracks. She turned left down Delmar Street and left onto Seaward Road, pulling up in front of the Cleary house. She was just a mother dropping off a home-cooked meal for her son; he had kitchen privileges. It was the most natural thing in the world.

Edna told herself this and other salves all the way to the top of the stairs and the first landing, and then on up to the second landing. She heard a television playing behind one door, a radio behind another, an argument behind yet another; ordinary people living ordinary lives, yet they seemed so exotic to her because they were completely unknown. She resisted the temptation to eavesdrop, and hurried up the stairs. As she arrived at the top floor, she ran through all the things he might say to her—at least, all the things he had said in the past. It didn't matter. She could slip past him and pop her offering into the tiny refrigerator. She'd be gone—reassured and gone—before he could tell her what he thought of her, how she couldn't let go.

Edna knocked on the door. His room looked over the back yard and the woods. A choice view, she'd once told him because she couldn't think of anything else to say. She knocked again.

If she'd made a lot of noise coming up the stairs, he might have looked out, seen it was her, and locked himself in, determined to ride out the storm of her attempted invasion. He was peculiar that way, shutting out the world in the most pathetically ineffective manner. But if he hadn't seen her—

He had to be in there. Where else would he be?

Edna rested her hand on the doorknob, gripped it and turned. The latch drew back and the door came unstuck from the jamb. For several seconds Edna Stine stood poised on her son's doorstep. She had never entered without an invitation of sorts, no matter how grudgingly delivered, but this was something different. An unlocked door bid her enter. Yet part of her knew he might not—probably would not—like it. He didn't seem to like much of what she did, and she had to just chalk that up to being his mother—it was the lot of mothers to have their best efforts unappreciated.

Edna pushed; the door opened, and she entered. The shades and curtains were drawn, giving a dark, gloomy air to the room. Only a tiny night light shone from the opposite far corner. Edna closed the door and felt along the wall for the light switch. The starkness of the overhead light blinded her for a second and she bent over, squinting and blinking.

"Miles?" she whispered. She looked around the room. He wasn't here. For a second she stood there with the casserole in her hands, not sure what to do, then tiptoed to the refrigerator. She slipped the casserole in and turned around. Somewhere in the house she heard a toilet flush and a door close. Ah, there he was, she thought. A doctor had once offered a prescription to tame her "imagination," he said, and now she thought maybe he'd been right. Why had she been so frantic? He was nearby and safe. A year from now she would laugh at this, she thought, and at herself for being so foolish. Well, maybe she wouldn't laugh at herself. She lowered herself onto a chair by the wall, sitting on his crumpled-up jeans and shirt, his outfit of the day before, left near at hand so he could wear it again. She looked around the room for other signs of how he was getting on.

A worn rug covered most of the floor in front of the armoire, a fading dark spot on one end recalling the motor oil that invariably showed up on his shoes when he was a teenager. The armoire seemed of a similar vintage—battered and tired, just barely functional. A suitcase peeked out over the top, and a towel was draped over a nearby chair. On the seat was a plastic CVS bag with a toothbrush sticking out. Convenient to keep it there, she thought. Right near the door when he had to go to the bathroom.

The walls were decorated with patches of light and dark and brownish lines, a record of all the pictures that had hung there and been removed. A single framed poster sat in one corner near a closet door, its shiny, brushed aluminum frame and bright colors a contrast to everything else in the room. She didn't want to think about why her son had it here or where he got it. Footsteps came up the stairs, slow and effortful and showing no effort to mask the noise.

It seemed to Edna that she had arrived where she was

meant to be—in a room that no one could actually live in but many did, with a son who couldn't make a life no matter how much she nagged him. Everywhere she looked she saw the detritus of all the lives of those who had lived here in the past many years: people hoping to stay just long enough to find something better, others praying they could hold on and enjoy this clean, dry place. The room seemed to teeter before her eyes, rocking like a plate placed on a child's head as he tried to balance it while he walked around the room. It was bound to fall.

The door flew open.

"Fer crissakes, Ma." Miles glared at her with his mouth open, his brow furrowed, an oversized T-shirt hanging down over a pair of sweats. He kicked off his shoes and circled her in the chair. "What're you doing here?"

"I was worried." She started to stand up, fell back onto the chair, then stood, and slipped past him toward the door. The rage glinting in his eyes scared her, and for the first time in her life she thought one of her own might be more like her ex-husband than her. Davy, the man she couldn't get rid of fast enough. "Just, you know . . . I left a casserole."

He swung his hand then pulled back, balling up his fist and twirling around in an angry dance of avoidance. He slammed his fist into the wall, then turned to her, breathing heavily and sweating. "I tole you, lee me alone." His words trailed away in incoherent syllables as Edna slipped out the door, pulling it closed behind her. She stumbled down the stairs, her knees wobbly and her breath uneven.

The Agawam Inn was usually hidden by thick foliage but this November, a sudden cold rain a week ago had shorn the trees of their leaves and the Inn now sparkled through the bare woods. Though it was nearly empty this time of year,

Reginald Campbell, reluctant owner of the Inn, had taken to burning a single light on every floor; to keep off a depressing chill, the neighbors claimed. Chandra Stine peered once again through the trees at the lights, then let the drapes fall into place.

Chandra was bored. Whenever she went out babysitting, she made sure to take along enough to occupy her for the long evening, but somehow tonight she had come up short. She had finished her homework about an hour ago, tried a little television, surfed the net, checked out the hotel lights— "Like a beacon," she had told friends—and was heading for the kitchen. None of the houses on either side were lit up and the only car that had gone by in the last couple of hours belonged to Mr. and Mrs. Faroli.

"Probably on their way back from the funeral," she said to herself. She didn't want to think about it more than that, because, if she did, she had to think about her brother too.

Chandra glanced at the heavy marble clock sitting on the mantelpiece. It struck the quarter hour with lovely chimes, and the hour followed with long bells that reverberated around the room. The first time it had happened she thought something was broken, and peered at it. She even remained in the room, trying to read magazines to pass the time to see if it did anything else strange, but the clock kept to its established pattern, and thereafter Chandra had to learn to live with it. She wondered how Mr. and Mrs. Griffin managed— and the two girls—but everyone else seemed oblivious to it. Only Chandra started when she heard it.

The refrigerator filled one corner of the kitchen and glowed inside like a magazine ad. Chandra liked looking at it but she liked rummaging through it even more. The Griffins had parties almost every weekend and the caterers left food neatly packaged for the rest of the week. The kids were growing up without ever tasting Spaghetti-Os or Hamburger Helper or Campbell's Chicken Noodle Soup. They were deprived, but it probably didn't matter, Chandra decided as she pulled out a container holding neatly arranged pieces of curried chicken on Melba toast. She headed for the microwave.

Seaward Road was pretty—*picturesque* was the more apt word—but neighborhood life seemed a bit thin. No one had children in school in town and the houses were far apart. The road rose and fell like a roller coaster, and if it had been laid out today, the developer would have stripped the ground of trees and leveled it. That might not be a bad idea, Chandra thought. She liked malls, and she had once been to the Midwest and was stunned by the flatness of it. You could see for miles. Of course, there was nothing much to see, so all that level ground was wasted. Except of course where they grew corn and things like that. Chandra popped her chicken hors d'oeuvres onto a plate and searched for a napkin.

"Hmm." She turned on the radio. She waited for the machine to make a sound other than static but nothing came from the shiny metal object sitting on the kitchen island counter. But a sound did come from behind her. She walked to the back window, her hand hovering over the light switch. As her eyes adjusted to the dark, she neared a window and peered into the back yard. This was a small, well-tended area that might hold three cars. But it led up into a woodsy area with narrow trails that twisted and turned from the train tracks to the ocean, through back yards and woods. Kids used to sit on the cliff just above the tracks and watch the trains go by, and some of them—certainly not Chandra—tried to hit them with well-aimed pebbles or rocks. The kids always managed to get away before anyone could catch them, disappearing into the woods or into Mrs. Cleary's back yard, a garden of rusting cars and old bathtubs and pieces of fencing and anything else a man might want to keep handy for a project.

Mrs. Cleary's was an anomaly. That was how people in town had described the place, particularly when they glanced around to see who might be listening, like a teenager with curious eyes and an intent look. Chandra mulled over the various stories she had heard about the woman and her house.

A widow who had rented rooms, Mrs. Cleary had been like a dozen other women in Mellingham in the 1930s and 1940s; forced to make a living in one of the few ways open to women back then. But as other women died and left their houses to relatives who sold them for single-family homes, Mrs. Cleary lived on, caught in a time warp of boardinghouses, bus trips to the city down the line, Saturday matinees with the ladies, and aprons tied over house dresses. When she died, her son and daughter continued the business without any changes except one—they cleaned up the back yard and put two picnic tables out there—with chairs, and one umbrella.

Most of the chairs looked like they were ready to fall apart if anyone sat in them, Chandra pointed out to her older brother, Miles, when she and their mother had been visiting, but he had pulled one from a shed by the side of the house, dusted it off, and dragged it over for Chandra to sit on. That was last autumn, when he invited Chandra and their mother over for a cookout. He made hot dogs on a grill and had potato salad from the Harbor Light Restaurant, where he washed dishes. You could almost see it from the front of the boardinghouse.

He was clean then—one of his sober periods—and Chandra's mother watched him grilling the dogs and telling her to have more Pepsi or more chips with a look of fey hope. He was clean. And this was the first time in—how many years? Ten?—sober, completely sober, and Edna Stine couldn't get over it. It was like all the hope she'd ever had for a normal family overflowed on that one day. She offered Chandra a little jar of relish with the plastic spoon sticking out as though it were caviar on a silver dish, then hovered over Miles, checking everything out with him first.

"This all right to pass around now?" She held up the jar of relish.

He nodded and let her hover. Standing back from the five-dollar cheap imitation Hibachi grill sitting on a board resting on two sawhorses, he studied the mustard, playing his role as dutiful host. No question was too minor for his careful consideration. He seemed to know that she needed to have one day that could pass as a real family day when no one got too drunk to stand up or started a fight or failed to show up or let her down in some other way. Just one day. That's all she needed and for the rest of her life she'd have an answer to that question; that one question that left her embarrassed, awkward, ready to rush into another story about traffic or the latest bargain at Christmas Tree Shops; that one awful question she never knew how to answer, "Do you have a family? How are they?" After today, after this afternoon in the back yard with hot dogs grilling, she'd have a story to tell about her children as adults—a son who was working and invited his mother and sister over for a cookout; a son who helped his mother into a chair and called her Ma, not Hey, or Old Lady, or something else. He had a job; he was clean.

And then came Labor Day.

It was always the holidays that wrecked it all.

Chandra peered out the kitchen window. Her family was pathetic. She could feel the raw night pressing against the glass. Eight-thirty. There wouldn't be anyone out there now. But she was wrong. A gaggle of kids she knew from school tumbled down the embankment and into the back yard, racing and cavorting across the grass until they reached the screened-in porch.

"Hey, Chan! It's us! Let us in," one of them called out. The screen door was locked with a hook, but that was enough to stump her friends. She switched on the porch light and opened the back door, standing well inside the porch.

"What're you guys up to?" she asked.

"Hangin'," one of them said.

"Yeah, come on. We been up to the tower gate and over to the beach," another one said. The tower referred to was an old stone building about twelve feet tall, used for storage of some sort dozens of years ago. No one was quite sure about its origins and it inspired numerous tales.

"I'm babysitting," Chandra said. "I can't leave the girls." She sniffed the air. "Are you guys smoking something?"

"We're not breaking any laws," one of them said. The others nodded and mumbled agreement. Two of them reeled away from the door and spun around the back yard, looking as though they were trying to launch themselves into the air.

"Philip? Is that you?" Chandra said, peering into the night.

"Yeah," a young boy said, his eyes sweeping past her dreamily.

"You look stupid," she said.

"Hey, I'm cool." He swung around and joined the other two stumbling around the yard.

"You guys should get out of here. If the girls' parents come back and find you here, I'm liable to get into trouble."

"And we don't want to get you into trouble," one of the boys said in a singsong voice.

"Just get out. Okay?" Chandra gripped the door and stepped back into the house. She wasn't sure how to get rid of them without getting into a fight, and she was afraid she'd lose any argument. All she could hope is that they'd get bored and move on. She had always thought Philip was all right, and wanted to count on him to help her, but he was the youngest one in the bunch and probably not up to challenging the others.

"It's all right, Chan," one of them said.

"Yeah, chill."

"Philip, you and your friends should get out of here." Not sure what else to do, she blinked the lights a few times. The kids drifted away from the house and began to prance and stumble around to the driveway and down the road. Philip was in the center of the crowd.

When the sounds of their erratic procession faded, Chandra walked around the house drawing curtains and checking locks on windows and doors. At the foot of the stairs, she strained to hear any sound coming from the girls' bedrooms. Nothing. The Griffins were due back by midnight. Normally she would settle in with a book or magazine, or watch some television, but seeing her friends and classmates like that had unsettled her. Philip's behavior was especially disturbing; he'd seemed so interested in theater and in doing something other than hanging around with losers. She'd really believed him when he'd told her he looked up to her. It had been an odd conversation—his telling her how much he admired her for what she went through, and her thinking that she wasn't that different from anyone else. But it had sounded so good to hear someone say all those positive things about her. Without realizing it, she'd started to count on him to be her friend on another project, but now, seeing him with that crowd, she subconsciously began to write him off. He'd take the other route, and that would be the end of their friendship.

Chapter 2

Wednesday Morning

Joe Silva hung up the telephone and rolled over, bringing his feet to the floor and sitting up. When he and Gwen McDuffy had first talked about living together, Joe had been the one with reservations.

"You don't know what it's like to get a call and have to go to work at three a.m.," he'd said. He'd been speaking metaphorically for the most part, since Mellingham wasn't prone to late night crime. But he knew the call was inevitable for anyone on the force. More than anything he'd wanted to be a man without reservations. He'd probably have to call her at lunchtime and change their plans for the weekend. He sat on the edge of the bed with his head in his hands, trying to think himself awake.

What was it Ken Dupoulis had said? Someone fell out of a window? Or jumped? Joe rubbed his face and stood up to stretch. Or was pushed, perhaps?

Fifteen minutes later, Joe was walking around the perimeter of the Cleary back yard; its residents huddled in bathrobes and coats by a corner of the house, Sergeant Ken Dupoulis hustling them back every time they oozed forward a few feet. An ambulance siren wailed in the distance.

"Over here," Ken said to Joe when he emerged through the crowd.

"Who is it? Do we know?" Joe asked.

"Miles Stine, age about thirty. Tenant." Ken paused,

looking around behind him. "He might have come up at the County Drug Task Force meeting. He's been in and out of trouble for years, grew up here, just out of Rehab. Friend of Ron Faroli." Joe nodded as the details of Miles Stine's life came back to him. Joe walked around the body, then knelt down to get a better look.

Miles Stein was sprawled on the ground atop the picnic table umbrella, onto which he had crashed, its tip crushing into his neck and killing him almost instantly. He was wearing a worn white T-shirt and navy sweats; his feet were bare except for a pair of dirty white tennis socks. He had rolled over after he and the umbrella hit the ground, and now lay with his eyes wide open staring up at the sky.

"Who found him?" Joe asked Ken.

"A woman on the first floor heard something." Ken nodded to a figure standing apart from the crowd, her face barely visible above the turned-up collar of her heavy wool coat. "She thought it was someone trying to break in and she went out to the hall and turned on the outside light. When she came back into her apartment to look out the window she saw him lying there. She only knew him as one of the tenants upstairs. He lived on the third floor." Ken looked tired, and Joe realized that this was probably the third extra shift he'd done this week. Since taking up hunting, he'd added on as many hours as he could, to extend his long weekends in the woods even longer. Joe wasn't much of a hunter, but he did appreciate the game Ken brought back and readily shared with his fellow officers: pheasant, quail, ruffled grouse. He was midseason right now—October 19 to November 30—and doing well.

Joe walked over to get a closer look at Miles.

"No tracks," Ken said. Joe nodded. "That's the first thing I thought of."

"Any other thoughts?"

"No obvious sign of alcohol."

"He just fell out of a third-story window," Joe said.

Joe rose and walked back along the lawn, making way for the EMTs who were approaching with their equipment.

"Let's take a look upstairs," Joe said.

"Sir, there's something else." Ken nodded to the woman wrapped in the coat who found Miles. "She says Mrs. Stine is here."

"And who is she?" Joe said, nodding to the woman in the navy coat.

"Her name is Carol Ann Summers," Ken said, "and she has a first-floor apartment at a reduced rent in exchange for limited managerial duties."

"Why is Mrs. Stine here?" Joe asked.

"Ms. Summers called her first thing; before she realized that maybe we might be interested."

"And Mrs. Stine got here before we did," Joe said. "She moves fast."

"Ms. Summers apologized for that."

"Let's go talk to her." Joe moved away from the body and introduced himself to the woman who managed the building. He had a vague idea of who she was, but he had never had any reason to notice her officially. He knew she was divorced, barely into her forties, appreciated a low rent, and had reduced the number of cars parked illegally on this part of the street. She had tried to spruce up the Cleary boardinghouse with a small garden of pansies the year before.

"Could we go inside?" she said after the introductions. "Mrs. Stine is inside also, but it's really cold out here. I don't feel well," she added after a glance in Miles's direction. Joe followed her into the boardinghouse and the front hall, where she paused and studied him for a second before saying, "Mrs. Stine came over tonight."

"When was that?" Joe asked.

"About eight o'clock, maybe."

"Did she usually do that?"

"Once in a while," Carol Ann said. "She was a meddler, though she meant well."

"Where is she now?"

"In my apartment."

"All right. Keep her there, would you? I have a few questions but I want to look at Miles's room first. Was she his only visitor tonight?"

"I didn't hear anyone else going up the stairs, and I usually hear anyone coming in late, well, after five; the stairs are old. I also tend to keep the door open just a bit after five or six, just to make sure no one tries to slip in."

"Slip in?"

"Sometimes some of the tenants will try to bring in a guest, you might say. And we're not exactly an apartment building. There are no overnight guests allowed."

"Does Mrs. Stine often come around this late?"

"No. She doesn't come often at all. I don't think they're close. It's not as though she's always popping in."

"So she hasn't been here regularly over the last few days or weeks?"

"No, not at all."

"Has he had any other visitors?"

"A few. I'd have to think about it for a bit; right now, I'm really tired."

"See what you can remember while I'm upstairs. And, stay with her, would you?"

Joe climbed to the third floor. He had known Miles through the network of men and women in recovery and drug officers keeping tabs on who was using what. In all the brief

reports about Miles he had never heard anything about insta-
bility that might lead to suicide. He knew that didn't mean
anything, but he was a little uneasy about this death. Men
didn't fall from windows at three in the morning without a
reason.

Joe pushed the door open.

"Would you expect it to be open?" Joe asked. Ken nodded
his agreement with the question.

The apartment was a single room, shabby and neglected
and used for little more than sleeping, from the looks of
things, Joe decided. He walked along the perimeter of the
room, skirting the bed after looking underneath it. Ken
looked behind a bureau and armoire before beginning to
search the bureau.

"He didn't own much," Ken said as he sorted through a
variety of T-shirts.

Joe walked to the window, which he noted was open. Neither sash, upper or lower, was broken or appeared damaged
in any way. Both sashes were unpainted; they had apparently
been stripped and returned to the frame without painting.
The lower sash rose and fell easily, with a light touch of Joe's
index finger; he pulled at both cotton cords, which felt tight.
All the panes were intact, and the frame was smooth and
painted. No matter how closely he inspected it, Joe could find
nothing wrong, no sign of damage or trickery or anything that
might let a man fall unsuspectingly to his death. It was a perfectly ordinary window. There was no screen top or bottom
and no frame for inserting one. He raised the sash again and
leaned out the window, trying to calculate if a man sitting on
the sill might fall over backward and land where Miles had
been lying, or would he have rolled to one side or the other.
Miles lay almost directly below the window, and centered.
He leaned out the sill, taking care not to smear any latent

prints, to get a better look at the clapboards, in case Miles had grasped at them on his way down, or scuffed one with his heel. But nothing.

Joe stepped back and ran his eye up and down the frame, noting the many layers of thick paint that had almost smoothed out the fluted woodwork. Other than the usual smudges from dirty hands, where tenants over the years had leaned against the window and peered out, there was no sign of any recent violence to the woodwork—no scratches showing someone had fought being pushed out, or tried to pull back from a fall.

The sill itself came up to an inch or so above Joe's knee, just right for using as a window seat. Joe knelt down and sought for fibers from socks, anything that might indicate how Miles had gone out the window—falling sideways, backwards, forward. But however he had gone over, falling down three stories, his socks left no threads Joe could see.

Disappointed, he took another look around the room before focusing on the tiny closet. It held the usual heavy shirt, winter coat, boots, and a laundry bag. On the top shelf sat a plain wooden box, roughly made, with well-worn sides and dulled finish. He put on a pair of latex gloves before lifting it down and setting it on the bed.

"Take a look at this," Joe said, stretching his hand over it to get a rough measurement. The box measured twelve inches by nine and was made out of pine.

"It's clearly handmade by one with knowledge but not great skill," Ken said. "Maybe by one learning the craft rather than a master of it."

"Where would you get something like this?" Joe asked.

"We made things like this in shop class in school," Ken said. "But I don't think they have those classes anymore."

Joe lifted the lid, admired the mitered corners, and let the top fall back on taut chains. The top tray held a few dollars, business cards for social services agencies, and some candy, which looked legitimate. Below the tray was a compartment holding a few letters from MassHealth and the Social Security Administration. That seemed to be about it.

Joe closed up the box and lifted it off the bed. He turned it around in his hands and looked at the bottom. "The interior is much too shallow to account for the exterior size," he said. He ran his fingers along the sides. On the left he felt a slight unevenness in the panels and experimented with pressure. Finally, one panel gave way, slipping in, and a panel at the other end popped out.

"Knew it," Joe said. He reached in, felt nothing, then held it up to the light.

"Looks like there might be something at the other end," Ken said. Joe managed to pull out a small sandwich bag, but it was empty except for a few grains of what looked like tobacco. He held it up.

"It doesn't look deadly, does it?" Joe said, turning the plastic bag around in the light, letting the grains sift from one side to the other.

"They never do," Ken said.

"What does it look like to you?"

"I want to say marijuana but I'm pretty sure it's not that." Ken drew closer and lifted an edge of the bag, trying to get a better look. "You're thinking . . . Those little grains." Ken peered at the bag.

"My first thought was they're not white, but it may be they're just contaminated."

"You're thinking about the pathologist's report on Ron?" Ken stepped back and nodded.

"If Ron had OxyContin in his system, he had to get it somewhere, and Miles was the one he hung around with." Joe turned the bag over in his hands. "And it doesn't take much. One OxyC pill, crushed, snorted; he'd be gone in no time."

"No word on who dropped Ron off at the hospital?" Ken asked.

Joe shook his head. "No, but it has all the marks of the usual friend's so-called help," Joe said. "What do you make of the box?"

Ken glanced at the box, then cast a disdainful glance at the rest of the room, stopping to take in the bright poster in the shiny silver frame. "It sure doesn't fit with the rest of this place, but then, that poster doesn't either."

"He probably picked up the poster and meant to sell it sometime. Sort of his bank account." Joe surveyed the harbor scene of bright boats bobbing at mooring, under a bright blue sky with feathery wisps of clouds overhead. A tourist scene. Joe turned back to the box. "This looks like something of his own."

"Could be a sentimental possession, something left from his high-school days," Ken said.

"I was thinking the same thing. It doesn't look like something he'd buy, more like something he'd keep from earlier years." Joe set the box on the bed. "About the only thing he's hung on to from the looks of it."

"What a crummy place," Ken said shaking his head. "Who'd think this dump would survive year after year."

"They probably won't much longer, not if they're forced to put in sprinklers." Joe bagged the plastic bag, labeled it, and handed it to Ken. "Let's hear what Mrs. Stine has to say."

Mrs. Stine perched on the edge of a chair in Carol Ann's living room, her eyes staring straight ahead, her hand working on the chipped paint on the wooden arm; on the floor lay a scurf of tiny white paint chips. After Joe introduced himself, she settled herself again, and resumed her nervous picking. All Joe could see of her face was a line of makeup near her ear.

"Mrs. Stine?" Joe pulled a chair closer to her as he began to talk. He knew she wasn't taking in any of his expressions of sympathy; they were just words, for which she was not ready. Tomorrow perhaps, but not tonight. She was too raw to hear them as anything but a mask over what she was really feeling. Right now the shock was too great. He moved on to his own questions.

"Edna? May I call you Edna?" A cautious nod. "You came to visit your son this evening," Joe said. "Is that right?"

She nodded. "I was worried about him."

"Any particular reason to worry?"

"I called him earlier and he didn't answer the phone."

"Was that unusual?"

She began to look him over, but in the abstracted way of those overwhelmed with grief. He suspected that she was finding her thoughts snagged on the color of his hair or the way his eyebrows reminded her of a character in a movie or of the grocery list she had left on the kitchen table; anything but what he was actually asking about. "Unusual? No."

"Was there something that bothered you especially tonight? Some reason that made tonight different?"

"I don't know. I was unsettled. He was so angry last time I saw him—it made me uneasy. I was worried about him. I wanted to see him and just reassure myself he was all right."

"Okay. So you came over here about, what, eight this evening?"

"Yeah."

"And then what?"

"I went upstairs. I knocked on his door but he didn't answer. So I pushed the door and it opened. So I went in." She paused, and her eyes looked less stunned.

"You went in."

"He wasn't there. There was a night light on."

"You're sure he wasn't there."

"Yes. I heard a john flush. So I sat down to wait for him."

"Did you do anything else?"

"I turned on the light. The switch is on the wall."

"Yes, it was on when we were up there just now," Joe said. "Then what happened? Did Miles return to his room?"

She nodded. "He came in and there he was."

"How did he seem?"

"Angry."

"Anything else?"

"Angry." She gazed at Joe. "He was angry, in a rage like. I brought him a casserole and I left it in the refrigerator—lasagna, but he didn't seem to think I'd done anything for him. I don't know what's got into him lately. I mean, he gets mad at me for pestering him, but not like this. He's been real angry at me. Like we're not even related." She drew her shoulders in, pressing her arms against her sides.

"Then what happened?"

"He told me to leave. I brought him a casserole and I put it in the fridge, but he was so angry. I just left. I was afraid he'd—"

"He'd what, Edna?"

Her eyes implored him, but for what was unclear. "He looked like he hated me. I just had to get out of there." She began to whimper, and Joe immediately moved to calm her.

"That's a fine wooden box he has up there," Joe said. "Did he make it?" She gave him a blank look.

"A box?"

"It must have been from his old woodworking class in high school, maybe."

"He didn't take that class," she said. "He didn't like working with his hands." She frowned. "I don't remember no box."

The Mellingham Community Center was lodged in an old warehouse on Delmar Street, which ran from Pine Street, facing the inner harbor, to Seaward Road. The brown-shingled building, with its multi-paned windows, was surrounded on two sides by fences and hedges, its chipped and darkening shingles for the most part hidden from the surrounding homes. Once the storage for a long-gone lumberyard, its loading docks and bays rustling with the noise of planks sliding in and out of piles as prospective builders searched for the unbowed board, the warehouse had been taken over and converted to a community center. What this meant to the town fathers who agreed to foot the bill, however, was that the building would be enclosed with interior walls—exactly four, and anything more was up to the Center trustees.

The Barrow building, named after the long-gone Barrow Lumberyard, stood two stories tall outside—and inside—except for a balcony that ran around all four sides and served to enclose offices and meeting rooms with a ceiling at one end. Except for the row of small offices at one end, the interior was one vast room, broken into smaller spaces by groupings of tables and sofas and occasionally tall screens. The corner claimed by the volunteer after-school art teacher tended to be cluttered and messy and generally chaotic, whereas the corner claimed by the Seniors' Book Group emerged from the surrounding distress as a tidy oasis of calm and color—a sofa draped in red fabric, directors' chairs with plaid cushions, ever-replaced potted plants and occasionally vases of freshly cut flowers. The interior of the Barrow was thus pretty much like Mellingham or any other small town along the New England coast: pretty in some places and not so pretty in others. It was one of the places Joe Silva had learned to keep an eye on, turning to it for clues to incipient trends or trouble in Mellingham.

It was also the first place a lot of townspeople would call to find out about Miles Stine. He had gone to meetings here, hung with friends, scrounged for free meals and taken advantage of free coffee, picked up a few odd jobs and, in general, made himself known. The town would be humming with news of his death, and Joe wanted to make sure the information, what there was of it, was accurate.

A police officer from the next town over opened the door into the central area, nodded quickly to her colleagues, and was gone; her regulation black shoes reverberating as she strode across the floor. Joe followed three other members of the Tri-Town Drug Force, with only Denny Clark behind him. The task force held monthly meetings on coordinating efforts to hold down drug use and keep an eye on the transient population, mostly by exchanging information. Their monthly meeting, just hours after Miles Stine's death, had proved to be fortuitous. Joe took up most of it with his brief report.

"I'll let you know as soon as I can," Joe said, scanning the large room before turning to Denny Clark. "Miles's friends will be uneasy until they know for sure." But Denny was barely listening. His gaze flitted across the large room. Joe's gaze followed his, but when Denny's didn't stop by the coffee table, where two young men were fixing cups of coffee, Joe frowned. Something else was up with Denny. He blinked and looked at the chief.

"What? Yeah, that's great. Appreciate it." Taller than Joe,

Denny had sandy blonde hair that moved back along his temples. He pulled at his cream-colored turtleneck jersey as though it were too tight, though it fell loosely around his neck.

"Dupoulis is working on this with me," Joe said.

"Yeah, good."

"I'm glad you know him already," Joe said.

"Well, I don't exactly know him, not personally I mean. I mean, he's the sergeant here—" Denny's eyes glazed over as he fumbled for the right word.

"By reputation," Joe said.

"Yeah." Denny nodded gratefully. "I've got to get that," he said as the phone rang. He lunged into his office. Joe strolled over to the coffee table where one young man in jeans and a light winter jacket was reaching over to every jar or cup and peering inside before moving to the next. His pale hair had a golden tinge, and the torn lining of his jacket straggled below the outer shell. The man's face was pockmarked around the nose and cheeks, as though he'd had an especially bad case of acne as a teenager and was just now getting rid of the scars. He kept turning in Joe's direction, but barely looked up as Joe took a Styrofoam cup and set it under the coffee urn. Joe pulled the lever and watched the cup fill.

"This is the only place in town where I can count on getting whole milk," Joe said. One of the men took his cup and wandered to the other side of the room.

"It's not as bad for you as they say," the man said. "More of those lies from the experts."

He raised his cup to his lips but never quite made it. "Is it true about Miles?"

"I'm sorry, yes. We found him this morning."

"What happened?"

"We're not sure. But he seems to have fallen from his bedroom window."

The young man shook his head. "He must've gone back to using." He looked up at Joe for confirmation.

"We'll find out if that's true, but we don't know anything yet." Joe finished stirring his coffee. "Do you have any specific reason for thinking he was using?"

"The word on the street, I guess," he said softly.

"Okay." How else would anyone know unless he wanted to implicate himself in the process? "You were a friend of his?"

"Yeah, well, more of Ron's."

"That's tough. What's your name?"

"Bernard Whitson."

"Well, Bernard, if you hear anything that might help us, I hope you'll let me know."

"Sure."

Joe left him there, holding his coffee cup and staring into the distance.

Steve Dolanetti tipped his head one way, then another, stuck his hands on his hips and began to tap his foot.

"I don't know. I just don't know."

Tiny stared at the sofa, trying to figure out what was wrong with it. He had been driving along minding his own business, thinking about the rumor he'd just heard about Miles, when he'd passed Steve out walking. Tiny had driven on by with a wave of his hand, stuck in his own thoughts, when he had by chance looked into the rearview mirror. He saw Steve standing in the middle of the street jumping up and down and waving at him, so Tiny pulled over to the side of the street and then backed up. He didn't bother waiting for Steve to come to him; he knew that would never happen, so he backed up. Steve leaned down to the window and peered in.

"Tiny, you are a godsend."

"I've things to do."

"I can't believe my luck—running into you."

"Why?" Tiny eyed him suspiciously.

"I just saw it. If you hadn't stopped, I'd have to leave it here." Steve was so pleased that he was grinning from ear to ear.

"Saw what?" Tiny knew he was being surly, but it was just eight-thirty and he hadn't had anything to eat yet and he couldn't get the news about Miles out of his head. And he still needed to wash up a bit and brush his teeth. "What's wrong with you, Steve? Haven't you heard about Miles?"

"What about him?" Steve stepped back and placed his hands on his hips.

"He's dead. Fell out of a window or something." Tiny started to blink rapidly as his imagination brought up an image of his friend falling from the high window.

"Gee, Tiny, I'm sorry. I didn't realize you were friends."

"We weren't really."

"Well, then . . ."

"It's just that when someone like you dies, I mean, me, it upsets me. I don't know."

Steve shook his head, this time with genuine concern. "In that case, let's think about something else and then I'll do something for you to make you feel better. You've come along at just the right time."

"Why?"

"Look! Over there!" Steve pointed to the other side of the street. There, amid boxes stuffed with debris and black trash bags stacked by a shiny aluminum light pole, sat a small upholstered sofa. "It's a sofa bed—for one person! I didn't think they made them. Come on!" Steve hustled across the street, waving for Tiny to follow him. Tiny parked and lumbered after his friend.

Tiny walked within four feet of the sofa, then stopped, hands in his pockets. He stared glumly at the piece of furniture as Steve poked and prodded, moving around it with an agility and enthusiasm that wearied Tiny.

"The frame is still good," said Steve.

"It might be dirty inside, real dirty," Tiny said.

"You're right." Steve looked aghast. "We can check." He threw himself onto the sofa, pushing aside the cushions in his search for a handle. He pulled up and the narrow mattress unfolded. He pulled it out toward the street and let the metal feet rest in the gutter. The mattress was well used but intact.

"It's old," Tiny said.

"I can replace the mattress. I know someone who can do that for me." Steve peered underneath and poked around some more. "It doesn't smell. That's so incredibly lucky."

Tiny kept his hands in his pockets while he leaned over the sofa and took a suspicious sniff.

"It's very important, Tiny, I can't tell you. Some smells get into the fabric and there's nothing—and I mean nothing—you can do about it. Mold, for one. And you don't want to sleep on anything with mold in it. If you don't have allergies before, you will afterward. And lung diseases. Mold is very bad for your lungs. Oh, I can't believe my luck. It's perfect." He was unable to take his eyes off the thing.

"Why would someone throw it out if it's still good?" Tiny asked. He wasn't enamored of furniture—or anything else—found on the sidewalks. It was an economic issue, not an aesthetic one.

"Well, look at it. Would you keep that fabric?"

Tiny studied the large floral pattern over blue and white stripes. "It's dirty."

"At the very least, Tiny, it is dirty. Anyway, I'll clean it up, and get a nice slipcover." Steve turned to his friend. "Can we take it to my place in your car?"

"My car?" Tiny said, trying to catch up with Steve's thinking.

"Yes, your car. It'll just fit."

Tiny turned to look at the vehicle in question parked across the street. "It will fit?"

"Of course it will," Steve said, waving away Tiny's objections.

"Looks kinda heavy to me."

"Well, yes, I suppose it does. It looks like a lump, but it will fit."

"Yeah, but think of my shocks. They're not great, you know."

Steve cocked his head to one side and seemed to be doing as Tiny told him: thinking about shock absorbers.

"Well, I can't do anything about that, but how about, as soon as we get it to my place I'll make you breakfast."

"What've you got?" Tiny asked, taking a step forward and startling Steve; Tiny rarely showed enthusiasm; he almost seemed afraid of it. But there was no mistaking his interest now.

"Ah, well, eggs and Canadian bacon and maybe toast. I have a few croissants in the freezer." He paused and tapped his index finger against his lip. "I do think I also have—"

"Toast and eggs and bacon?"

"Ah, sure. You got it," Steve said, closing up the bed and piling the cushions back on, careful not to look directly at Tiny.

"Can I use your shower?"

"Huh?" Steve turned around and gave Tiny a blank look. "My shower? Oh, Tiny, I'm so sorry, I didn't think. How stupid of me. 'Course you can."

The prospect of a hot meal and a hot shower brought out Tiny's enthusiasm and within a few seconds he had his arms wrapped around the middle of the sofa and was trotting across the street with it. Steve hurried along behind. The sofa fit into Tiny's '88 Chevy wagon—just barely—after Tiny moved around some boxes and frayed grocery bags. It and Steve bounced along precariously on the short ride to Steve's apartment. It took longer to carry the sofa up the narrow back stairs and into Steve's one-room apartment but Tiny managed without too much grumbling over Steve's insistence on helping. As soon as Tiny deposited the sofa along the wall, he looked around for the bathroom, but Steve's wail of dismay called him back. Tiny moved the sofa. Steve clucked. Tiny moved it again. So now it sat along one wall of the large room while Steve tried to decide if this, the third arrangement worked.

"What do you think, Tiny?"

"It's okay." Tiny moved toward a narrow door standing ajar.

Steve turned and smiled indulgently at his friend, then caught himself. "Oh, Tiny, how thoughtless of me. Go! Take a shower and I'll start cooking. There's an extra toothbrush in the cabinet if you need it and clean towels in the closet. The only thing I keep in a closet." He winked, then sighed when Tiny looked blank. "Just go take your shower."

Tiny's face softened and he headed into the small bathroom. Steve could hear his friend's elbows bumping into the wall that made a narrow corner by the door and his boots hitting the floor as he dropped them. It was far too cramped for anyone to use as a dressing room, but these macho guys, Steve thought, were far too modest to undress in front of an almost stranger. With a last look at his new acquisition, Steve turned to his galley kitchen and pulled open the refrigerator door.

"Hmm. Eggs and bacon and toast." He pulled toward him a gray egg carton in which he was storing a variety of bits of glass—he had once been told that a good beachcomber could find semi-precious stones like amethyst and he had set out to try, picking up all sorts of bits that looked like something but remained a mystery to him. He wiggled the half-empty milk bottle and put it back on the shelf. "So how creative am I?"

Steve had his answer as soon as Tiny sat down at the wrought-iron dining table and started to eat without even bothering to ask what it was. He kept his eyes on his plate, as though each bite had to be carefully watched lest it disappear on its way to his mouth, stolen by a sly enemy. Steve watched with growing relief and satisfaction.

"Hmm, you were hungry," Steve said. "I thought you were living over at—what's that place?"

Tiny shook his head, and swallowed hard. "I had to get out. I haven't been working so much and I can't get the deposit together for another place right away."

"So what're you going to do?" Steve asked, looking worried. He liked Tiny. The man had no taste, little sense of humor, and not a single intellectual gene in his body, but he was a decent guy who didn't inflict his problems on others, and he was honest about them. He'd treated Steve well since their first encounter in an AA meeting.

"I've been trying to figure that out. Behind the Laspac warehouse no one would notice a car late at night but they have a regular patrol coming around. So I tried the beach parking lot but some old lady was already calling the cops when I got there, drove out one car early and sure wasn't gonna let me stay."

"Oh, Tiny, you can't mean to sleep in your car all winter." Steve leaned forward to get a better look at his friend, who kept bobbing away, as though reluctant to show his face.

"Well, maybe it won't be that long. I can go farther down the shore and pull off into one of them old fire roads. No one goes down there much anymore."

"Not when it snows. You could get stuck," Steve said, but Tiny picked up his fork again, no longer paying any attention to his friend. He had noticed a few scraps left on the serving platter and was reaching for them. Steve's glance drifted from Tiny to the new sofa filling almost one quarter of the floor space. He couldn't do it; couldn't bring himself to make the offer, but he sorely wished he was someone who could.

"I don't mind living in a car," Tiny said, "not as long as I can get clean. I hate being dirty. You know, sweaty and grimy in the morning from sleeping."

"Yeah," said Steve. "I certainly wouldn't like that." He cast a speculative eye on the bathroom door and lapsed into a meditative mood.

The Community Center was prone to echoes when it was empty or nearly so, which to Ann Rose's mind had the advantage of keeping the few visitors aware of each other's wandering presence. She could hear Denny Clark rummaging in his office—a familiar sound that had led her to think of him as a furry gray field mouse who had moved into a house with tolerant owners for the winter. Even a resident dog would probably find him inoffensive.

Ann gave herself a mental shake. She had started to let her mind drift along such paths more and more lately—putting all her friends and relatives—especially relatives—into the guises of animals. Her sister was a kangaroo, cheerily hopping from one interest to another; her husband, a large contented seal that moved seamlessly, gracefully, from work to relaxation; her neighbor, well, her neighbor was a woodpecker. It occurred to Ann that she had a lot of woodpeckers in her life. She mentioned this one day to a friend who asked if she were in therapy. That's when Ann thought she'd be better off keeping these thoughts to herself.

Ann didn't see how her casual imaginings could seem pathological but then she had no idea what went on in other people's heads. What sort of thoughts did other people have? She had this idea that everybody else was thinking unusual, distinctive, unique, creative, funny, exciting thoughts, and she carried this idea—that people held vast stores of lore secret in their minds—until she arrived in college. Assigned Virginia Woolf's *The Waves* in an English class, she was stunned to discover her own thoughts flitting across the page. The memory no longer shocked her. Instead of discovering during college how vast and rich the human race was, she came away with the impression that human beings were ordinary, prosaic, and often small; their minds filled with little plots to embarrass those who have a little bit more in life than they do, schemes to get around a rule or restriction, dialogues they would have if they ever encountered that odious little person in that odious little drugstore, assuming they got up the courage to confront said odious little person. All in all, college persuaded her that people could be incredibly disappointing.

A cup of Lapsang Souchong tea provided a welcome distraction from her mental meanderings and she waved the aromatic, steaming cup beneath her nose. Her mind was wandering everywhere while her fingers fiddled with pen and paper. She must be more frustrated than she realized. She set the tea aside and examined what she had written.

At the top of the sheet of lined paper she had written "Tutors and Literacy Volunteers." Below that she had listed four names; hers was one of them. That was the problem. She couldn't get past the stubborn gut feeling that her friends might say yes—probably would say yes—to donating a few hours a month to tutor disadvantaged local students. But they wouldn't feel the same about helping out semi-literate adults. Kids, even when they were teenagers, tended to be cute (or cutish), fun, sweet, eager, easy to guide. Whereas illiterate, or semi-literate adults tended to be, well, adults. Sometimes they had managed to create successful lives without anyone ever finding out about their handicap, but more usually they had tripped over their illiteracy every step of the way down their path in life, and ended up with all the problems of the disadvantaged. Her friends had their limits. Ann sighed and propped her head up on her hands.

"That doesn't sound good."

"Oh, Denny." Ann leaned back in her chair and tried to smile at him. "I'm just trying to put together an expanded tutorial program."

"Not optimistic?" Denny leaned down to read over her shoulder. Ann shook her head. "Maybe you're looking at the wrong crowd."

"What do you mean?" Ann Rose had spent much of her adult life creating volunteer services for those in need, usually by drawing in all her friends and acquaintances who had a few spare hours during the week. They often said they had no time but unless they held down a full-time job, she didn't believe them. Now Denny was suggesting she'd been going about it the wrong way.

"You look at the people who are available," Denny said.

"But maybe you should try the ones who'll benefit the most. Literacy is good for the economy, the country."

"Well, sure, but—" Ann was drawing a blank. "So?"

"So how about local business people? The Rotary. The Elks. The VFW?" Denny sat on the table, dangling one leg and waiting while Ann absorbed the idea.

"I suppose I could ask to speak at their meetings and make a pitch," she said. Denny nodded vigorously. "And I could use your pitch about it being good for the economy—all that." In truth, she never thought about whether or not something was good for the economy or the country. She never got that far. She got as far as whether or not it was needed. Did she see someone limping along in life because someone, somewhere along the line had failed him—or her? If there was one, then there were probably others. And that decided her. She supposed the idea had crossed her mind that overall her programs were a good idea but she had never worked them up into a philosophy. But here it was, handed to her just when she needed it.

"Denny, that's a great idea," Ann said. "You're a life saver."

"Glad to be of service," he said with a bow.

Ann quickly jotted down Denny's key phrases and then, over the next half-hour, filled the sheet of paper with names of people to contact and notes of things to do. Every now and then she paused and glanced back up at the top of the sheet, where Denny's words were recorded.

That's what we wanted from him, she thought. She recalled the deliberations of the Community Center search committee, their concern about getting someone who could be both a catalyst as well as a leader; someone who would set a standard for programs and services but also guide others to create their own. They were at a crossroads, they said; there were so many groups using the Center now that the new executive director had to be able to negotiate all the pitfalls of small-town life and its politics.

Denny Clark had won over the committee, Ann recalled. He wasn't a mouse back then. He was something else—but that was before she was into characterizing people as animals. He had won them over and brought all the groups together into a cooperative whole. It was just in the last few weeks he'd started to seem mouse-like—burrowing, flitting around with those jerky movements that small creatures make.

Ann turned her paper over and began to scribble on the back, trying to remember who among her husband's friends belonged to which organizations. Denny might know; she could ask him later.

In all the time Denny had worked at the Center, Ann had never actually worked with him. She knew very little about him except what the search committee had shared. He came from a small social service agency in the southwest somewhere, had divorced his wife and taken a year off for health reasons, then set up a federally funded program for at-risk youth. The kids liked him but he didn't try to be their buddy—that was the assessment. He had good boundaries, in the lingo of the day, Ann thought.

But he had become a mouse.

If I knew him better, she thought, I'd ask him how things were going, but that seems so personal. She scribbled some more, losing herself in the planning, a fresh path to renewal for dozens of strangers. Dozens, she thought. We can reach dozens. Maybe hundreds. Good grief. Are there that many who can't read in this neck of the woods?

Chapter 3

Wednesday Afternoon

Joe didn't realize how tired he was until he looked at his wristwatch and saw both hands pointing to twelve. The tiny flash of surprise was quickly followed by relief—he hadn't missed Gwen McDuffy at the Harborlight Restaurant, at least as far as he knew. He pulled his car into the parking lot. A year ago he might have thought he was living in two separate worlds, as his feelings for Gwen deepened, but now she was the factor that informed all his thinking and feeling. He found himself anchored when he hadn't even known he was adrift.

"Hey, there," he said softly as he came up behind her. He let his hand slide across her back as he leaned down and gave her a quick kiss on the lips. Her chestnut brown hair curled around her ears, and she gave him a warm smile.

"Here." She pushed the menu across to him. "Mary Anne was asking me what I was going to have for lunch today and I told her I didn't know so she started telling me about this couple she knew—I guess she worked for him one time way back when—and, anyway, they always had the same thing for lunch. The two of them. They always had toasted cheese sandwiches with tomatoes. She couldn't get over it—and they had enough money to have whatever they wanted. She talked about that practically all morning."

"So now you have to have a toasted cheese sandwich with tomatoes," Joe said, picking up the menu.

"Oh, you!"

A large man, round and solid with a long white apron and his dark hair slicked back, strolled along the booths waving an ordering book in his hand. He had no pencil in hand or in a pocket and didn't stop to take any orders until he reached Joe and Gwen's booth.

"Hello, there, Chief."

"Badger," Joe said with a nod. "Gwen already ordered a toasted cheese sandwich, if I'm not mistaken."

"You're not." Badger treated Gwen to a broad smile and a wink.

"And I'll have an East Ender."

"You had that last week," Badger said.

"I know. I like them."

"Keep at him, Badger," Gwen said. "His cholesterol is going to go through the roof." She spoke with a smile that barely concealed a twinge of distress.

"I use low-fat ingredients," Badger said, not entirely happily.

"It's not that bad," Joe said after Badger departed.

"I'm sorry, Joe. I'm just feeling cranky today." She pulled the water glass toward her, but didn't drink, her fingers wrapped around the cool glass. "I had a call from the school today." Joe stiffened.

"Philip?"

"How did you know?" Gwen leaned forward. "Have you seen something I didn't?"

Joe shook his head. "He's a teenager."

"That's not it, Joe."

"I was going to talk to you, but I wanted to talk to him too. Ken told me a couple of days ago that he'd seen Philip

lieved to find himself listening to a tale of youthful enthusiasm unfolding.

"Gai something," Gwen said. Joe began to laugh.

"Gaiato?"

"That's it. Why? What does it mean?"

"It's Portuguese for rascal. Gaiato O Gato," he said with a
grin. "Sort of like Cleverly the Cat, or Rascally the Rodent.
You know, Gwen, that's pretty good. I didn't realize he'd
been picking up so much of what I say."

"You know, now that I think about it, that's downright
scary."

"So what's the rest of it?" Joe asked.

"Well, the story is about this cat and the man he lives with.
The man lives alone and has lots of toys including a fancy
train set that he has set up all over the house, tracks going in
one room and then into another. On and on and on."

"And?"

"One day the man brings a girlfriend home and she pats
the cat on the nose and then decides to move his water dish.
Well, the cat doesn't like that at all and goes off and hides."

"And?"

"So after supper the woman decides to go upstairs and
play with the train upstairs and the cat sees her coming and
jumps out of his hiding place and screeches at the woman,
lands on the train button, turns the thing on, and frightens
the woman so much that she screams and falls over backwards. Falling down the stairs to her death." Gwen finished
in a breathless rush. "Joe, it's not funny."

"Yes it is."

"Joe!"

"All right, but it's certainly not animal abuse."

"I thought he wanted a pet," Gwen said.

"Obviously he sees more potential in Gaiato than you do."

week, there was some talk about Miles being involved, but we don't know anything more than that—just rumor. They hung around together, and with a couple of others. And plenty of people around here knew them."

"That's two unnatural deaths in less than a week," Gwen said. She waved to Clara and called out, "Coffee?" Clara waved back from behind the counter. "Do you think she heard me, or does she maybe think I'm just being friendly? How long has she been working here, anyway?"

"How old are you?"

"I'm not going to get my coffee, am I?" She shook her head. "So what do you think happened to Miles?"

"Hard to say. His mother went over to see him yesterday evening."

"Why?" Gwen asked.

"To take him a casserole and make sure he was okay."

"You're kidding me."

"Gwen, you know—"

"As well as I do that—"

"—people do the strangest things—"

"—and have even worse excuses. Yes, Joe, unfortunately, I do. People are crazy."

"I'm going to have to wait for the toxicology tests to come back, but I have a few ideas." Joe turned around and waved to Clara at the counter. Immediately, she leaned over and smiled at him. "Two coffees," he said.

"I'm disgusted with you," Gwen said when he turned back to her.

"It's a man's world."

Joe was used to dealing with all kinds of grieving parents—with mothers so distraught that their sobs kept them from breathing, fathers crumpling from a linebacker to a water boy—but Edna Stine was one of the most surreal he had ever encountered. When he had finished interviewing her earlier in the morning, she had refused medical treatment, and had even refused to let someone drive her home, insisting she was perfectly all right and would manage on her own. He couldn't force her to accept help, so he had let it go. When he came out of the Harbor Light Restaurant and watched Gwen march across the tracks and up the hill to her office, he turned into the parking lot and saw Edna hovering near his jeep. She began inching her way toward the front of the car as he approached.

"I thought we could talk," she said as he came nearer.

"Let's go back to the station, then."

"No, no, it's not that important. Just a little thing."

"All right, if you're sure. What is it you want to say?"

"He was clean," she said. "I want you to know that. He was clean."

Joe nodded and waited.

"I get worried when he doesn't answer the phone," she said. "But I know he doesn't 'cuz I'm a pest too." She took a deep breath and exhaled. "I suppose this is the time I should have known it was different. Some premonition. But I had no idea, no premonition. No idea. None." She would hoard this thought in the coming years, a secret shame that she had lacked enough of the maternal instinct to know when her child was in trouble, or worse. "He was clean, you see. That's why I didn't suspect anything when he didn't answer the phone." She looked into Joe's face as if to make sure he was appreciating the importance of her news. "Just got out of the Discover program a couple of weeks ago."

Joe's gaze remained steady. She was tired, weary, but she showed no sign of breaking down and sobbing. Maybe it was hanging around with some guys he shouldn't know." Joe hunched forward, to get a better look at Gwen's face. "Hey, honey, it's not serious. He's just veering a little off to one side; we'll get him back on track. He's a good kid—just testing the waters a little."

She looked up at him. "Joe! I can't stand even thinking about him getting into trouble. It makes me come unglued."

"You? After all you've been through." He reached for her hand and rested his on it. "Come on. This time you're not alone either." She sighed and let him take her hand.

"You know, he begged me and begged me for weeks to get him a cat. Remember?"

"I remember," Joe said, leaning back and getting comfortable.

"I thought he was going to finally learn about taking care of things—a pet you have to feed and clean up after. I thought he was ready for that." Gwen ran her hands over her face.

"He's done okay, hasn't he?" The last thing Joe wanted to hear was that Philip was becoming cruel to an animal.

"He's been studying the cat—just watching him—and it was driving me crazy. I couldn't figure it out." She leaned her head on her hands and sighed. "It really seemed so odd, so I kept watching him watching the cat. You know, Joe," she said, peering up at him, "he was following the cat around as though he were up to something." She sighed. "Well, I finally found out why." She looked around as though help had to be within sight. "I came across something he wrote."

"Something what?" Joe leaned forward, his arms resting on the table.

"He's given Boots a new name and put him in a short story about a man who has a cat."

"What's the cat's name?" Joe asked, beginning to smile. Gwen had given him a good scare about Philip, but he was re-

lieved to find himself listening to a tale of youthful enthusiasm unfolding.

"Gai something," Gwen said. Joe began to laugh.

"Gaiato?"

"That's it. Why? What does it mean?"

"It's Portuguese for rascal. Gaiato O Gato," he said with a
grin. "Sort of like Cleverly the Cat, or Rascally the Rodent.
You know, Gwen, that's pretty good. I didn't realize he'd
been picking up so much of what I say."

"You know, now that I think about it, that's downright
scary."

"So what's the rest of it?" Joe asked.

"Well, the story is about this cat and the man he lives with.
The man lives alone and has lots of toys including a fancy
train set that he has set up all over the house, tracks going in
one room and then into another. On and on and on."

"And?"

"One day the man brings a girlfriend home and she pats
the cat on the nose and then decides to move his water dish.
Well, the cat doesn't like that at all and goes off and hides."

"And?"

"So after supper the woman decides to go upstairs and
play with the train upstairs and the cat sees her coming and
jumps out of his hiding place and screeches at the woman,
lands on the train button, turns the thing on, and frightens
the woman so much that she screams and falls over backwards. Falling down the stairs to her death." Gwen finished
in a breathless rush. "Joe, it's not funny."

"Yes it is."

"Joe!"

"All right, but it's certainly not animal abuse."

"I thought he wanted a pet," Gwen said.

"Obviously he sees more potential in Gaiato than you do."

"Boots," Gwen said. "His name is Boots."

"I think you'll have to go along with Philip; it's his cat."

"I wish you'd take me more seriously."

"I take you very seriously, Gwen."

"I'm sorry. I'm just feeling moody. It's amazing how overwhelmed I feel all of a sudden." Her green eyes softened, and the furrows in her brow disappeared. "I got him a pair of socks this morning with golf clubs on them. Before I got the call from the school. I was thinking how cool that he and I share the sock thing."

"What're you wearing?" He leaned out into the aisle to get a look at her feet.

She stuck her foot out and wiggled it. "My Elvis socks."

"Serious socks, huh?" Joe said.

"For serious collectors only." Gwen managed a rueful laugh. "Tell me it'll be all right, Joe." She lowered her voice, and he was afraid she'd begin to cry.

"It'll be all right." He raised her hand to his lips and kissed it. "Promise." With you, he thought, I forget I'm a policeman, and I'd promise you anything anyway. "Who called from the school?"

"His home room teacher. He failed a big test last week, and missed one more this week—he didn't show up at school to take his test, Joe. He didn't show up. Philip never got anything less than a B-plus and he failed one and didn't even show up for the other. I feel like tying him down to a chair and not letting him up until he's twenty-one."

"I'd have to arrest you for child abuse."

"He's never done anything like this before. Never."

"We'll talk to him. Tonight."

"I'm going to completely lose it and yell at him."

"No, you won't."

"I'm sorry. I'm being a jerk."

"No, you're not. You're a mother."

"And you're a policeman." She took a deep breath. "Let's get away from my problems. I'm sick of listening to me even if you're not. I heard the sirens early this morning. I almost called you, but I figured you were busy. What happened?"

"Miles Stine. Did you ever know him?"

She shook her head from side to side while she repeated the name softly. "I know the family. There's a teenage sister, closer to Jennie's age than Philip's. Chandra I think her name is."

"Chandra and Miles. There was a third child, an older brother who's also dead."

"Too bad. What happened to Miles?"

"Apparently he fell out of a window early this morning, around three, and died when he hit some lawn furniture. Apparently, I say, because there's no sign of why he went out the window."

"Where'd he live?"

"Cleary's. Third floor."

"Whew. That's quite a drop. Those old Victorian houses always seem so much taller than the ordinary three stories."

"Hmm." Joe leaned back as the waitress placed a large plate in front of him and a smaller one in front of Gwen.

"If he was living at Cleary's he wasn't doing too well, was he." Gwen reached for her sandwich. "I should watch what I say, shouldn't I?"

"I wasn't going to say anything," Joe said, smiling smugly. "That's probably your quota of fats for the week."

"In that case I'm going to enjoy it." She took a big bite. Joe didn't try to make sense of her muffled comments after that.

"Miles was a friend of Ron Faroli's, from what I've learned. When Ron was taken into the emergency room last week, there was some talk about Miles being involved, but we don't know anything more than that—just rumor. They hung around together, and with a couple of others. And plenty of people around here knew them."

"That's two unnatural deaths in less than a week," Gwen said. She waved to Clara and called out, "Coffee?" Clara waved back from behind the counter. "Do you think she heard me, or does she maybe think I'm just being friendly? How long has she been working here, anyway?"

"How old are you?"

"I'm not going to get my coffee, am I?" She shook her head. "So what do you think happened to Miles?"

"Hard to say. His mother went over to see him yesterday evening."

"Why?" Gwen asked.

"To take him a casserole and make sure he was okay."

"You're kidding me."

"Gwen, you know—"

"As well as I do that—"

"—people do the strangest things—"

"—and have even worse excuses. Yes, Joe, unfortunately, I do. People are crazy."

"I'm going to have to wait for the toxicology tests to come back, but I have a few ideas." Joe turned around and waved to Clara at the counter. Immediately, she leaned over and smiled at him. "Two coffees," he said.

"I'm disgusted with you," Gwen said when he turned back to her.

"It's a man's world."

Joe was used to dealing with all kinds of grieving parents—with mothers so distraught that their sobs kept them from breathing, fathers crumpling from a linebacker to a water boy—but Edna Stine was one of the most surreal he had ever encountered. When he had finished interviewing her earlier in the morning, she had refused medical treatment, and had even refused to let someone drive her home, insisting she was perfectly all right and would manage on her own. He couldn't force her to accept help, so he had let it go. When he came out of the Harbor Light Restaurant and watched Gwen march across the tracks and up the hill to her office, he turned into the parking lot and saw Edna hovering near his jeep. She began inching her way toward the front of the car as he approached.

"I thought we could talk," she said as he came nearer.

"Let's go back to the station, then."

"No, no, it's not that important. Just a little thing."

"All right, if you're sure. What is it you want to say?"

"He was clean," she said. "I want you to know that. He was clean."

Joe nodded and waited.

"I get worried when he doesn't answer the phone," she said. "But I know he doesn't 'cuz I'm a pest too." She took a deep breath and exhaled. "I suppose this is the time I should have known it was different. Some premonition. But I had no idea, no premonition. No idea. None." She would hoard this thought in the coming years, a secret shame that she had lacked enough of the maternal instinct to know when her child was in trouble, or worse. "He was clean, you see. That's why I didn't suspect anything when he didn't answer the phone." She looked into Joe's face as if to make sure he was appreciating the importance of her news. "Just got out of the Discover program a couple of weeks ago."

Joe's gaze remained steady. She was tired, weary, but she showed no sign of breaking down and sobbing. Maybe it was a relief. How long could anyone, especially a parent, live with the knowledge that someone's death was inevitable? When it finally came, it had to bring a tragic sense of relief as well as sorrow.

"You're thinking about the business of Ron Faroli last week. That oxy stuff," she said. She huddled inside her coat; light brown swales of dried dirt covered the toes of her black laced-up walking shoes. She's shrinking, Joe thought, right before my eyes.

"Yes." Joe nodded.

She dismissed it with a short jerk of her head. "Chandra got up and went to school this morning. I could hear her making herself breakfast, like it was any other day of the week; she's strange, that girl. I don't know what's wrong with her; she doesn't seem to care about her brothers. She just went out the door. The house feels odd. You know, right after someone dies, there's that last while when they're still with you, still around. You can feel them in the house. It's not re-membering. They really are there."

"I'll take you home," Joe said.

"I don't wanna go home." She began to move away from him, putting more of the Jeep between them. "I thought maybe Chandra could take me for a drive. I don't think it's a good idea for me to go home. I'd be there alone and I just don't want to be alone inside right now. I'm not afraid of being alone, it's not that, but this is my last boy. What am I supposed to do now?" Beads of sweat sprouted along her hairline.

"Do you have a family doctor?"

She shook her head. "If I need anything, the clinic helps me."

"Maybe I should give them a call."

"I'm all right. It's just—" She glanced up at him. "It's just that at a crisis, when I get so scared, I'm afraid I'll mess my pants. I don't know where I get that. Fear, you know. It does strange things to you." She straightened up.

"Tell me what was happening in his life," Joe said. He knew she could take one of two paths—she could claim the memory of her dead son as she needed or wanted him to be, wreathe his image in the smiles of childhood and the dreams of a mother's heart, or she could open herself up to the person Miles Stine had become, accept the uncomfortable truth of his life and give him the dignity of truth and honesty—and not bury him with hatred and bitterness. Joe wouldn't take anything she said today in the aftershock of her son's death as definitive, but it would be a warning.

"You don't believe me." She held her loden coat together with both hands, interlocking her fingers and confronting him squarely.

"He had some trouble a few days ago. With Ron Faroli." Joe spoke as softly as he could without whispering. He towered over her but her stalwart stance seemed to say, 'I'm as tall as anyone, as good as anyone.' He knew that stance, especially among women who had at one time "worked out"—as his aunts called it—women who took day cleaning jobs when times were precarious but who had no intention of letting anyone treat them differently because they cleaned other people's houses. It was a defensive pride that had died along with their Sunday hats and gloves. Edna Stine had worked out, Joe knew, and he recognized that stance.

"I have nothing against Ron Faroli," Edna said. "A good family. Nice people." She ducked her neck inside the collar and rubbed her cheek against the thick wool. "But he was no angel. I told my boy to stay away from him. I told him there was nothing but trouble ahead for him." She pressed her lips together. "I told him. Don't think I didn't warn him." She grew stiff with the need to convince Joe.

"I'm sure you did, Mrs. Stine." He waited for her to grow calm again. "He and Ron took together, didn't they?"

"I don't know anything about that," she said, looking around as though she didn't want to be seen with Chief Joe Silva. "Miles had a bad back. He took pain pills sometimes; that's all." She leaned against the car door.

"Do you know how they got them?"

"He was just out of that detox program, you know. They don't cure bad backs, you know."

"I didn't know much about Ron. Were they good friends? Ron and Miles?"

"I wanted Miles to make something of himself, but he could barely think about next week, let alone next year," she said, her voice drifting. She began to button her coat, each bone button awkward in her cold fingers. She tugged on one and Joe realized her hands were trembling. "Ron didn't want to go to college, you know, but his father pushed him. Always pushing him, Ron said."

"And Ron didn't like that."

She shook her head. "George is bitter. You never hear him talk?" She glanced at Joe, surprised, waiting. "He's real bitter. No reason for it, not really. He went to BU—wanted to go to Harvard or some other big name school, but couldn't get in, I guess. Feels cheated. He never says it in so many words but you can hear it sometimes. He wanted to be on that town committee about historical places but no one appointed him and he didn't know how to ask. Too proud to ask and too stupid to figure out how to get on it. Kept telling everyone the committee was just for Harvard types. You can hear the anger something fierce in him when he talks. You just listen sometime."

"And that drove Ron away?"

She nodded again. "You got to be careful with kids. They always hear what you're trying not to say."

At any other time Joe would have agreed and thought how wise and sensible this hardworking woman was, how honest and aware, but all her wisdom didn't seem to have done her any good.

Edna Stine rubbed her cheek against the collar, like a child with a special blanket, her hands in her pockets, lost in her thoughts until Joe touched her elbow. "Let me drive you home." She shook her head.

"My car's right over there." She nodded to the old black hatchback at the other end of the parking lot. "I just want to go for a drive. I need to think."

It bothered him mightily that the small town of Mellingham had known two deaths in less than a week, both of them of young men with drug histories. In each dead face he could see Philip—the boy who had become like his own—and the danger he faced, the slide down and down, with nothing to break his fall. Joe had made a comfortable life for himself away from the tumult of his own family, as though the intensity of their love and life had been too much for him; as though he had been made differently. But now, as he thought about Philip and Gwen and the two dead men, Joe knew he was just like anyone else with something to lose.

Joe pulled out of the parking lot, headed over the tracks, turned right and in less than a quarter of a mile turned right again onto Seaward Road. The Cleary house seemed to have settled back to normal, with the only signs of the morning's events being the ruts the ambulance and police tires had left in the soft earth. He was just driving, getting a look at the town from the new perspective Miles Stine's death had given him; his sense of place shifting to accommodate this new burden of tragedy and ugliness.

Joe turned right and headed down Delmar Street and slowed as he passed the Community Center. Bernard Whitson was standing out in front just staring ahead, as though he were watching something across the street or trying to remember where he was headed. Joe knew that vacant look in drunks, who seemed so anaesthetized by booze that they couldn't climb out of themselves into reality. He had a sinking feeling that this fellow wasn't going to make his first month's anniversary. Joe pulled the police car over to the side and walked back to where Bernard stood.

"Bernard," Joe said when he was a few feet away. "Something wrong?" The air felt damp and the young man wore only cotton slacks and a quilted cotton shirt; his hands hung down at his sides, but his eyes seemed clear. "You can't stay here, Bernard."

"I was supposed to meet Miles this morning and I guess it's all hit me. What am I going to do?" The young man was pale, and Joe could see the shock beneath his apparent vacant look.

"Let me take you home."

Bernard looked like he was about to cry, and all Joe could think of was a little boy he had once known who, when he finally understood his father was moving out, had stood stoically in his bedroom door watching, turning away when his mother told him to go do something else and turning back as soon as she was gone; his little chin trembling beneath his clenched teeth, his hands balled into fists at his side.

"You were close to him?" Joe said.

Bernard nodded. "He did a commitment the first meeting I went to. He—He—He was powerful." Bernard drew his hands up against his shirt jacket and brushed them down again, hunching over and crushing the fabric into his fists. "He helped me."

It was worth hearing, that plaintive elegy from the dispossessed—he helped me. In a matter of weeks, perhaps even days, the only thing anyone would remember about Miles, outside of his family, would be the way he had lived his last few weeks and the way he died. Bernard might write his friend's epitaph, but few would hear it. Joe stretched out his hand to squeeze Bernard's shoulder as the other contorted his face in an effort to conceal his anguish.

He was just a boy, thought Joe, nowhere near the emotional age of his body, a child in some ways. After years of drugs, his body had reached age twenty-three, but Bernard was where he had been when it all started, in his teens. He was still an adolescent, whether he understood that or not. Right now, Bernard was facing the greatest gamble of his life, one that he might have no way of controlling—would he remain an adolescent all his adult life, or would he take that leap into maturity that sometimes happened to addicts after they'd been sober and clean for two years or more? Joe stared at him, wondering, wondering. Did the boy have it in him?

"I'm sorry," Joe said. He didn't know if this death would lead to good or bad. Bernard shoved his fists into his pockets and swung around.

"He's dead," Bernard hissed. "He just got clean. He had everything going for him—a place to live, a chance at a real job. You should have heard him talk—he knew what we needed to get it back together. He never treated anyone different—respect, all the same for everyone."

"Bernard, you said he was clean. Are you sure of that?" Joe waited. "We found something in his room."

"I don't believe you."

"We found something," Joe said.

"No pills. He swore off them. He told me. Miles wouldn't lie to me about that. I know how it is. He was telling the truth. I know he was."

"When did you last talk to him?"

"Sunday, no Monday. The day before the funeral. The pills—oxy?—they really scared him. He didn't think Ron took them seriously enough."

"Did Miles tell you that?"

"He wouldn't take them. I'm telling you." Bernard looked up and down the street, then pushed his hands deeper into his pockets and hunched over. This is it, Joe thought, the little confession.

"Miles told me he was frightened—all that time in rehab scared him because he met some guys. Nothing scared them." Bernard paused. "He wasn't going to do anything that wasn't legal, he said. He only got legal stuff. He said he could get just as much kick from legal stuff."

"No pills?" Joe gripped Bernard's shoulder and pulled him closer. "Just what he could get that was legal. You're sure he said that?" This was beginning to cut deeper than Joe had expected. No town, no matter how well off its residents, was immune to the drug plague, and sometimes the more affluent communities had a tougher time of it—their youngsters could afford to buy the best, and often did.

"No, Chief, he wasn't a liar. A drunk and a thief, maybe, when things went bad for him but he didn't lie about it." He stopped, turned as though he would retch, and reached out a hand to steady himself against a maple tree. His face was red hot. "Yes, okay, he was, he was those things. That's what we are. Me too. I'm a drunk and a loser. It's what I am."

"Don't bother talking like that."

"It's the truth. Ron's parents didn't blame him." He peered up at Joe.

"Say that again," Joe said.

"Ron's father was angry, sure, but Miles told him he didn't take that OxyC with him. He wasn't into that. He didn't take anything illegal." Bernard's shoulders squeezed tighter and tighter together.

"Miles told you this?" Joe said. "That's good news if it's true."

"He wouldn't lie to me about that. He said Ron's father came by one day and told him he didn't hold nothing against him."

Joe recited exactly what Bernard had said, trying to find the trap in it. It just didn't sound like George Faroli—to seek out and forgive the man who had contributed to his son's death—unless Miles had somehow convinced him he'd had nothing to do with it.

"Miles took Ron to the emergency room, didn't he?"

"Yeah."

"Where were you?"

"I wasn't around," he said, turning away.

"Still high somewhere? I need to know what happened, Bernard. You're not snitching on anyone. I need to figure out what happened to Miles."

"I wasn't doing anything illegal."

"Why so careful all of a sudden?" Joe asked. Most addicts blocked out the dangers so successfully that he wondered if they even understood English when they were using.

"Miles had a real scare a couple of months ago. He tested positive for HIV, but it was a false positive. After that he was terrified of getting HIV or Hep C or syphilis or anything. He'd tell everyone about it—not to use the needle. He had all sorts of ways to get high without the needle, he said, and the best part was they were all legal."

"You keep saying that, Bernard, but I'm not hearing any reason to believe you."

"He told me I was stupid to be drinking—alcohol'll kill you faster than anything else, he said. He meant it. He said he could use coke and live to be ninety. But he had something better and it wouldn't get him into trouble." He stopped to take a deep breath. "He thought alkies were jerks, just killing themselves. And needle junkies—taking stupid risks." The deeper he fell into recollecting his conversations with Miles, the more calmly he spoke, matter-of-factly, as though he were listing the standard features of a new car—nothing special about any of it. Miles Stine looked at the various classes of drugs pragmatically—some were safe, some were not; some were legal, some were not.

"You're going to have to convince me, Bernard," Joe said. "I don't know anything that's going to do what you say and still be legal."

"I don't remember the exact name of the stuff," Bernard said.

"Sure, you don't," Joe said. "Okay—"

"I mean it. It was from Mexico. He got it off the Internet," Bernard said, growing alarmed that Joe's suspicions might mean trouble. "Salvia something. I'm not lying, honest!"

The desperation in Bernard's voice was convincing—at least for the moment.

Salvia something, Joe thought, wondering if this was just one more calculated lie all tricked out in the most confusing conversation he'd had in a long time.

The AA meeting was not supposed to begin until 5:30 p.m., but the vast floor of the Community Center was dotted with pairs and small groups of men and women who had begun to gather as news of Miles Stine's death spread. Denny

Clark slid his chair back to get a better look through his office door and, with his lips moving slightly, counted twenty-three people.

This was a large AA meeting, the largest in town, and would probably be larger for the next few weeks. Every afternoon at 5:30, men and women stopped on their way home from work for the meeting that most, if not all, credited with saving their lives and their sanity. When Denny had proposed the meeting a few years earlier, the Community Center board members had been caught off guard and visibly squirmed, but eloquent pleas and calm explanations that such meetings would not interfere with the business of the Community Center had carried the day. The AA meetings were approved for three nights a week.

After the first week there were the usual complaints about traffic on Delmar Street and an influx of out-of-towners (two), but local families were surprisingly quiet. Since children under fifteen had to be out of the Center on those days by five instead of five-thirty or six in the evening—the hour to which the Center hours had dragged on and on—Denny had expected to hear complaints from all age groups. Instead, it seemed that kids were arriving home at five, or soon thereafter, giving their families a chance to get a good look at them in daylight. The AA meeting was having unexpected benefits.

Two more men came in the door, both carrying briefcases and chatting to each other while they doffed their coats on the way to the coffee table. In another minute they were juggling coats over one arm, with a briefcase in one hand and a cup of coffee in the other. Denny pushed his hand against the wall and rolled back to his desk. He didn't lead the meeting; he didn't even attend, and if he was working in his office when the meetings began, he merely closed his door and waited till the end.

He especially liked the opening prayers; he had probably heard each one a dozen times but each time he heard an opening prayer, it seemed new to him—completely fresh and original and profound, and he pondered it throughout the evening until he forget about it. He had once taken a course in anger management—and he knew all the tricks on stepping back, hearing your feelings, ways to distance yourself—but in the end he had still been angry. The prayers, on the other hand, seemed to calm something deep inside him and they never felt sentimental or phony, as his Sunday church experiences often did. He knew one form of help wasn't any better than another intrinsically, but that didn't change how he felt.

The scraping of chairs across the wooden floor signaled the imminent beginning of the meeting. A man dressed in jeans and a heavy navy blue sweater stood up and shoved his hands into his front pockets. The group grew quiet and Denny closed his door. He was careful not to let it click shut. He pulled his chair up to his desk, exhaled softly, and waited for the person reading the prayer to begin.

The meeting was much as Denny expected it to be. A few members wanted to talk about how devastating Miles's death was for them, how it frightened them to get back on track with meetings; some new faces nodded especially vigorously. Others were harsher, pointing out that both Miles and Ron Faroli had thrown their lives away—getting off one drug just to get onto another.

"I'm telling you. He lost his way. Wouldn't—"

"Who?"

"Ron."

"I'm talking about Miles."

"Guys, let's get back—"

"You know what I heard?"

"It's gossip, guys. It won't help."

"He'd switched. Heroin."

"I don't believe it."

"True. No shit. I'm telling ya."

It took awhile for the leader to get the group back on track, but the new members were bursting to talk. A woman stood up to speak and waited for quiet. She wore black from the neck to toe, except for pink underpants that peeked out above her hip pants. These times Denny was glad he stayed in his office.

The gals came dressed to kill—hot, hot, hot—and he found them a massive distraction. When they hung around after the meetings—paying no attention to him but distracting everyone else just as badly—he found himself gruffly hurrying everyone out so he could close up. "It's late," he said no matter what time it was. They dressed to get attention and they got it.

Sometimes he chastised himself for eavesdropping on the group; other times he justified it by telling himself that he had to know what was going on; monitoring was part of his job. And sometimes his need for something larger and kinder in his life slipped through his defenses and he wondered if he'd ever get past the pride that held him back. Would he always settle for life on the fringes? Always be afraid of throwing himself into things? He was the big guy, the one with all the answers, the one everyone came to for help. He couldn't stand the idea of seeing himself as he really was—frail, like every other human being. So he sat in his office, soaking up what he could instead of showing a minimum of bravery and going out there and sitting in a chair with everyone else.

The chairs scraped across the wooden floor. Denny didn't know how long his mind had wandered into the darkness of his past. He heard a soft rap on his door.

"Yes?"

"We're just cleaning up," a man in worn jeans said. "I meant to give this to you earlier." He handed over an envelope with a number of bills in it. Denny took it without looking at it.

"Thanks, Malcolm." He folded the envelope and wrapped an elastic band around it, then dropped it into a cash box, which he locked in a drawer.

"Some of the guys are taking Miles's death pretty hard," Malcolm said.

"I didn't see much of him lately," Denny said. "He was in here a couple of days ago and seemed pretty crabby. I thought it was because of Ron's death."

"What a waste," Malcolm said, shaking his head. "He sure let a lot of us down. But, hey, we do what we can. How's his family taking it?"

"It's just his mother and sister," Denny said. "The older boy went the same way. It has to be hard."

"The little shit," he said softly, a note of affection in his voice. "Couldn't hold it together for a week." Malcolm went off shaking his head. A slap on the back for a few long timers and he was gone, the front door slamming behind him.

It bothered Denny too, but not for the same reason.

Joe watched the computer shut down while he picked up the telephone and punched in Gwen's number. Over the last few months he and Gwen had settled into a routine that was not allowed to be comfortable though it was comforting for both. Each had reasons, or so went the rationalizations, to avoid the trap of comfortableness but in truth each was afraid—for different reasons—of the intimacy that ushered in such a condition in a relationship. Gwen was a bit edgy—still soured from earlier failures—always fearful that something would catch her unawares and she'd lose her children, as they

seemed to her. They had grown into bright, energetic teenagers, but they hadn't fallen into rebellious patterns—at least
not until now. They had always been good kids who seemed a
bit wary of the world, perhaps absorbing some of Gwen's un-
ease. With Gwen's news today at lunch, Joe knew dinner this
evening could be rough. Still, knowing that he was going to
see her in a few minutes left him feeling warmer and easier in
his skin.

"You need anything?" he asked her when she picked up
and said hello.

"Less gray hair," she said.

"How about something edible?"

"I made Toucinho do Ceu," she said. "Am I saying that
right?"

"This afternoon?"

"I was thinking of making it. I'm upset." She sighed. "You
like it, don't you?"

"One of my favorites, but I don't think I've ever had it in
the middle of the week. It's a fancy dessert."

"Decadent, aren't we?"

"How about an Irish dessert some time?"

"Do you have any idea what an authentic Irish dessert is
like?"

"I guess not." He rang off, and was filled with Gwen's ambivalence about Philip and the coming evening. He stood up
and let her uneasiness slip away; Philip was a good kid, and
Joe wouldn't let anyone else's doubt change that opinion.
Gwen was having a little trouble separating her past from her
present, in his view.

Joe pulled his car onto Main Street and turned left, to
head toward his own house, pulling into traffic just behind
Paula Faroli. Her right-hand signal light lit up and she turned
into the driveway for the Sara Meya Funeral Parlor. Joe

slowed, holding up a single car behind him, waited thirty seconds, then turned into the same driveway. By the time his car crept into the parking lot, Paula Faroli was disappearing into the Funeral Parlor. Joe parked and followed her in. He paused in the entryway, listening for voices. When he heard them he entered a room that he knew Paula would have to pass through on her way out. Last night it had been filled with people and flower arrangements; today it was silent and empty. He moved along the perimeter, slowing as he reached an open door.

"Just this photograph, Mrs. Faroli," a young woman said. Joe thought it must be the secretary.

"Isn't that something?" Paula Faroli said. "I was sure I'd left another photograph. I thought you were sending this one over to the papers."

"We did," the woman explained. "They scanned it and sent it back. I was going to call you tomorrow. It'll be in the paper this Friday. They said they'd do a nice piece."

Joe almost sighed aloud. The secretary was being thoroughly compassionate and helpful, the last thing Paula needed. He had passed her a couple of times in the town today hurrying intently on one errand or the other. She didn't need compassion; she needed a good bracing wall against which she could fling her own anger and pain and confusion at the loss of her only child.

"Well, I guess I left it somewhere else," Paula said. Joe heard her shoes hit the wood floor as she approached the open door. She almost fell over as she veered to avoid bumping into him.

"Oh, Mrs. Faroli." The secretary hovered. Joe sent her off in search of a glass of water.

"I'm really all right," Paula said, grasping her head with both hands. "Really."

"Yes, you are."

85

She glanced up at him, startled perhaps by his matter of fact tone. "I am."

"I know you are. I wouldn't have stopped otherwise," Joe said.

Paula drew the lapels of her coat together and tugged the collar into place; she brushed her right hand down the front. "I've left things all over town—I feel like a hobo parking my belongings in little hidey holes until I need them. It seemed so messy; I just thought I'd clean up a bit."

"I'm sorry about your son, Ron."

"Thank you."

"It was a surprise to us too," Joe said, watching for her reaction. "I thought you should know that."

"Thank you." Barely a whisper. "He was better, wasn't he?"

"We try to keep a close eye on anyone getting out of Rehab, someone who might be struggling. It's for their sake as well as our own," he said when he saw a quizzical look on her face. "People can change their lives. Sometimes they have one bad experience and that makes them want to be different. And sometimes they just wake up one morning and want life to be better, something to enjoy."

"That's what I kept waiting for, hoping for," she said.

"You had no clue anything was happening?"

"Not a sign. George and I were stunned. At first we thought it had to be a mistake. I'm sure every parent thinks that—no one can believe their child is gone and gone from drugs—it's so dirty, so wasteful. There are lots of ways of refusing the truth—some of my friends are experts at it. They fight with every professional they meet and keep records of every encounter. When one of my friend's husbands had a stroke last year, she followed his case like an investigative journalist, even sat in the OR with notebook in hand. They must have hated her. She took all that as a sign of how well she was coping. But one morning, early, a nurse called to tell her he was gone, just slipped away. What do you mean he's gone? He can't be. Are you sure? That was her reaction. Anger. Disbelief. She was so used to fighting, she just wasn't ready." Paula took a breath, exhaled slowly. "Can you imagine the nurse not being sure? Excuse me, ma'am; I'll just double-check that. May I put you on hold? Thanks. Be right back." She began to rub the palms of her hands together. "I'm being catty. Truth to tell, I wanted to say the same thing. Are you sure? You must have made a mistake. But of course, they hadn't. So then you start to accept it."

"How about George?"

She nodded. "George—It's been harder for him." The hands grew still and drifted into coat pockets. She tossed a strand of hair away from her face. "We heard about Miles today. Poor Edna. George thinks we should do something for her." Her voice trailed off, as though she wasn't quite sure of what she was saying.

"Both boys were friends, weren't they?"

"Do you think they have friends when they're like that? I mean, you know, the way normal people have friends?"

Joe studied her brown eyes, steady on him, waiting for—what?—a comforting lie or the comfort of the truth? "The bond is always drugs. The palling around with someone is a byproduct."

"Yes. I knew that."

"I'm glad to see you're not holding any kind of grudge against him."

She shrugged. "George said we should forgive him. Odd, that. I've never heard him talk like that before, but that's what he said."

"Other than Miles, was there anyone else he hung out with?"

"No one special I ever heard of." She offered a wan smile. "The truth? I'm not the one to ask. I knew nothing about him. He was a stranger. A body walking around with my son's name and his voice—a complete stranger to me." She closed her eyes against the rising grief just as the secretary came up behind her holding a glass of water. Joe gave a shake of his head and the other woman backed away.

"Do you want to sit down?" Joe asked. She shook her head.

"I made all the mistakes—I did everything you're not sup-posed to do. I lectured him, didn't trust him and then bailed him out whenever he got into trouble. Even when he was a little kid. I couldn't let him breathe. He turned on me once, told me he hated me, it was my own fault he ended up the way he was, if I really wanted to know." She caught her breath. "He was pretty ugly, I can tell you."

"When was this?"

"About ten years ago. Not recently, if that's what you're wondering." She shook her head. "Later, maybe a month after that, I was trying to find out where he was living and he told me. 'Look, I like my life. I'm not giving it up. Okay? I don't want to be saved.' He was filthy, living in squalor some-where and he liked it. He liked it. That's how angry he was with me. Us."

"And then he just changed?"

"I don't know how it happened, what brought it about, but I've always wondered. He never confided in me. Or in George. Maybe he saw too many people dying. I really don't know."

"Do you know where he was the last few months?"

"No, except that he was around here. He came back, said

he was straight, nothing illegal for him, and just wanted to be left alone." She inhaled and caught her breath. "I passed him on the street here and I was so startled at seeing him that I didn't know what to do. He walked right past me. I didn't know what to do."

"When was the last time you saw him?" Joe asked.

"At the hospital. In the ICU." She paused. "They let us see him there, as though . . . He was gone, of course." Her lips and chin began to tremble; she was barely holding herself together now.

"And the last time you could talk to him? When was that, Paula?" He spoke loudly, to jolt her back into the moment.

"I don't know, a few days ago. George and I were coming out of the drugstore. He was coming down the sidewalk just stepping into the street and he looked up at me and George and said, 'Mom, you'll never guess.' He looked just like he did the day he won an award in high school. 'Catch you later,' he said." She took a deep breath to steady herself. "He was talking to us like, like normal parents. Like he was normal and we were all just like anyone else."

"What do you think he wanted to tell you?"

"I don't know. It doesn't matter. Not to me, anyway." She started to turn away. "But George. Poor George. He keeps asking me, What do you think it was? Constantly. He's obsessing over it. Maybe it was this, maybe it was that. No, George, it's probably something so insignificant, so unimportant."

"So you really have no idea?"

"Joe, it doesn't matter. It was probably about getting a good deal on a second-hand car. Who cares now?"

"It might help, Paula."

"With what?"

"Well, first of all, we have no idea how he got the pills he took. OxyContin is so dangerous that a lot of drugstores refuse to carry it. How Ron did things is pretty much a secret to everyone. We know almost nothing about his life."

"Oh." She looked blank. "I never considered it. I just took it for granted that you knew those things, whatever you needed to know. I sometimes think you know more than the rest of us do about what's going on."

Joe ignored her comment. "We've checked with every drugstore in the area, asked them to look over their prescriptions. We've checked on the street. Nothing."

"Does it really matter now? I mean, he's dead."

"We have to find out, Paula. It might also help us figure out what happened to Miles."

"Poor Edna." Paula sighed, then pulled her coat tighter around her. "You know, she's lost two boys to drugs. Two. Doesn't seem possible."

"If you think of anything that might help us, anything at all, I want you to call me and let me know. Promise me you'll do that, Paula. No matter how unimportant or minor it might seem. Will you do that? Paula?"

"Joe, Joe, you're as bad as George. It can't matter, don't you see? He's gone."

Chapter 4

Wednesday Evening

Three months ago, Joe Silva had expected a period of awkwardness when his upstairs neighbor, in the two-condo house, was forced to accept her new physical limitations after a fall. A daughter appeared at Joe's front door, announced her plans for her mother, Mrs. Alesandro, and abruptly disappeared back upstairs, where the only evidence of her presence was the noise of closets being emptied and boxes packed throughout the weekend.

Joe had taken to checking in on her, expecting to hear a few grumblings and confused memories and a final reluctant agreement to move, but instead Mrs. Alesandro spent her days on the telephone calling doctors and nurses and health facilities. She seemed to be always walking around her condo with a telephone pressed against her ear. Joe heard her when he left for work in the morning and when he arrived home in the evening. After three weeks she had traced her dulling mind to one pill, her wobbly sense of balance to another, and her unexpected falls to a pair of orthopedic shoes with unevenly wearing heels and faulty soles. She did not break any bones in her fall, was not on the precipice of massive disintegration from osteoporosis and had no intention of going anywhere. Bruised and confused, she survived everything—her fall, her family's good intentions, and the medical establishment's erratic attentions and neglect—by sheer force of will.

He hadn't realized how concerned he was about her plight until his mother called late one Sunday evening, reminding him they hadn't spoken in over a month. As he began to fill in the gaps, she stopped him and said, "Mrs. A, the lady above. Tell me how she is first." Like elderly women everywhere, his mother and Mrs. Alesandro needed to hear that the other one was all right; it gave each woman a boost. So Joe had two reasons now to check in on his neighbor: her health and his mother's.

"I thought I heard you." Mrs. Alesandro stepped back from the door, opening it wide and ushering him inside. She turned to wobble back to her armchair, using a cane walker, which she rested against an upholstered arm. "I want to hear what's been going on with that poor boy. Miles Stine."

"So you've heard." Joe shut the door behind him and walked over to another armchair.

"You look beat. How about something to drink?"

"Not right now, thanks."

"Of course. It's Wednesday." She pushed herself deeper into her chair. "Well, tell me before you run off."

"What tells me you know as much about this as I do, Liz?" Joe had taken to calling her Liz one day after hearing her reminisce about her youth. It seemed to him that here was a woman whose body belied her livelier, youthful soul. She became Liz to him, but to no one else.

"Always was a troubled family," she said. He nodded while he pushed a few pieces of kindling back onto the pile of wood for the fireplace. She had had it converted to gas a year ago, against her daughter's protests ("But it's so inauthentic!") and used it whenever she felt like it, which could just as easily be June as December. She kept the wood around to satisfy her daughter's aesthetics. "Yes, Joe, that is an interesting fireplace," Mrs. Alesandro said, calling him back from his reverie.

He laughed and sat back. He wasn't going to tell her what he was thinking about.

"What do you know about the family?"

"She's a townie. Family moved around the area for work, I guess. She married a townie—Doug Stine. He wasn't much, but they were young."

"Too young?"

She nodded. "He got tired of the responsibility, I suppose. Just took off. I think he sent some money for a while, then probably nothing. Edna never seemed to have enough for anything. She's had the same job for years. Works at that little private clinic near the corner of Trask and Main." Mrs. Alesandro paused, cocked her head to one side, and studied him.

"Liz?" he prompted her.

"I always thought she could get a better job, but she never seemed willing to try. Seemed afraid to set out for more." She frowned, as though she didn't quite approve of her own judgment of this woman.

"Did you know all the children?"

"Oh, sure. The way you know children in town not the right age for your own or your grandchildren."

"Was there anything unusual in Miles being friends with Ron Faroli? Other than the way drugs bring people together."

"They're not so different, if that's what you mean."

"How so?"

"You look at the two families now, and they seem to belong to two different parts of the town, but they grew up pretty much on the same level, if you know what I mean. And if Doug had stayed—or George Faroli hadn't—those two gals, well, life could have been very different for both of

93

them." She paused, then started to speak again, then stopped before saying, "I sometimes wonder, though, if we really do have any say in how our lives work out."

He leaned his arm across the back of the barrel chair, crossed one foot over the other, and lapsed into silence. "Now you're getting philosophical. And that's a position not very popular these days."

"You mean there's no such thing as luck. What you have is what you've earned?" She spit air and shook her head. "This country's got too much money. Doesn't know what to do with most of it."

"Not many people would agree with you."

"What do I care? I'm old." She leaned back and waited, but when Joe's attention returned to the fireplace, she said, "What's bothering you, Joe?"

"You're not surprised about the drug problem in Mellingham," he said. It wasn't a question.

"My grandson is in college. His parents want to live the good life and have everyone notice that that's what they're doing. How did I ever produce such offspring?" She shook her head. "Watching them scared me so. So I made sure that boy heard things he had to hear."

"Good for you, Liz."

"You think I'm talking about drinking and driving, but I'm not." She took a deep breath, as though she were about to yell at someone and needed the oxygen. "I know you don't mean to be patronizing, Joe, but most people don't even see me anymore. No one notices women as soon as we hit middle age. We could get away with just about anything because we don't matter to people now. I could shoplift my way up and down Newbury Street in Boston and no one would even notice. An old woman is the perfect thief. We're not noticed; we're ignored. We're not even considered people anymore.

But we're the ones who know what's really going on. We know as much as you police do, and don't you think we don't. You sit at Bingo or a bridge game or making pies for a church supper and you listen to the other women gossip. We tell each other everything, and we know the worst of what's going on no matter how delicate we try to be about it.

"What's out there these days is pretty bad. Kids have to be trained to watch out for what's out there. None of this 'own your feelings' stuff. The world's too dangerous to let them make up their own minds. I took my grandson down to the Senior Center where they had that talk on HIV spreading among retired folk in Florida. I told him the two of us were in the same boat. Well, that got his attention believe you me."

Joe opened his mouth to speak, but could only smile. She was definitely a Liz. "How did your daughter and her husband take that?"

"You're absolutely right, Joe. She was furious. 'You shouldn't be talking to him about condoms.' She thinks he's not even doing—those things, if you know what I mean."

"The parents are often the problem, especially when they think they're protecting their kids."

She hissed and waved her hand, as though driving away a fly. "She's a prude. My own daughter. She'll have to get over it if she's going to cope."

"What about Miles and Ron?"

"Ron and Miles were headed downward a long time ago. Edna was too weak, too wishy-washy to do anything about it, and I suppose she wasn't any worse than most other moms, but still, she could have done more. No one wants to believe their kid could get into trouble. And George and Paula were too blind, too wrapped up in themselves. They're not bad people, just not as smart as they might have been." She snorted. "It's an indictment, isn't it?"

"An indictment?"

"Of us. The richest, strongest country in the world, the best time to be alive in all of history, and our kids want to lose themselves in drugs." She pulled her sweater tighter across her chest.

"When you put it that way, I guess it is an indictment." He took a deep breath and changed the subject. "But I have to give them some credit."

"For what?"

"I've talked to Paula and she hasn't a bitter bone in her body, at least not that I can tell, not for Ron's friends. The word on the street is that George and Paula aren't holding any grudges."

"Is that the truth?"

"I've heard it twice today, once from Paula."

Mrs. Alesandro frowned while she thought this over. She began to chew on her lower lip while her frown deepened. "I'm very impressed, Joe, very impressed. Aren't you?" She waited for him to answer. "Aren't you the least bit surprised?"

"Some," he admitted. "Some." He changed the subject again, and this time Mrs. Alesandro let him talk for several minutes before interrupting him.

"What's really bothering you, Joe?" she asked.

George Faroli could hear the rustling and occasional bump from his den on the first floor. All day he'd been listening to his wife moving through the house on one project or another. He had thought it a good idea to stay home the day after the funeral to be with her, but as the day wore on he grew lonelier and lonelier; the pain sharpened by the pull to follow his son. George wanted to go to work in part to get away from himself, but he didn't want his employees to feel self-conscious, as he knew they would. Marley would be the most natural but he was the kind of big go-ahead-and-talk guy who sometimes scared George. He didn't want to think about what life might have been like if their positions had been reversed.

George had spent years silently resenting being tied to the family business, never having a chance to strike out on his own. Then one day, he wondered if he could—if he could strike out on his own and do something—and he realized he couldn't. His time had come and gone. Opportunities postponed year after year had vanished in a brief moment, a moment that had come and gone and he hadn't even noticed, hadn't even realized that this was the last day, the last hour and last minute when he could walk out the door and be someone else; live a different life, make the change that nagged at him in the early morning hours before he was fully awake. After that realization, he clung to his job like a sick man hanging all his hope on a second opinion. And Marley. Marley had never seemed to be anything but an ordinary employee, but he became, after that day of realization, all that George wasn't. Marley had everything a man could want, George imagined, and in his lonelier hours he built up Marley's life into unreasonable, irrational proportions. George knew his fantasies were just that, but he couldn't stop them. And because George had created this image in his mind, he couldn't bring himself to show weakness in front of Marley—or any of his other flaws. So he stayed alone, at home. In a day or two he could go in and things would be less awkward.

Paula had a different way of coping. She had gone into overdrive the minute they walked out of the funeral home.

Everywhere she looked, something needed to be done. A glance into the coat closet discovered old snow boots and a basket of mittens that needed to be sorted through, and by eleven o'clock, as George was urging her to give it all up and go to bed, she was screwing in hooks along one wall. George had long ago forgotten he'd even purchased them—another project lost in the mist of good intentions.

Once Paula got started on something, she was relentless and oblivious. George called to her a couple of times Tuesday night but knew she wouldn't answer. He was listening to the sound of his own voice with no expectations whatsoever. And today was no different. Since early morning, she had washed all the washable floors and vacuumed everything else, changed bed linen, cleaned out closets, sorted laundry into half a dozen piles. The linen closet had been stripped and re-organized. Meanwhile George grew increasingly morose.

He hadn't wanted her attention last night, but today he wanted her to look at him with the same need for comfort he knew was in his eyes. But she never even looked at him. She went on scrubbing, rummaging, arranging, while muttering one-syllable replies to his comments or questions. Perhaps her need was as great as his, but he had no drug to mask it.

"That's a silly question, George. I'm doing this because the cupboard is a mess. Has been for months. I just haven't had time."

The envelopes of old family photographs, childhood awards for most improved intermediate swimmer, best young citizen for 1981, reports from the town finance committee for 1992, and more were all jumbled together on the floor while Paula wiped down the shelves and laid down new shelf paper.

"I thought we could go for a walk," George said staring at her back. All his married life he had wanted to take care of her, be a good man in his family—he didn't know how to want anything else—but today none of that seemed to matter. He could hardly remember who he was the day before.

"I'm too tired, George." Paula shoved a box of trophies onto the top shelf.

"A short walk and I'll help you with all this." He looked at the debris of their lives scattered at his feet. Paula turned around and looked at him.

"I'm not doing too well, am I?" she said. Her hands hung limp at her sides, the veins in the backs of her hands bulging, her facing glowing with a warm sheen.

"Let's take a walk."

"When I'm coming down with a cold, I get a burst of energy, as though my body knows I have to get everything done now because I'm going to be out of commission for a while, but this—" She looked at the boxes stacked up all around her. A look of panic flitted across her face. "Oh, George."

He reached out and took both her hands in his.

"I wasn't much good last night, was I?"

"No?" He shrugged.

"I paid no attention to you. Just had to hammer away at those clothes hooks and that closet."

"It looks great."

"Sure it does." She glanced down at the roll of shelf paper. "I knew we should have made him come here." Her eyes began to fill and her cheeks and nose turned pink.

"Don't, Paula. We didn't know."

"If he hadn't gotten mixed up with that—"

"Now, Paula, easy. Edna's hurting too. Like us."

"Yes." Barely a whisper. The tears slipped down. It was all he could do to keep the rage buried; it frightened him that he could actually feel it down there bubbling, sloshing around, looking for a way out. "Nobody should have to go through this."

"We'll get through it," George promised.

"I'll make dinner. Okay?"

"No walk?" He needed to walk, to get out of the house and breathe fresh air and know the world was still out there. Inside the house, sitting in his den, he felt Ron's life—his wasted, unhappy life—reproaching him, his death closing in on him—but outside, walking in the cold autumn air and looking up at the sky, he could feel the world was whole and Ron was still a part of it somehow. Outside, walking in a neighborhood with other people living their own mixed up, blessed lives, he could feel the real world, larger than his troubles, kinder than his thoughts. Outside George didn't feel cut off from his son, severed for life from his own soul.

"I feel so raw," Paula said. "I don't think I'm ready to have people looking at me. I don't want to see their faces and know what they're thinking. I'm not ready." She wiped her hands on her slacks and stepped over the piles and left the room. She was calmer now; the period of frenetic energy was over, which meant that whatever was left undone would remain where it had fallen for another week or more. For the next few days Paula would move like an automaton through the house.

George pushed the boxes aside with his foot, and returned to the den. He closed the door and sat down at his desk. This room had been a refuge, a place of comfort and quiet over the years. The dark wood built-in shelves were filled with a motley of books and magazines, and his favorites—local history books—sat on the shelf nearest his reading chair. His old desk was much too large and awkward for today's cubicle offices but he kept it out of habit.

This was going to be a difficult period but there was no reason it had to be harder than it already was. He reached for his address book, found the number he wanted, and picked up the phone. He could hear the muted voices from a television—the evening news—as he punched in the numbers. Before the call could connect, he pressed the off button and rested the phone on its cradle. No. Not tonight. He wouldn't—couldn't—go there tonight. He looked across the desktop, over the scattered papers, the collection of clay sculptures Ron had made as a child, oil weeping from the unfired clay, at the sun-bleached color photo of Ron at age thirteen, at the broken tokens from an old Monopoly game. Then he reached for the telephone.

A single lobster boat was working its way through the inner harbor, a lone figure in a yellow slicker at the wheel. The evening mist was settling into thick layers and in an hour or so Joe wouldn't be able to see anything passing along the same channel. The evening would be cold and damp.

Joe removed his gun and holster and locked them in a desk drawer; he wasn't one for looking back on an accident that might easily have been prevented and saying, if only . . . if only. If his behavior was part paranoia, so be it.

He had his shoes and socks off and was about to undress and turn on the shower when the phone rang. Joe walked across the bedroom and lifted the receiver. A year ago he had picked up the receiver of his cordless phone to make a call and heard Mrs. Alesandro having a satisfying gossip with a neighbor. The insecurity of cordless phones came home to him with a smack—they had been talking about Gwen McDuffy—so now whenever he wanted his calls to remain private, at least on his end, he used the older phone, the one with the cracked cradle and too-short line.

"Sorry to bother you, sir." Ken Dupoulis's familiar voice floated into the room. "I was just talking to Kyla up at the hospital." Since deciding to rack up as much time as possible in the early part of the week, so he would be free to hunt on the weekends, Ken Dupoulis's social life had morphed into long telephone calls from work. Since Kyla also worked long hours at a nearby hospital, it seemed a good match. She was a good source of news too.

"And she had something to pass on," Joe said, feeling his heart sink at the thought of canceling his evening with Gwen.

"She sure does," Ken said. He was a little too eager for drama sometimes, but otherwise managed to keep his head, in Joe's view.

"What is it?"

"It's about Miles Stine."

The minute Ken said the name, Joe knew it had to be so; no surprise, just a quiet sense of validation for a prediction he had not articulated even to himself.

"You're not surprised, sir?"

"Not really. What did Kyla have to say?"

"She was working in emergency earlier today when they brought in Miles Stine's body. It was shunted off to a lab, where everyone expected an autopsy in a week or so." Ken paused to answer a muffled question. "Sorry about that."

"No problem. What about the autopsy?"

"That's just it. There may not be one."

"No autopsy? Kyla's sure about that?"

"That's why she called. She wanted to know if the rumor was true and what we were up to, more curious than anything."

"Did she say why the autopsy was cancelled? There must have been a reason unless he was under a doctor's care and there was something going on we don't know about."

"Well, that's what Kyla was thinking."

"There has to be more," Joe said.

"The doctor who saw Miles, maybe a week ago for something, was in the emergency room when he was brought in and shunted him off, then nothing happened, and that's when Kyla and the others started talking."

"There has to be more to it than that," Joe said. "We're talking an unexplained death here."

"There is more," Ken said. "And from the sounds of it, the oddest reason you can think of, sir," he said with a note of wonder in his voice. "I made Kyla repeat what she'd heard a couple of times because it made no sense if you think about it. It's only rumor, but the nurses tend to know what's going on."

"And the reason?"

"The family doctor had just seen Miles after he got out of rehab and had talked to him since then and knew he wasn't in great shape, so he's ready to certify death from an accidental fall—and this is the surprise—just to save Mrs. Stine, his mother, more grief."

"This is an act of compassion?" Joe said. "I don't believe it. The doctor is dropping the ball and pulling a few strings—he has to be—and he says it's just to save Edna Stine some discomfort. Is that what you're telling me?"

"Seems a bit of a stretch to me," Ken said, "but yes, that's it. He said he was a nice kid and he didn't see any reason for looking for something that wasn't there. A little bit on budget cuts and a little bit on time and a little bit on compassion—all rolled up into a decision not to autopsy."

"What'd you make of it?" Joe asked.

"Seems odd. I mean, I don't get the idea so many people like Mrs. Stine. I don't mean they dislike her; it's just she's not a local favorite, the kind of person people go out of their way for. All I can figure is maybe she's got connections through that clinic where she works."

"Get the name of the doctor, Ken. I'd like to talk to him before he signs off."

"Will do." Ken paused. "Any chance he did a preliminary and wants to save himself any more trouble?"

"If he did I want the report. What about the plastic bag?" Joe asked. Dupoulis perked up at Joe's tone of voice.

"We should get something there," Ken said.

"Get me what you can," Joe said. "I'll be at Gwen's if you need me."

Joe Silva pulled his Jeep Cherokee into the small parking lot behind Gwen McDuffy's apartment building. The lights were off on the first floor, which meant the owners were away at one of their never-ending card games. A few years ago, a bedridden neighbor had started a game to get friends to visit her, and the idea had taken off like crows after a crumb. Card games moved from house to house throughout Mellingham. Even a stubbed toe was enough to get a trio or quartet of visitors almost any time, day or night. Some people never seemed to need sleep.

Joe turned his key in the back door and pushed it open. From deep inside he could hear the commentator on "All Things Considered" nattering away about a photography exhibit. Joe closed the door behind him and climbed the stairs to the second floor; he called out as he crossed the hall to the kitchen and dropped his jacket onto a chair before passing on through the dining room.

"Hey, there." Gwen greeted him from the living room, where she was piling newspapers into a paper bag. "Do your newspapers multiply spontaneously the day after recycling day?"

"Mine wouldn't dare do anything like that," Joe said. "You're in a better mood."

"There must be something wrong with me." She gave him a fey smile.

"I'll take those." He picked up two paper bags and carried them to the small alcove at the top of the back stairs. The kitchen smelled of onions and spices cooking.

"I thought you'd be too busy with Miles Stine's death," Gwen said, following him into the kitchen.

"But you cooked anyway."

"I did. What can I say? I love my rut." She put her arm around his waist as he leaned down to kiss her lightly on the lips. Her mouth was soft and warm, and he felt himself tumbling.

"And the charges?" He wanted to stop himself whenever he asked that question. He was alternately amused and annoyed at how predictable human beings were, especially himself. He visited Gwen for dinner—and more—every Wednesday evening, and as soon as he kissed her, wondered where Jennie and Philip were. He wouldn't have thought he was so middle class, so bourgeois in his morals, if he hadn't watched himself again and again. But he knew it was more than that. He was well past fifty now, and though he understood and appreciated the role of convention in ordinary life, he no longer felt he had time for it. But he wasn't sure Gwen could understand that yet; she was younger, in lots of ways.

"Jennie's at her mentoring program and Philip is probably trying out a half-dozen video games between reading pages of his chemistry book." Her green eyes flashed with pain and fear.

"That's not so bad," Joe said, walking over to the stove. He restrained himself from taking lids off pots and peering in with the inane question, what is it?

"I told him we had to talk tonight."

"How did he take it?"

"He gave me a look of contempt that I thought would kill me," she said. Joe could feel his spine tingling. He had never been able to accept the disrespect children showed their parents—it was his Achilles heel.

"I'd like to get my hands on the parents of some of his friends," she said, shaking her head, arms akimbo. The old passion flared in her voice. "What the hell are these kids doing?"

"*Quem canto de galo em minha casa, sou eu,*" Joe said with a laugh.

"You're making fun of me, aren't you?" She crossed her arms.

"No, I'm not. You know I wouldn't." He put his arms around her. "Just relax. It'll all work out."

"Okay, so what does that mean? That was another one of your Portuguese sayings, wasn't it?"

"The one who sings in my house is me," Joe said.

"Meaning?"

"Meaning you rule the roost in your own home."

"You bet I do." She gave him a light pat on the chest. "And there's nothing wrong with that."

"No, there isn't." Joe moved to lean against a counter while Gwen released her emotions on the unwitting pots.

"I'm scared," she said. "As long as that's clear."

She opened a cupboard and rummaged through its contents, her back to Joe. She had told him once she wouldn't let herself go stale, no matter what happened. And she wouldn't, he knew, because of something deep within her: a drive to live, to feel and draw into her world as much as she could. It gave him that feeling of vertigo, to think of who she was behind the protective covering of her two young charges.

"So how was the rest of your day?" She turned to him when he didn't answer. "Something wrong?"

"No, nothing's wrong." He smiled at her. "Miles Stine's

death has a few surprises for us. Did you ever know him?" She shook her head. "He grew up here, got in trouble here, elsewhere, got out of rehab, seemed to be clean, but I can't say one way or the other. Ron Faroli was his best friend and got into trouble with that new painkiller, OxyContin, that some of the other towns are having so much trouble with," he quickly added when Gwen looked blank. "Someone took him to the emergency room—probably Miles—but apparently didn't have any problem himself."

"Why the other towns and not us?"

"Because our two pharmacies refuse to stock it. We got a flyer on it early on, and I made a point of talking to both pharmacists. They were glad to get the jump on what could have been a huge problem."

"Is it bad?"

"Ron Faroli died from it. And then, this."

"So it's a painkiller?" she asked while stirring.

"Potent."

"So as long as the drugstores don't stock it, we're okay?"

"Not exactly. We're behind the spindrift but still on the wave. There's nothing special about Mellingham; it just takes trends longer to reach us."

"Could Miles's death be from the same time with Ron Faroli? Maybe it didn't hit him hard right away?"

Joe shook his head.

"It couldn't be a delayed reaction?" She transferred rice to a serving bowl.

"I don't think so. I found a plastic bag filled with something; he had it hidden in some kind of box."

"Hmmm." She ladled pieces of chicken with onions into a serving bowl. "So you've really got it sorted out in your head; you just haven't been able to take the time to write it down?" Gwen turned around to look at him, the chicken sending up a

107

soft plume of steam, her green eyes sparkling. This was why he was always ready to talk things out with her. She pegged him each time.

"Is that a question?"

"Do you want a beer or wine?" She carried the plates to the kitchen table and arranged them while Joe pulled a Sam Adams from the refrigerator and opened it. He poured the beer into a glass as he walked to the table. Gwen settled on one side, touching each serving bowl as Joe slid onto the bench opposite her. The apartment was one of a half-dozen in town built during the 1930s, when kitchens came equipped with built-in kitchen tables and benches, glass-fronted cupboards, and ceiling lights in every room.

"So what are you going to do?" Gwen served herself from a dish of broccoli and cauliflower.

"I'm going to try to find out what was in the bag," Joe said.

"You mean, it wasn't obvious?" Gwen frowned and lowered her fork. "You know, if I found a bag of something near a dead body I wouldn't even wonder why it was there. But that's me. There'd be one reason only in my mind."

"And that would be?"

"Overdose. An ex-druggie, not long out of rehab? Overdose for sure. What else?" She liked the cauliflower and served herself another portion.

"I'll bet most of the town thinks just the way you do if they know about any of it—and I'll bet they do." Joe reached for his glass.

"So why are you suspicious?"

"Some of the things I've heard," Joe said.

"Like what?"

"One of the people Miles hung out with insists he was clean. He's adamant about Miles getting clean, staying clean, and even going so far as saying he wasn't going to use anything unless it was legal." He returned to his dinner, giving all his attention to Gwen's cooking.

"You know that sounds so odd," she said.

"Exactly. Why is he stressing that whatever he's doing is legal?"

"Makes you think it wasn't," she said.

"There's something else that keeps coming up," he said.

"More?"

"He seems to have been very angry recently, but no one knows why." He reached for his beer. "This is good, Gwen." He heard himself saying her name, and understood why she preferred this to the casual endearments couples adopted when they drew close; hearing your lover say your name could be far more intimate than being addressed as honey or dear.

"Good, I'm glad. Can you find out why he was angry now?"

"I can try. It might have something to do with his experiences in rehab, but he's been out long enough to not be angry in the way people have described. He's been belligerent, pushy, in your face kind of angry."

"Is that how he was before?"

"Not that we knew," Joe said, wondering if it was possible for his men to have missed something so obvious. He didn't think so.

"Maybe it was something he was taking," Gwen said, looking over the refuse of her well-prepared meal. She looked up to see Joe studying her.

"Maybe indeed." He grew thoughtful.

Gwen gave him a quick look and turned her attentions to her own cooking again.

"So what about Philip?" When she didn't answer he lowered his fork and studied her. "What's wrong, Gwen?"

"I don't want to be one more problem in your life," she said; she began to pick at a piece of chicken, turning it into threads.

"That isn't possible," he said.

"Yes, it is." She pulled her hands into her lap, and hunched her shoulders. "I couldn't stand your job, Joe. I have to be honest about that. I admire what you do, I love you for it—well, not just for that," she said with a smile, "but I couldn't come home to the same problems I work with all day long. I know you don't mean—"

"That's not how I see it," Joe said. "No one today can raise kids without having to face this stuff. That's just the way things are. I could sell cars and come home to worries about quotas and lawsuits and the rest of it."

"It's not the same." She looked wildly around the table. "I'm not sure what to do—I just want all this trouble to go away."

"Let's talk to him. Now."

"I'm having a meltdown, aren't I?"

"Yeah."

Joe drew a glass of water from the kitchen tap and walked through the apartment as he waited for Gwen to finish clearing the table. She had told him one evening, before either one knew how deeply involved they would become, that her first priority were the children—Jennie and Philip—and she simply would not consider a serious personal relationship for herself until they were safely grown. At first Joe had admired her without reservation. But now. Well, now there was a twinge. He recalled her words sometimes when he awoke late at night and heard her breathing softly beside him, the little whistle in her exhaling reminding him of his mother's cat. He and Gwen had gone too far past her initial pronouncement to discuss it, but neither one seemed ready to admit it.

He could hear her voice in the background whenever he spoke to his sisters and brothers, hear Gwen's laugh when he called his parents, see her ironic smile when he listened to his nieces and nephews talk about their school projects. The family knew there was something different in him—Gwen did too. They both knew. He'd have to make it formal soon. Hell, he wanted to make it formal now. What was he waiting for?

Philip slouched into the living room in pants that rested somewhere near his crotch and a sweatshirt that hung down to his knees. His hair was spiked because it was dirty, not because it had been arranged that way. His face was beginning to break out into a mild case of acne, and his eyes were tired and suspicious. In short, he was what passed today for a typical teenager, of the more frightening variety. His hands reaching down to his pockets, he fell into a chair.

Gwen glanced at Joe and settled herself on the sofa. Joe sat beside her.

"Your teacher called me from school today, Phil," Gwen began, leaning forward, her hands clasped in her lap. "She said your last report was signed but she thought, maybe, I should come in and talk about this one anyway." She paused. "I don't remember signing anything, Phil. But she told me what it was and then about this new one." Again, she paused, swallowed, and took a deep breath. "It's not very good."

"Yeah."

"I want to talk about your grades," she said. Joe could see how nervous she was getting, but he didn't want to interrupt her, even to offer her the small comfort of a hand on hers. She took another breath. "Look, Phil, your grades are falling apart and you're cutting classes and not studying."

"So?" He spoke without looking at her.

"I don't like what's happening," Gwen said. "Unless your grades improve and things get onto an even keel, you're going to get grounded."

"Fuck you!"

In a nanosecond Joe had crossed the short distance between them and his hand was cradling Philip's neck. Philip pressed himself into the soft upholstered chair, his eyes wide with fear and confusion. "She is your mother, Philip." Joe spoke softly, and Philip looked even more confused. "You should never speak to her like that. You love her. She loves you." His mouth open, Philip stared at Joe. "Sit up. Now." Joe stepped back. Philip pushed himself up higher in the chair, and Joe squeezed the boy's shoulder affectionately. "She is your mother. You understand."

Neither Gwen nor Philip seemed to know what to make of this turn in events. Braced for anger—to receive and to give it—they blinked at each other, then both turned to watch Joe as he returned to the sofa. He reclaimed his place on the edge of the conversation and waited for Gwen to pick up the thread of her questioning.

"That's what I wanted to say," Gwen said.

"Okay? That's it? So, can I, like, go now?"

"Not yet. I want you to tell me, Philip. What're you using?"

"I'm not doing anything illegal, Mom. Honest." The belligerence and suspicion were gone, replaced by the uncertainty of a boy repeating his arguments but without passion.

"I've heard something like that earlier today," Joe said. "Salvia?" Philip started, then nodded slowly, his eyes on Joe throughout. "Show me."

"What?" Philip glanced at his mother, then back at Joe.

"You've got it here, haven't you?" Joe said.

"You've got it here?" Gwen repeated in a thin, high voice. Joe placed his hand on hers.

"Some. Just a little left over from the other night."

"What other night?" Joe asked.

"Tuesday."

"When you were out with your friends?" Gwen asked. "You said you were going out to see Chandra. She was babysitting."

"I did, but. . . . but she wasn't interested."

"Show me," Joe said. Philip pulled himself out of the chair and led Joe to his room, a small bedroom at the front of the apartment, just off the living room. He pulled open a desk drawer and extracted a cookie tin. He pried off the top and held the tin out to Joe. Joe picked up a small plastic bag with some dried, crushed leaves. "I'll take this, if you don't mind."

"It's not illegal," Philip said.

"Where did you get it?" Joe turned the bag over in his hands.

"I don't remember."

"Philip."

"I know my rights," Philip began.

Joe gave him an amused look. "I'm sure you do, Phil. But I don't want to hear anything like that out of you. It's not necessary." Joe shook the bag and watched the crushed leaves tumble and rearrange themselves. "Who sold it to you?"

Philip stared at the bag, as though the little treasure were about to slip out of his hands forever. He glanced up at Gwen hovering in the doorway, then at Joe, who loomed over him. The boy's nose began to run, and he swiped at it with his hand. "It was Miles Stine. He said it was legal," he said, his voice beginning to rise.

Joe turned around to look at Gwen. "He may be telling the truth," he said to her. "Come on back out into the living room, Philip. I think you can help me."

Chapter 5

Thursday Morning

The telephone rang four times between seven and seven-thirty in the Mellingham Police Station, prompting Joe Silva to set down his morning coffee and roll his chair to the doorway. He called out Steven Maxwell's name and slid back in.

Maxwell had asked to go back onto a day shift as soon as his daughter was old enough to go to school in the morning. At least that was the reason he gave Joe, who thought the other man probably got tired of trying to match small socks in a myriad of colors and get them onto smaller feet. In the last three or four years Joe had learned, thanks to Maxwell, that not all shades of red and pink could be worn together, among other mystifying facts of outfitting little girls. Maxwell appeared in the doorway.

"Local reporter," Maxwell began without preamble. "He thinks there might be something in the deaths. At least that's how he's putting it."

Joe nodded. "I was wondering when we'd hear from them."

"I told them neither death was more than an accident as far as we knew," Maxwell said.

But the reporter got more than that, Joe knew. He had given Maxwell the job of PR officer because he always looked like he was recalling a funny story. He was always on the verge of a smile, and remembered the odd bits of information about people that made them feel important, special, singled out for all the right reasons. When he talked to reporters or visiting officials from other parts of the country, he gave everyone the feeling he was trying to give them a little something more than what was on the agenda. He was probably giving them less, Joe mused, but no one else knew that.

"How long are we going to hold onto that?" Maxwell asked.

Joe glanced at his phone with the red light blinking. "I'm on hold for the boy's doctor. The nurse is tracking him down now." Joe sighed.

"Sir?"

"Hmm?"

"They're bound to find out about Miles's personality change—all that sudden anger."

"I know." Joe slid back into his office just as a voice came onto the speakerphone. He picked up the receiver and heard the doctor on the line. "Dr. Meyers?"

"What's your concern about this patient?" Dr. Myers began. Brusque, in his forties, Dr. Andrew Myers belonged to that generation which had enjoyed a smooth ride for almost his entire career. He had never known much of a struggle; coasting through college on grade inflation and beginning his medical practice in the booming eighties. Since he had never struggled, he regarded most of the world's population as losers. He annoyed the hell out of Joe, who was afraid if he had a serious car accident he'd find himself in the semi-competent hands of someone he'd been rude to.

"He died just days after his friend, Ron Faroli, died from taking OxyContin," Joe said.

"Hmm. Yes, I know."

"Did you know him?"

"The Faroli man? No. You think there's something odd about his pal dying about the same time?" Dr. Myers spoke with that distracted air that said he had something else going on, and Joe heard pages rustling in the background. A voice murmured, and the doctor gave an okay.

"Look, Dr. Myers. There was a bag of something that looked like you might smoke it," Joe said.

"Well, there you have it. Anything else?"

"Did you look at the body?"

"What are you asking?"

"It seems there might be something else going on."

"I've gone over the paperwork that came along with him. It looks in order."

"Are you planning on certifying this as an accidental death?" Joe was still looking for the one spot that would prick the doctor's interest.

"That's the general idea. He fell out of the window, from the sounds of it, in a fit of anger or intoxication."

"Have you looked at the body?"

"I was Miles's doctor. Both he and Ron came through here a week ago. Maybe more."

"I mean yesterday or today. An autopsy."

"Do you really think that's necessary? I mean, think how long that could take? Look, Chief Silva. Haven't the parents been through enough?"

"He only has a mother as far as I know. Mrs. Edna Stine."

"I was thinking of the Farolis too."

"Because of . . ." Joe left the sentence unfinished.

"George is a great guy. He's right about how hard this kind of thing can be on other parents, on Paula, for instance. Better to get it over with."

"You've spoken with George then?"

"I think that was pretty decent of him, calling. He didn't have to take the time. After all—well, look—"

"After all?" Joe said.

"Well, according to my information, Miles was—" Dr. Myers stopped in the middle of his sentence. "There was that bag with him."

"The bag of unidentified materials. It should have been turned over to the state lab for testing," Joe said. He heard a heavy sigh.

"A small evidence bag?"

"That's it. Any idea what was in it?"

"No. But you think—"

Joe waited. The other man's breathing was steady. A paper crinkled.

"I'd better track it down." The doctor sighed. "I won't call George Faroli back. I'll just take a look for myself."

"How soon can you get the body over for an autopsy?"

"I'll call them now." His voice dropped and Joe could hear him writing, and then speaking to someone nearby. "I'm sorry, Chief. I didn't realize . . ."

So, thought Joe, the man might be human after all.

Chandra Stine was known in Mellingham, when she was known at all, as the quiet one in the Stine family and the local townspeople speculated at length on the reason. Any explanation would suffice as long as it was mildly interesting and kept the conversation moving; no matter that it veered from the obvious—she was a teenager who knew when to lie low.

The speculation wasn't necessarily unkind. In a small town, everyone had to accept the inevitability of being the subject of discussion. So far, despite her infamous brothers and sometimes cranky mother, Chandra Stine had escaped with most of her reputation intact. She was shy and laconic.

But the flip side of that perception was also inevitable. There would come a time when the tall teenage girl who held back—standing along a wall twirling a lock of hair around her finger while she sized up the others in the room, ignoring the way her glasses slid down her nose—would push herself away from the wall and demand center stage, or at least a place on it. The time would come when she would think about putting herself first instead of crouching outside the line of fire.

On Thursday morning that time had come.

Chandra Stine paced between two trees planted like sentinels on the sidewalk outside the Community Center while she waited for someone (she had expected Denny Clark) to open up and turn on the heat. The late night chill had left lacelike sheets of ice in small puddles, and they crinkled like breaking glass as early morning commuters hurried past her to the train station. Sodden, rotting fall leaves, turning brown in the gutter, were dusted with icy dew and also crinkled underfoot, but no one else seemed to notice. For Chandra, the noise was unnerving, sounding like a world shattering around her. She was nervy this morning, edgy and nervy and very likely to say the wrong thing. She would have to be sure to say as little as possible but still get her point across.

She knew Ann Rose had a meeting scheduled for eight-thirty and liked to arrive early, so Chandra paced between the two trees, scuffing up the sloped macadam around the tree roots and down to the level sidewalk again, pacing back and forth; to the extent she could remain calm enough to walk in a measured manner. It was as though all the energy suppressed by a wariness of her brothers' distorted lives had at long last broken through and her body could barely channel it out into the world. She pulled off her backpack and clutched it to her chest, bouncing on the balls of her feet and picking at the nylon seams as she kept an eye on the front door barely ten feet away from her.

"Good morning, Chandra."

"Oh!" Surprised, Chandra spun around as Ann Rose passed her and unlocked the front door. Chandra scurried in behind her.

"Oh, Mrs. Rose. I'm so glad you're early," she said following the older woman through the large room as she flipped on lights, checked the heat, pushed in a chair, collected a two-day old newspaper and dropped it into a recycling bucket, turned on a light, threw away a dirty napkin, and headed on to the galley kitchen at the rear. Chandra followed her with halting, mincing steps. "Oh, Mrs. Rose."

"Chandra." Ann turned around to face her. "Aren't you supposed to be on your way to school? I thought you told me you had an early morning class."

"I do, and I'm late but I'll be all right." Chandra stared at the older woman, leaning forward, willing her to understand without having to be told.

"Did you want to see me?" Ann asked.

The teenager confronted her destiny in a sudden unexpected moment: a turning she thought she would sneak up on and snatch, like a child capturing a butterfly, gently, easily, with nothing to keep the butterfly from continuing its fluttering within her cupped hands. But of course, life wasn't like that. "Chandra?" Ann repeated.

"It's my mother," Chandra began, still clutching her backpack. She swallowed hard.

"Oh goodness. Is she all right?"

"Yes, she's fine. I mean, she's not hurt or anything like that."

"Well, good. That's a relief. I'm so sorry, Chandra. You've been through so much."

"I meant—" She halted, looked around at the large, airy space. "She's very—ah—thinking about Miles and of course it all brings back Jacko." This wasn't at all what she meant to say. She started out with a clear image in her mind of how this conversation would progress, but then words came out of her and veered off into another direction. It didn't make sense to have one thing in her head and another thing taking shape in front of her. Her language was letting her down.

"Yes?"

"She takes things hard." No, that wasn't right either.

"Both of her sons. Your brothers." Ann placed a hand on the girl's arm and squeezed. "It's hard to keep going but I guess you just have to. You know, I'd be glad to help if I can."

"Would you?" Chandra thought Ann Rose was the most wonderful person she had ever known.

"Of course, dear. It's hard to keep going when something so awful happens, but you have to. Your brother wouldn't want you to lose all the good things in your own life," Ann said.

"Yes, you do have to keep going, don't you?" She took a step closer to Ann.

"I'm sure your mother is very proud of you and the way you're handling all this."

"I guess so." Chandra had stopped thinking about how her mother viewed her years ago, and hearing the idea come out of Ann Rose's mouth made it seem even stranger.

"Are you keeping up with things in school?"

"I'm trying to," Chandra said. "So far I'm okay."

"If you need any help, you know you can always let us know here and we should be able to help you out."

"Really?"

"Of course, Chandra. And don't be afraid to ask."

"I'm in a theater group. At school. We're doing Dickens's *Christmas Carol*."

"How lovely." Ann smiled. She was used to teenagers and she thought Chandra a particularly nice specimen.

"I have a speaking part," Chandra said, looking directly at Ann. "One line, that's all. But it's an important one. That's why I didn't want to give it up. It's important."

"I'm sure it is," Ann said. "And you should continue with it. It'll be a good distraction for you. That's the kind of thing that gets you outside yourself and you'll cope better while you're doing this." She reached for the coffee pot, found that it had been washed the night before, and put it down, and reached next for the coffee filters.

"We had to sign on in pairs."

"That's nice." She plopped the coffee filter into the basket, and began to measure out enough coffee for a full pot.

"Pairs. Two of us. We had to sign on in pairs. One student. One parent." She stared at Ann, willing her to understand.

"That's nice." She slid the basket into its slot and reached for the pot. "Probably a very good idea, too. As I recall that play calls for a lot of actors."

"That's why we had to sign on in pairs."

"Good thinking on the director's part."

"Well, actually we had to sign on as one student and one adult, actually. Doesn't have to be a parent. Has to be an adult. It's because of the large number of roles—the director has to make sure he has enough people—you know all those parts to fill." She looked even harder at Ann.

"Oh, I see." Ann nodded. "I see." She frowned. "And since your brother's death, your mother probably won't want to think about being in a play."

"Yeah, like that. She can't even focus right now. It's very confusing at home."

"I'm so sorry, Chandra. That must be very disappointing for you." Ann filled the pot with water.

"Mrs. Rose?" Chandra took a step closer. "It can be any adult."

"That's nice."

"And you're the right age."

"Excuse me?"

"You're the right age. You're an adult. And you're smart. You can remember when to come on stage and when to stay in the wings and stuff like that."

"Well, thank you, Chandra. That's very nice of you, but I don't think I could—"

"Yes, you could. I checked. I wasn't sure what to do, and I thought maybe I could talk one of my friends into it, but the permission form said it had to be another adult. But it can be any adult. Anyone I know who is willing to make a commitment to the whole play. I made sure it could be any adult just so you wouldn't be embarrassed in case someone said no. I didn't want your feelings to be hurt."

Ann shook her head. "Chandra, that's very considerate of you, I'm sure, and I'm very flattered that you'd want me, I really am, but I couldn't possible agree."

"Why not?"

"Well. . . ." Ann began to look confused and stuttered. "I can't just show up, Chandra," she began. "I suppose you really want to do this. Couldn't you wait until next year when things have settled down?"

"I may not be here next year," Chandra said, and began to wring her hands.

"Oh, Chandra," Ann said, "I can see it means a lot to you."

"Please, Mrs. Rose. This is the only thing I've ever wanted this much. I've been planning this all year since last Christmas when I helped with the costumes. It took me months to talk my mother into it and now she can't even remember who Dickens is."

"Yes, I can understand that," Ann said.

"This is the only thing I ever really want to do. No one really understands—well, maybe Mr. Clark—but I'm going to act in college. It's all I think about all day long. I make up scenes of me in one play, then another—all the different roles. I try out accents. Meryl Streep works really hard at it—and I listen to people—the way they talk. I get the sound, the way words bump along in different people's sentences. People have such odd ways of talking. I try to pick up as much as I can and imitate them, get inside the way they think so that their words come out sounding like them. It's really interesting."

"I'm sure it is." Ann looked a little taken aback by all this passion. "I'm glad Mr. Clark has been supportive."

"Huh? Oh, yeah. He thinks I should do anything that takes me out of my family situation. I think he really understands how things are for me." She grew thoughtful, tilting her head to one side and chewing on a cuticle; she dropped her hand and wiped her fingers on her slacks, pulling in her chin and making her soft neck crinkle.

"That's good you feel you can confide in him."

"Oh, I don't. I didn't mean that at all." Chandra straightened up, shaking her head. "He just started talking to me a few months back about how I should stay away from Miles and his friends and go in a different direction." She checked her fingers and the offending cuticle.

"Did he now?"

"Yeah, like he thought I was going to do something dumb,

124

and besides Miles is my brother. I resented it a lot, totally huge. I mean, like, you know—it's personal."

"Yes."

"But after a while I was sorta glad." She snorted softly. "It means someone understands how it has to be for me. This is absolutely perfect for me too."

"I've never been on a stage before," Ann said. "I'm not sure how I'd feel about that."

"It won't be hard. They have people to direct us and everything. Besides, I already know my line. You wouldn't have to worry about that at all. Really."

"Well, that's impressive. You've already studied your part?"

"Oh, yes. I'm so ready." Chandra's face turned a warm pink.

"Well, aren't you good!" Ann said.

"And they have the costumes and the makeup. There's practically no rehearsals. It's so easy. There's nothing to it. It means so much to me—"

"Well . . ."

"Mrs. Rose, this is everything to me." She squeezed her backpack so tightly against her chest that the seams cut deep into her smooth soft skin, but she didn't notice any of it.

"Oh, Chandra." Ann sighed, looking anything but happy. "I suppose it's doable."

"Oh, thank you, Mrs. Rose. Thank you, thank you. This means more to me than you'll ever know." With that rush of heartfelt gratitude, she bolted for the door. "I'm late for class," she called out.

The Community Center was usually humming by mid-morning as people dropped by for a free cup of coffee, to make a phone call, or just see what was going on. Joe Silva knew that Bernard would be there until he found a job; his sponsor was the active kind, full of ideas of how a newcomer should spend his time, and Bernard was the passive kind, in need of a push.

Bernard mumbled a greeting as Joe approached the table, and continued pouring sugar into his coffee. Joe and Bernard were alone in the coffee corner. Across the room Ann Rose was thumbing through a large book, her brow furrowed. Nearby someone—Denny Clark, it sounded like—was setting up a meeting on the telephone. In our little bubbles, Joe thought. People die for lack of human contact, lack of feeling cared for, but put us together and we hide in our separate worlds. Busy with nothing, really.

"My sponsor said he could get me into Solidarity House down in Dorchester but—"

"But what?" Joe asked.

"Ron said this was a nice town and I'd be okay here. Him and Miles knew the ropes around here and I figured I'd be better off someplace where I had friends." He sipped his coffee while Joe mixed a cup for himself.

"So you and the other two were close," Joe said.

"Oh yeah," Bernard said, as though challenging a particularly heinous idea. "We were together all the time. Like that, we were." He brought his fingers into a tight fist and clenched it in front of himself.

"But not the night the two of them took OxyContin?"

"Well," Bernard glanced at him.

"You don't have anything to worry about. I just want to know what happened."

"I left early. Sort of hustled out. They didn't offer me any."

"You were there with them that night? You and Ron and Miles?"

126

"Yeah. We'd been hanging together. Had a pizza and just hanging. It was shitty out. Rainy. Cold. So I was just going on about whatever and then they wasn't talking and then they just asked me where I had to meet someone, so I figured it was like that. They had something and they weren't sharing."

"Short supply?"

"Yeah."

"Anything else?"

"No."

"Miles wasn't angry about something?"

"Nah, not then. He was the way he always was. He had a—" He looked at Joe and paused.

"Go on."

"Nothing. He wasn't angry or nothing. He was the way he always was."

"Nothing unusual in his behavior? Nothing he might have been hiding?"

Bernard shook his head. "They were tight. I knew it. I wasn't so close to them."

"Anyone else with you that night?"

"Not after the pizza."

"Who was with you for pizza?"

"That big guy. Tiny. He came over and had a piece. He only had a couple of dollars so he didn't get one for himself."

"That it?"

"Yeah. Just the four of us for pizza. Then Tiny went off somewheres." He began to rub his left hand down the front of his jacket again and again. His fingers grew stiff and his entire hand seemed a clump of flesh and bone, nothing that had ever been useful, with feeling. It was something Joe had noticed about some addicts when they became distressed: they lost coordination in a non-dominant limb, or stumbled more, or revived a childhood stutter. Joe waited while Bernard regained his self-control. The cup in his right hand trembled, a few drops sloshing over the side. He put the cup down and picked up a stray crumpled napkin and wiped up the coffee spill on the table.

"You must have looked back on that night thinking you were pretty damn lucky." Joe spoke softly, unsure how this young man would react to his probing.

"Lucky? They're both dead. I have no friends now." He picked up the cup and gulped down his hot coffee, oblivious to its temperature. "I have to go." Without another glance at Joe, Bernard tossed his cup in the trash and bolted away from the table. With jerky, awkward steps, he crossed the room, his fists in his coat pockets and his shoulders hunched over.

Steve Dolanetti tugged at his shirt collar until it settled into an even band of blue around his neck, above the dark navy of his sweater. As he turned this way and that in front of the mirror, he pondered the blue handkerchief just peeking out of his back pocket. Too much, he decided, and pulled the offending item from his pocket and tossed it into a tall bureau standing in one corner.

This will have to do, he decided. He kicked the toe of one sneaker against his ankle, then switched feet and did the same again with his other foot; he was stalling. He hated running shoes—and running—and even long walks in the bracing air made him feel nauseated. The great American drive for health seemed to him an obsession bordering on mania: a new form of mental illness that would rise to the top of the list—or page one of the DSM IV—if so many health care professionals weren't themselves so infected with the disease. How else could one explain the bizarre behavior of a man who chose to race around the neighborhood in the early morning darkness instead of enjoying a cup of homemade chai and eggs benedict in a dining area set with the best in china from a George Jensen gallery? They were nuts. That's all there was to it.

Steve leaned on the doorknob, looking back at his small domain. It represented a choice, as he constantly reminded himself. Boston was too stressful for him now—he needed calm, and that required distance. He had achieved both, along with a new kind of stress. He supposed it was inevitable—the fates laughing at him. Steve took one last look at himself in the mirror.

"Well, nipples to the wind," he said and headed out the door.

A private person who found it easier to entertain an audience of one or ten than to engage in honest conversation no matter how mundane, Steve had settled into a quiet life in Mellingham expecting to remain private, unknown, in control. But just as that veneer began to crack and crumble in a particularly contentious AA meeting, Tiny Morley, in his quiet way, had turned out to be a stand-up guy.

Tiny. With his short hair that at first made Steve nervous and edgy. All he could think of was Skinhead, neo-Nazi. The words hammered in his head his first few weeks in Mellingham—disrupting conversations in the checkout line at the convenience store on the other side of the post office, tripping him up as he strode into the parking lot or across the street. He'd take a deep breath and tell himself it was nothing, just a bad hair day and it would grow out—he could wait. And then in more rational moments, he could laugh at his own absurdities.

Not every baldy was a neo-Nazi. And wasn't it his moral duty to challenge stereotypes and heinous assumptions? Of course it was.

Then one day Tiny surprised him, and when Steve thanked him afterwards, Tiny nodded his big head and blinked a few times and said, "Wanna drink?" Steve went along to the Loblolly Bar, where both men had Cokes, and Steve wondered what he was doing in a bar with a man who looked like a lost biker. He'd never been into the leather scene—masochism had no appeal for Steve—but as Tiny began to talk about his troubles in Mellingham (and life in general), Steve began to listen. What he expected never happened—Tiny never rushed to let Steve know that he was straight, had a dozen girls in his past and one or two in his present. He was not aggressively insecure in his heterosexuality. Nor did Steve feel the need to reassure Tiny that he, Steve, wasn't the least bit interested in him sexually or romantically—even if truer words etc., etc. Steve relaxed. Tiny was different. He was okay.

Steve was just heading up the long hill to the beach when he felt the breeze following him. He glanced up at the sky, hoping it wasn't going to rain—there were a dozen places where Tiny could discreetly park his car with little fear of the police pushing him out—at least as long as no one complained. Steve estimated that he could check out most of them in a three or four hour walk, but not if it rained. He had worked into his schedule a quick stop at the Community Center, for a short visit with his social worker, but that was mostly for the sake of appearances. He knew where his life was going, and he was glad to have help in keeping up with all the documentation he needed for his disability and other programs, but his mind was elsewhere.

Steve couldn't figure out where Tiny had disappeared to or why. His regular schedule had just evaporated over the last twenty-four hours, leaving Steve hanging, literally, out the window waiting for his ride to the mall. And then came the

rumor that there was something odd about Miles's death yesterday morning. It made everyone uneasy. Steve couldn't sit
still and wait; he had to locate Tiny if only for his own peace
of mind.

Not at the beach. Steve stumbled up the rocky cliff path
and along to the first wooden bench. He glanced up and
down the long, white beach, but saw no one, not even a retired couple walking their dog. The wind cut through his
sweater and he felt the uncontrollable need to sneeze just because he was out in all this raw air. He tickled the top of his
palate with his tongue to keep from sneezing and took three
deep breaths. It worked, but there was still no Tiny. He
slouched down the low hill back to the road. A few minutes
later he was heading down an old dirt road, running off West-
erly Road, that led to an abandoned construction site. A high-
flying executive had started the mansion of his dreams only to
lose it all in an investment scandal that left him nearly broke
and many of his new best friends "embarrassed." At another
time Steve might have devoted a good twenty minutes to a
satisfying fantasy in which he got even for all the little people
who were hurt—the carpenters who weren't paid, the hard-
ware store stuck with two dozen special order door pulls—
just by his own cleverness, but today he didn't have the heart
even to put together a few choice words about all of that. He
only wanted to know if Tiny and his station wagon were concealed behind a pile of rubble.

Nope. Nothing at all.

Steve swore. It would be just like Tiny to have discovered
a new spot and have said nothing to anyone; to keep it just for
himself.

No, it wasn't, he admitted. It wasn't anything like him.
Tiny was an open book. That was his problem—he'd never
developed a protective social skin, and he needed one; lordie

did he ever, almost more than anyone else Steve had ever known.

Steve made his way through back lots and little used garages behind businesses. His legs ached, his hands were cold. Tiny had been worried about Miles, and now Steve was worried about Tiny.

A few minutes before noon Steve turned down Delmar Street and headed for the Community Center.

Joe Silva leaned into the doorway of Denny Clark's office, expecting to see the other man sitting in his chair, but instead the chair seemed to wiggle on its own. Joe drew the obvious conclusion and knocked again, calling out Denny's name. The office desk chair rolled away from the desk and Denny emerged.

"What?" he began. "Lost my damn mouse." He pulled himself up with the aid of the desk edge and dusted off his knees. Then he reached down and picked up a thin electrical cord from which dangled the aptly named item. Denny scowled at it and laid it on the desktop. "They're as much trouble as the real ones sometimes." He motioned Joe to a seat and dropped into his own chair, his legs and arms sprawling. Khaki slacks, white shirt, beige sweater and limbs flailing—he looked like a potato left to sprout its waxy yellow roots in a dark drawer. "So what's up, Joe?"

"What's the word about Miles?" Joe asked. Denny was one of those people always willing to talk—just give him a topic and let him go. Except sometimes. Joe pondered the discrepancies as Denny dug into the rich soil of memory fertilized by imagination.

"Well, it takes all that effort to get clean. You know, the guys go into a pretty intensive program—in some of them they're never alone. They're in group after group after group.

All day long. There's no escape, no afternoon in front of the tube. No driving around letting off steam. I mean, you know, these guys face some pretty intense work. And it's not easy. The second anyone suspects any BS they're all over you. That can be frightening to someone who's been hiding from himself for years. Pretty scary. Tough guys who are basically strangers to themselves—they've been numbed by drugs for years—they have to face being human and how it feels and that's frightening. It makes some of them real angry." He shook his head. On a roll, Joe thought. On a roll, propelled by the sound of your own voice. "Real angry. And that's their first experience with feelings."

"Angry enough to kill?"

"Whoa?" Denny stared at him, his face blank. Joe repeated his question. Denny ran his tongue over his lips before swallowing hard. "Is that what you think?" His voice was low, soft.

"I'm wondering what you think, what the rumors are."

Denny glanced at the open door just as Joe reached over and shut it.

"I never thought about it," Denny said. He swiveled in his chair and turned to look out the window. Outside, the gray November day sharpened the outlines of the old train station across the tracks. A young couple dressed in jeans was skylarking on the platform; one or the other peering down the track for the anticipated train. "I see people as angry as they can be sometimes, but I've never thought, this was it. This one's going to snap." He turned back to Joe.

"Did you ever hear anyone express any animosity toward either one of them—Ron Faroli or Miles Stine?" Denny's eyes widened in shock for a few seconds. He shook his head from side to side.

"But that doesn't mean anything," Denny said. "Anyone

who's been a user knows a lot of unsavory people. It's the way things are. Both of them could have run afoul of some pretty scary types."

"Tell me about them and their friends."

"You know most of it."

"Refresh my memory."

Denny glanced at Joe. "Let me see. Ron Faroli was older than Miles. Went to school here. His parents had plans for him—not the usual, following on with the store," Denny began. He spoke in a smooth narrative, as though he had prepared this presentation, and Joe was struck by how clearly and deeply Denny obviously thought about this group of visitors to the Community Center. He described Ron's unremarkable life and his entry into a Boston college, neither prestigious nor marginal, and the beginning of the end in his mother's eyes.

"Paula felt strongly about what? Who he was hanging out with? What he was doing?"

"Yeah, all that. She started nagging him to live at home, keep up with his old friends, see more of the family. That sort of thing."

"How do you know this?"

"He complained about it regularly in some of the groups. He came to AA sometimes, and sometimes NA over at the church."

"So his issue was his family."

"But it went deeper than that," Denny said.

"Go on."

Denny lightly clasped his hands in front of him. "If Ron had been one of a large family, he would have been the black sheep. There was something wrong with him."

"Like what?"

"He had no feelings for anything. He could hurt people

without any sense of remorse. He gave me the creeps sometimes."

"And this nagging drove him deeper into whatever he was
toying with," Joe said. "And Miles?"

"Miles. Not much hope there. You've met his mother?"
Denny glanced up. Joe nodded. "She'd drive anyone around
the bend. Shouldn't say it, I know. Don't mean to be unkind." He paused and cleared his throat, as though about to
begin again.

"You were saying about Miles," Joe said.

"Yeah. Ron and Miles were friends for years. Don't know
how they first got together, but it was a known thing—they
were pals. I sort of think they met in school here, but they
wouldn't have been friends back then. At least I don't think
they were. Anyway, it could have been here in town they first
met. Could have been in Boston. But once someone starts
using, you may not know, I may not know, the family for sure
probably doesn't know—not right at first, anyway— but the
guys on the street know. They could have been friends for
years and most of us here in town wouldn't have known."

Joe scribbled a note in his notebook and leaned forward in
his chair. His belt felt tight and he was tired, not from any
physical exertion or from lack of sleep. He felt weary. There
was something draining about listening to stories of lives
wasted.

"That's a blow," Denny said. "It's hard for any family to
accept. At first they feel foolish, can't believe their child
could be doing something like that."

"Then what?" Joe wanted to hear where Denny would go
in his reverie.

"Anger, denial, accusations. The works." His breath was
heavy, his eyebrow twitched. "And then they want to know
why the police didn't stop it. Half the time people are furious

with you and you go out there and fight for them anyway. I guess this is what it means to serve and protect."

"That's exactly what it means," Joe said as he got to his feet.

Chapter 6

Thursday Afternoon

Joe Silva believed in going about things methodically, but it was getting harder and harder. The two deaths in two days had been so obviously accidental on the surface that he had little, actually no, evidence to justify a full-scale investigation.

"We're not making much progress, are we?" Ken Dupoulis said. He'd finished a submarine sandwich some time ago but still looked hungry.

"Two men who both claimed to have gotten clean die within a matter of days of each other, and everyone is surprised. It's unnerved some of Miles's friends, that's for sure," Joe said. He tipped a coffee cup toward him, looked at the now cool dark liquid at the bottom, and seemed to decide against it, pushing the cup away. It was time for lunch, and he was torn between heading off at once for something to eat and following through on some of his ideas.

"You don't really want to say what you're thinking, do you?" Ken said.

"Let's try out some of my wilder thoughts," Joe said, swinging around to face Ken in his chair. "Let's say that someone is out to get the druggies in this town. Just suppose," Joe added when he saw the look of consternation on Ken's face. "Who are the likely candidates and why?"

"Users or executioners?"

"Both."

"That could be a long list, Joe. I mean, that five-thirty AA meeting is pretty crowded. You're not thinking everyone there could be vulnerable?"

"Probably not everyone, but I want them checked out. I want to hear what they think about this business with Ron and Miles. Talk to any of the members who knew them."

"That's a lot of people." Ken paused. "That's maybe a dozen."

"I'll agree with that." Joe waited. "And the executioners?"

"No one name pops up first, but I suppose there could be a lot of people with motives," Ken began. "I mean, if you look at the big picture, lots of families have lost someone to drugs or because of drugs. Think of the Kenningtons—their daughter was killed by a DUI."

"Yes, and her father was barely coherent at the trial."

"And those kids cruising in Boston last winter got pretty beat up when they landed in the wrong club."

"I was thinking about less obvious people also," Joe said.

"Meaning someone who doesn't stand out," Ken said, nodding. "Someone we would never pick up on unless he or she did something to tip their hand. "You're thinking of someone in particular," Ken said.

"I'm starting to think of a lot of people, but I've got one on my mind for this afternoon, that's for sure."

"Who?"

"Denny Clark." Joe thought about his earlier conversations with the man.

"Any particular reason?"

"Something about how he was talking this afternoon. I'm wondering if I missed something on his resume."

"That's easy enough to check, if you want me to get on it. Anyone else?"

"Last week, when I called all the pharmacies about OxyContin, they were adamant they didn't stock it in the store—all the chains around here had the same answer," Joe said.

"We don't have any independents left, do we? Maybe one in the area. Twenty minutes from here."

"That's right."

"And there's only one other possibility," Ken said. "The Mellingham Clinic." He shook his head doubtfully. "They keep a pretty low profile. But I suppose they could carry OxyC, like a drugstore."

"The secretary I spoke with last week insisted that they don't," Joe said. "It was a brief conversation, just checking on the basic facts, but I keep wondering. The director was out all last week, so I didn't get to talk to him, find out if he had any ideas on the subject." Joe stood up and reached for his jacket. "He's back late tonight, so I'm supposed to see him tomorrow morning. Call over and confirm the appointment, would you, Ken?"

"Sure thing."

"Right now, I'm going to track down that feeling about Denny Clark."

Joe recalled that initial interviews for the new director—including that with Denny Clark—had been conducted partly in Town Hall, to accommodate certain committee members on tight schedules. Gordon Davies, Town Clerk at the time, had not wanted to wander far from his office and had prevailed upon the others, including Ann Rose, to meet in a basement conference room. The committee members had further accommodated themselves by keeping their files of resumes in a little-used file cabinet and Joe had a suspicion as well as a hope that the files were still there. As he headed over to the Town Hall, he remembered them all sitting around the conference table: Gordon Davies, tall and gangly, with his moth-eaten beige sweater tucked into his pants, ready to shoot down any sign of enthusiasm before the candidate had duly earned it; and the board member who showed up in a silk suit and kept checking her watch for the first half hour of the meeting.

The pneumatic door wheezed shut as Joe entered the stairwell to the basement in Town Hall. He pushed open the conference room door and crossed to the opposite corner where a series of file cabinets held the reports and records of town commissions with no offices of their own—the arts council, beautification, housing initiatives, volunteer clean-up brigades. Joe pulled out the top drawer in the first cabinet and riffled through the papers. Nothing. He shut the drawer and pulled out the next one, wondering that none of them were locked. Security in town offices had been a major topic when he had first arrived, and he had spent considerable time trying to persuade the board of selectmen and a few others that greater effort should be made to secure town offices and records. Some efforts had been made, but not all those Joe had thought necessary. He worked his way through the files. Somewhere along the line he had changed, given in, capitulated, been outfoxed, and he hadn't even noticed. Town Hall was little more security-conscious now than when he'd first arrived. He slammed the drawer shut, its metal frame sliding smoothly into place. In the hall outside, three women burst into noisy chatter as they left for lunch.

Joe found what he was looking for in the middle of the last cabinet, second drawer from the top. A file labeled in tidy small lettering "Com.Ctr.Appls. 2000" bulged with papers in various pale colors as well as white. He pulled out the file and placed it on the conference table: he'd forgotten there had been a large number of applicants. Gordon Davies had remarked on it.

"Are we in a recession or something?" Gordon asked.

Ann Rose had recomposed herself to deal with this onslaught. "We're fortunate to have so many applications."

"Probably think we're not smart enough to see through them," Gordon growled. "People looking for a sinecure."

"We want to like at least one of them, Gordon," Ann said through clenched teeth. "That's what we're here for." Joe recalled the familiar chuckle that went around the table. The discussions had been lengthy, mostly to satisfy Gordon and two board members, but most committee members had picked out their favorites on the first day. A few had been sidelined by poor references, but Sergeant Dupoulis had vetted the finalists and noticed nothing suspicious in any of the applications. Joe turned over one page after another until he came to Denny Clark's—Dennis J. Clark. Joe drew out the cover letter and resume and returned the rest of the file to the cabinet.

For the next several minutes Joe studied Denny Clark's resume, considering the earlier career steps of the executive director—counselor, manager, lecturer on community activism. There was something about his earlier conversations with Denny that told Joe something was amiss but the resume seemed ordinary, the record of a man who had made it to the top of a low hill in his neighbor's back yard. Always up to something, Joe concluded, dropping the resume on the table. The papers floated away. Then Joe reached out his hand and slapped it down onto the sheets, pulling them closer to him. He stared at the record of Denny's job change in the early 1990s—a lateral move, his only one.

Five minutes later, Joe was in his office, on the telephone

to a halfway house in Connecticut, wondering whether or not anyone would remember a counselor from over ten years ago.

"You probably should talk to—" the man's voice paused, hummed "—Ralph Patch is probably the one to talk to." Joe had explained his inquiry into the employment of a man some years back, but there was no "ah ha" of recognition. Joe waited while a call for Ralph echoed in the background.

"Yo!"

Joe waited, growing less optimistic.

"Yo!" The voice was loud. "Ralph Patch here."

Joe introduced himself and again explained his inquiry into Denny Clark's employment. Silence. Joe waited.

"Lemme look here. You wanna wait?" Ralph sounded tired, as though life in a halfway house was exhausting.

"Sure." Joe began to sign letters while he listened to sounds of humming from the receiver.

"Got it," Ralph said. "Dennis J. Clark. Counselor. Licensed social worker." He began to read in a mumble.

"And?" Joe prompted.

"Yeah," the man said. "I heard about him. So who are you again?"

Joe explained himself a third time and began to wonder if he was going to have to go through the local police station.

"Yeah. Dennis Clark was here. He left." Joe waited. "You wanna know why he left, don't ya?"

This sounded promising. "There's a gap in his resume back then."

"Yeah, there would be," Ralph said. "He did six months, then six more on probation. Yeah, I heard something about him when I started a few years ago."

"What's the story?" Joe waited. "Is confidentiality an issue?"

"No, not in this case. It would be if you were calling about one of the boys, someone who graduated here and moved on to something, but with an old employee? Nope, we don't have any kind of exit agreements like in some places."

"So what can you tell me?"

"It's not pretty. We're a halfway house now, but we were a sober house back then. Anyone who just got clean coming out of detox could apply. We have ten rooms. Dennis was the counselor here. He lived off site with his family. According to what I have here—and it jibes with what I've heard—Clark caught one of the ex-residents—someone who'd broken the rules about using and had to leave—hanging around his daughter and nearly beat the guy to death. Thought the guy was trying to sell drugs to his girl. He served time, Clark did. Had to take an anger management course—they were pretty new back then, not as polished as they are now. But still, they're a good thing. We have people here who get a lot out of them."

"Good, okay," Joe said, trying to stem the tide of irrelevant information. "Well, that explains the gap," he said. "Anything else?" Joe asked after a long pause.

"I was gonna say no, just looking here in the file. But—"

"But?"

"I remember hearing about this. Not Denny's name, but the guy he beat up. He's sort of a warning lesson for the counselors here. It was the housemate who really stirred things up. If something out of line happens here, we used to just take the guy aside, whoever it was, and try to solve it. But this case really upped the ante, if you know what I mean."

"Spell it out for me."

"Mark the guy's name was. He went to a lawyer, who went to the cops, who went to the you name it. Everyone was in on it. It led to some good changes, but it made some things harder. Teenagers aren't afraid of anyone these days. They know the law is on their side no matter what, and if it ain't, they know how to twist things around. It's a tough job, trying to pull kids back from the brink, and this case didn't make things any easier. Mark was out for blood and got it."

"So Denny did time when he might have expected— what?—a slap on the wrist?"

"Yeah, and maybe a week off to cool down."

"That must have been quite a surprise to him," Joe said. "How did he take it?"

"Pretty good, pretty good, from the looks of this." He shuffled a paper. "They sent him to someplace easy and he did his time and got out. I didn't know him, but I can tell you all that because he kept in touch with some of the other staffers here, sort of trying to clear his name, I guess."

"I appreciate the information," Joe said, ready to ring off.

"So what's he doing now? Not in more trouble, I hope."

"No. We've got a situation up here and we're just checking out any gaps or inconsistencies," Joe said, "just checking." It wouldn't stop Ralph Patch from imagining the worst but right now Joe didn't care. He was recomposing Denny Clark's image as the quiet, somewhat deferential Community Center director.

Ann Rose was always efficient and prompt in her dealings and wherever she went, she went with purpose. Joe knew the type and braced himself as she crossed the village green, heading straight for him, and intercepted him just as he was descending the steps.

"I suppose you're in a hurry, Chief Silva." She smiled up at him. Her L.L. Bean jacket flapped open in the cold air and a scarf fluttered around her neck. She began to rise on her toes.

"I have a few minutes," Joe said. Ann Rose had never

called the police for anything more important than to warn them of an upcoming party at their house. "Is there a problem?"

"Well, no. Not for me, anyway." She planted her feet firmly and took a deep breath. Beyond, the harbor was turning slate gray and a thick low wave—the wake of a small motorboat—moved toward shore. "It's about Chandra Stine," she said in a lowered voice. "Well, sort of."

"Is she in trouble?"

"No, no, nothing like that." Ann sighed. "I'm sure you know what her situation is, with her mother all at loose ends over Miles's death. It can't be an easy situation. Anyway, she waylaid me at the community Center this morning. She was probably late to school because of it." Her voice drifted off.

"And what did she want?" Joe was too hungry to listen to a ten-minute digression. His thoughts were consumed with prosaic meals like meatloaf and potatoes, or grilled chicken and baked potatoes. He was getting hungrier and hungrier by the minute.

"She wanted me to help her with a play. It's more complicated than that. What it is, is in order to be in the holiday production of *A Christmas Carol* she has to have a parent. It's a way of getting enough adults in the cast. Anyway, she has to have an adult, not necessarily a parent. And from what she said, her mother just doesn't seem to be up to it." She shoved her hands in her pockets and started to pace in front of the station. Joe had no choice but to follow her.

"What's the problem?"

"I'm not sure there is one," Ann said.

"But something's bothering you."

"Her brother has just died and I know they weren't close. That's not news. They were several years apart—she barely knew him as an adult." Ann paused.

Joe wondered just how much it mattered to Ann that Chandra barely knew her dead brother and perhaps hardly understood her feelings about him. A chill lifted from the water and curled around them.

"Are you worried about Chandra's doing something in reaction to her brother's death?"

Ann shook her head and pressed her lips together. "It's not that. I'm just wondering—"

"Yes?"

"Well, some time ago, I guess, someone told her to stay away—" She turned directly toward him and planted her feet a steadying two feet apart. "There's no rumor that she's been in trouble, well, using, is there?"

"I haven't heard anything about Chandra Stine, but the police often don't in the early stages. But I'll be on the lookout from now on."

"I don't mean that at all."

Joe waited. You can't take back a suspicion, he thought, not from a police officer. The cold was beginning to seep into his back and shoulders. He wished she'd just get to the point; he was starting to think about clam chowder. It would be so much easier if he could just interrogate the woman without any courtesies—he'd know in a matter of seconds what was bothering her.

"What I mean is—Chandra's confused, that's all."

"That's your concern? You're worried that she's having a bad time of it and she might do something foolish?"

"Well, yes, but—"

"That's understandable, Mrs. Rose. You can suggest she talk to someone, make sure she has people around her who can help her if she shows signs of falling apart or doing something foolish." He waited, but she pressed her lips shut and looked around her. "There's something else, isn't there?"

"Some weeks ago Denny Clark told her to stay away from her brother and his friends—I certainly understand his saying that, though I do think it was ill advised. Children are so loyal to their families when challenged by outsiders, even when they think they're terrible to them or impossible to understand. It must have set up the most incredible conflict in her. She just seems so confused now—sort of clutching at whatever holds some promise. The other day when I was talking to her about something, nothing important, she interrupted me with some bizarre question about salvation and did I know about it and then went right on talking about something else. And then she showed no feeling at all about her brother—" She glanced at him. "I'm rambling, I know. But I heard that certain kinds of behavior are a sign of drug use and I was just wondering—" She took a deep breath, and he could feel her pulling for him to finish her thoughts.

"You were wondering if she's behaving irrationally for a reason? If Denny Clark knew something he wasn't telling you?"

Her eyes seemed to sharpen their look on him, now that he had identified her real concern. Joe thought back to his last telephone call, and the Denny Clark he had discovered in Connecticut. No one was ever what they seemed, but it was a shame that truth so often worked against an individual, instead of for him or her.

"She seems a perfectly nice girl," Ann said.

"And as far as we know she is," Joe said. "I can get you some pamphlets on signs of addiction and use of certain drugs if you want." Ann nodded, her eyes widening.

"That would help, I suppose." She didn't look like she believed her own words.

"Was there something else?" Joe asked after a slight pause.

She looked around at the quiet street and the occasional man or woman walking briskly down the sidewalk. "Actually, I just wanted to pass along some information. I had no intention of getting drawn into her life. I mean, she has her own life with her family even if it is a mess right now. I don't think I should get involved, do you?"

"It sounds like you already are," he said.

"I'm not sure it's right for me to be fussing about."

"We have to worry about the kids here in town," Joe said. "They're our kids." An image of Philip and then Jennie came to mind and he couldn't help wondering what would happen to either one of them in the future if someone didn't care now.

"Yes, yes, it's just a duty. That's all." Ann looked unconvinced and it was obvious to Joe that what was really bothering her was still unspoken. She might not have even figured it out herself, though it was transparent to Joe.

"And if you learn anything more, let me know. But I think you can feel safe about Chandra. I think she's just a teenager trying to make her own way in a family that doesn't offer her very much in the way of guidance and stability."

"That's for sure." Ann spoke with such relief that Joe felt sorry for her. And then he felt heartened for Chandra, for having someone like Ann Rose to take an interest in her. But Dennis J. Clark was an entirely different matter.

Joe Silva eased his foot off the gas pedal, flicked the right-hand turn signal, and turned up Pickering Street, giving the patrol car just enough gas to climb the gentle rise. He wasn't in a hurry—in fact he preferred not to exceed ten or fifteen miles per hour. The neighborhood of modest bungalows and colonials was once nothing more than a quiet street leading into a small town, but in the last few years it had become a

148

front, a façade, an outer layer of camouflage protecting grand estates located in the woods behind, on land that had not been surveyed in over a hundred years—until two or three years ago, when developers understood what lay shrouded in the neglected woods. The modest homes lining Pickering Street marked the front boundaries of estates owned by families that expected never to be bothered with ordinary traffic, never to wonder who was passing by on the sidewalk, never to need to place a call to the police for anything more than a special detail for parking at an anniversary party or a child's birthday party.

Such were their expectations.

And then there was Steve Dolanetti.

The calls had come in while Joe was talking with Ralph Patch and later with Ann Rose: a strange man had been seen walking along private lanes, public streets—walking and paying close attention to certain driveways. Could the police check it out?

Joe knew it was Steve Dolanetti by the physical description one homeowner had called in—*tall, walks like a dancer, well dressed but, well, he's walking, you know.*

Yes, Joe knew, and pulled the cruiser onto the shoulder halfway down Pickering Street to let a line of cars pass while he scanned both sides of the street. Steve was looking for something—or someone—that much was obvious. Joe had an idea that Steve was part of this drug mess that was splattering Mellingham with blood; the ugly and pathetic mess that most Mellites like to believe could never touch them. Joe pulled up opposite Rockholm Lane, considered the way it turned and rose into the woods—an area still relatively undeveloped on this end of Pickering, with old dirt fire lanes dissolving into narrow tracks with trees blown down across them every fall after hurricane season. He turned and headed up the road;

then turned right onto a dirt lane, backed out, and paused. He'd guessed right.

From the other end of Rockholm came Steve Dolanetti, his long legs stretching out gracefully, his arms swinging away from his sides, his head swiveling from side to side. He halted, bent his knees and peered into the trees, then pushed himself up and walked on. At one point Joe expected him to lift a branch to get a better look, but Steve managed to avoid getting quite that close to the natural world. The police cruiser drifted onto the lane and parked. Joe stepped out of the car and rested his arm on the roof. Steve stopped and blinked at him, bringing him into focus.

When two people meet unexpectedly, and both know why they are there in that unusual spot, they do not tumble into the rote behavior of social niceties. Neither man spoke for almost a full minute. Steve looked around him, still hopeful. Joe gazed at the woods, thinking about how different they were from the small town just a quarter mile away. The leaves shimmered silver and gold in the breeze, drawing Joe's gaze upward.

"We had a few calls this morning about a stranger out walking through neighborhoods—not the usual jogger type," Joe said.

Steve lifted one eyebrow. "I would never jog."

"We also got a call about a car parked overnight off Spring Street—down Old Town Lane." Joe ran his hand through his hair. He felt like an interloper here in the woods—all this life going on around him—the trees bowing and shaking to each other; animals hunting, stalking, fighting, eating, sleeping, mating; rocks falling loose and gliding down hill; brooks working their way through mud banks—all this world, and he had no more consciousness of it in his office than he had of the other side of the moon. He and this world were entirely separate—he had no effect on it whatsoever. He might be no more than a pebble kicked up by a doe making her way down an embankment, looking for water. He remembered Steve, and looked across the cruiser at him.

"Get in the car. You can ride over to Tiny's with me."

"I've been looking for him."

"I know."

"On foot." Steve drew close to the car, an air of wonder overriding—just barely—a note of grievance.

"I know all that. Now I want to know why," Joe said. He opened the back door and Steve clambered in. Joe slid into the front seat and looked into the back. The mesh screen was sitting on the floor of the back seat and Steve was trying to settle in with his feet beneath or beside the screen.

"I don't want to put a hole through your screen," Steve said.

"You won't." Joe waited. "Why're you looking for Tiny?"

Steve ran his eyes over the back seat. A tall blonde man who could fade away among the browning oak trees and gray fall landscape, he tipped his head to one side, then brought it up again, as though stretching a muscle in his neck. "He's a friend of mine."

"More than usual?" Joe waited. Steve had that feral look of a man interrupted in his hunt by reason, cold clear reality; a man beginning to see that his fears could seem foolish and surreal.

"What's that supposed to mean?" Steve sat bolt upright in the back seat. "You know, Chief, it seems to me that there are certain things that the town of Mellingham could do for some of its citizens."

"Where's this going, Steve?" Joe looked at him in the rearview mirror. "I asked you about Tiny."

"Yeah."

"Tell me."

"I'm not used to this sort of thing. I mean—" He looked around, tripped up by his own thoughts. "Tiny's living in his car and I just wanna make sure he's okay."

"Why wouldn't he be? Afraid we'd arrest him?"

"No." Steve blushed and looked away. "I mean yes." He seemed to consider this. "Hey, that's not a bad idea. Could you? I mean, would you do that—just for a few days?" Joe ignored this.

"Why're you looking for him?"

"I told you."

"Come on, Steve."

"That's it, just me worrying."

"It has to do with Ron Faroli and Miles Stine, doesn't it?" A doe moved among the trees to the right of the cruiser. Joe let it drift on the edge of his vision—an intrusion into his world that made him wonder which world was real. Tiny living in a car and two of his friends dead? Or a doe drifting around them like a ballerina? Steve sneezed.

"I'm allergic to grass," he said, looking at the trees outside the car window. "Nature doesn't agree with me."

"So you moved out here to Mellingham?" Joe smiled.

"I thought the water might help," Steve said. "How was I to know you'd have so many trees?"

"Lots of towns are on the ocean," Joe said. He didn't like being hustled, and even though Steve wasn't a danger to anyone anywhere, it mattered that he wasn't being entirely honest.

"Well, life in the city is rather expensive," Steve said.

"So it was all a matter of rent," Joe said.

"Well, not entirely. I mean, there are other considerations. I was thinking about rent more than anything else, I suppose."

"You suppose?"

"You mean other considerations I might have had," Steve said. Joe's hands rested on the steering wheel, his head turned just enough to see Steve out of the corner of his eye. "Well, yes, I suppose there might have been other reasons."

Joe turned a little more. "Is there anything I should be aware of?"

Steve sighed and leaned back, his hands resting on his lap. "No. I came out here because I needed a place to live that felt safe; somewhere where my ex-lover wouldn't think of looking for me. At least, not while he was cooling down and picking up someone else."

"Not a nice man, your partner?"

"No, not really. In fact, he was pretty awful when he got in a state. Men can be very mean and spiteful—no offense, Chief—"

"None taken," Joe said.

"It's just that he got so awful—threatening to make my life miserable if I didn't—Well, never mind. I didn't want to go through all that crap about filing complaints and—"

"And looking ridiculous to your friends," Joe finished for him.

Steve stared at the back of Joe's head, his hands frozen in place. "Yes." He swallowed, and turned to look out the window. "It's very pretty here. And the town doesn't have a reputation for being unsympathetic to—well, outsiders."

"Gays?"

"Exactly. So, I thought I'd be all right."

"You will be," Joe said. "Put on your seatbelt."

Joe put the car in gear and started off; the car rocked over the mounds and gullies worn into the ground. Neither man spoke as the car inched toward Pickering Street, where the ordinary world of fear and death closed in on them again.

"You're worried about Tiny, aren't you? And it has nothing to do with your own life, right?"

"Right."

"Okay. So you must think there's something wrong about Miles's death, and maybe Ron's too."

"No—"

Joe turned around and glared at him.

"Okay, okay." Steve sneezed. "Miles was clean. And after he got out of detox he swore he'd never use anything illegal again. That's what Tiny said." Steve's voice caught in his throat.

"I think it's time we found Tiny." Joe stepped on the gas and pulled onto Pickering Street.

Joe headed down Pickering Street and turned right onto Spring Street, with its older houses sitting closer to the road; their back yards blending into the woods beyond. The woods were becoming an illusion in most parts of Mellingham, shielding housing developments that in a few more years would shoulder their way into view. Trees would be cut for more aesthetically satisfying landscaping; lawns would be extended, roads paved. People had to live somewhere, was the now common refrain.

The street was wrapped in an afternoon stillness that would shatter soon, with the arrival of the school buses. Tiny wouldn't stick around as the school closing time approached. He was smart the way unintelligent people often are, with a canny survival instinct and the ability to disappear at will. Joe turned left onto what looked like a long dirt driveway between two houses and followed it across a field and up a low rise into the trees. He slowed and turned left again, to follow a bumpy track deeper into the woods.

"I'm glad you found me," Steve said. "I can't bear the

thought of having to cover this much territory on foot." He peered through the front window, absorbing the images of a little-known section of Mellingham. "I might not have found him for days. My shoes couldn't take much more."

Joe sighed. "What're friends for?"

"He can't be too much further," Steve said leaning over the seat. "His car can't take too much bouncing." He gripped the seat and peered ahead over Joe's shoulder. "How'd you know he'd be here?"

The track rose into the trees, veering along hard ground, around boulders, and between thick shrubs. As the track widened, and grass filled the center strip, Joe turned into a clearing, swung the steering wheel to the right and parked. Grass brushed against the undercarriage. Opposite them, in a grassy corner, sat Tiny's old station wagon. The back was hanging wide open, and small cardboard boxes were arrayed on the ground in front of the car.

Tiny stood up from a small, makeshift table and started to walk backwards away from them while Joe climbed out of the cruiser and turned to open the back door for Steve, who struggled with a door handle that wouldn't open from the inside. So, he's never been put in a police car, Joe thought. Good to know. Steve climbed out, embarrassed and surprised by the experience.

"I hope no one thinks I've done anything wrong," Steve said.

"No one noticed you with me," Joe said.

"You're sure?" Steve said, visibly relieved, as he followed Joe around the car. "Hey, maybe they'll think we're friends." Chuffed by this thought, Steve missed Joe's amused glance.

"Getting ready to move out, Tiny?" Joe spoke with a studied casualness as he approached Tiny, and Tiny visibly relaxed.

"It won't take me long, Chief," Tiny said.

"Take your time, Tiny. No one's hurrying you." He tried to give the appearance of being just as interested in the landscape as he was in Tiny.

"Okay. It won't take me long to get this packed up."

"You probably don't want to be around when the kids come screaming home. They give you a hard time?" Joe was within three feet of Tiny's table now.

"Nothing much," Tiny said, glancing at the table and back up at Joe.

"I'm glad to hear that, Tiny, I really am."

"It's okay," Tiny said.

"Good, glad to hear it. We spend a lot of time in the schools trying to teach kids to be respectful and considerate of others and how important that is to a civilized society."

"They're okay. Really. I'm okay."

"Good. Let me know if you have any trouble, Tiny. Let me know. I mean it." Joe knelt down as he spoke. "I mean it." He glanced upward and Tiny nodded, yes, he would let the chief know, at least he intended to at that minute. Who knew how he'd feel when the time came?

"I've been looking for you," Steve said.

"He's been scaring the neighbors," Joe said and smiled.

"Yeah, he'd do that." Tiny grinned.

Joe reached out and touched an arrangement of acorns, twigs, and dried berries decorating the top of a closed basket. Nearby sat a picture frame similarly decorated. A cardboard box was packed with newspaper-wrapped objects that Joe surmised to be more of the same.

"What are they?" Steve asked, peering over Joe's shoulders. He began to wrinkle his nose, not in disapproval, but as an expression of thinking.

"Very nice," Joe said. "You do nice work, Tiny." He stood up, arms on his hips. "Where do you sell them?"

"You sell them?" Steve gaped at Tiny. Joe sometimes wondered at the way some people could go through life without ever noticing what was going on around them.

"There's a shelter near Boston takes stuff guys like me make for to sell in their thrift shop. I sell a couple a week. It's a few bucks."

"You never told me that," Steve said, visibly hurt at his friend's secretiveness. Tiny shrugged. "Tiny, I am so impressed."

The three men stared at the array of forest materials and the decorated basket and boxes: these lowly carriers of dreams and self-respect, of youthful promise and tattered dignity, of incongruent gifts and reality. Tiny had kept these secret from his one true friend, even as he had kept hidden from himself his fragile hope to be something other than an alkie living in a car in the woods. There were lots of reasons why men stayed away from a homeless shelter, but Tiny had kept his to himself.

"How about some help packing up?" Joe said. Steve leapt forward and gathered up the basket as though it were an abandoned kitten.

"How much do you want for it?" Steve asked.

"It's not for sale," Tiny said.

"But, Tiny—"

"I mean, you can't buy it from me," Tiny said. "I have to sell it through the shop. If I don't keep my sales up, they won't take my stuff. This one's sure to sell."

"Oh." Steve cradled the basket in his hands. "Oh," he said again. "I don't have a car. How will I get there?"

"I'll take you over there."

Joe let the two men negotiate while he pushed boxes into

the back of the station wagon. It didn't take long for the three of them to pack up the rest of Tiny's materials. Tiny slammed the back shut. He had walked across the clearing, back and forth, scanning every square foot for evidence of his camp or for material for his crafts. As Joe watched, he guessed this exercise wasn't for his benefit; that Tiny was indeed conscientious about where he camped during the day. If he left evidence of his presence for the neighborhood kids to find, it wouldn't be safe to return later in the evening for the night.

"All set?" Steve asked, growing restless. He kept looking around him as though he expected wild animals to jump out of the trees at him.

Tiny nodded and opened the car door.

"One thing, Tiny," Joe said. "Help me out here if you can. I keep thinking about Miles Stine's death. It seemed pretty unexpected, wouldn't you say?" Tiny glanced over at Steve, who was studiously tying his shoelaces.

"Yeah, maybe. He fell out a window, so what?"

Joe waited. "You weren't surprised?"

"Yeah, I was surprised."

"Why?"

"Why would he fall out a window? He was alone, wasn't he? So no one pushed him. He just fell out the window. He didn't jump. He was bragging about how he was clean and legal. Him and Ron."

"What's this about his being angry about something?"

"I dunno, Chief."

"What was happening with him? Help me out, Tiny."

"He was turning on people—getting after them no matter what they said. He had a lot of mouth on him the last few days. I don't know why, considering how nice everyone was to him after Ron's death," Tiny said.

"What do you mean people were especially nice to him?" Steve asked, standing up to join in the conversation. "Except for Mr. Faroli, I didn't think anyone was thinking about Miles. He was getting pretty scary."

"Mr. Faroli was nice to him? How? What did he do?" Joe asked.

Tiny glanced at Steve, then shrugged. "I didn't think it was that big a deal. But what he did was, Mr. Faroli told him he knew how he felt, losing a friend and all that."

"Mr. Faroli did that?" Joe asked. "I'm impressed."

"So was Miles," Tiny said.

"Who told you this?" Joe asked.

"Miles," Tiny said. "He thought it was crap because the last thing Mr. Faroli said to Ron was something about staying away from the house when they weren't there. And then after Ron dies he comes over all kind and understanding and sad— all shit, you know what I mean."

"What changed Mr. Faroli's mind?" Joe asked.

"Dunno. But Miles said the old man came up to his place, at the Cleary's, and told him he knew he was hurting because it always hurts to lose a friend and he wanted him to have some of Ron's effects, and that was that."

"He probably just wanted to get rid of them," Steve said. "Didn't want to have them around."

"You're sure that's what he said?" Joe asked Tiny.

Tiny nodded. "That's what Miles said."

"I remember the Farolis going away on a trip and asking us to make sure no one got into the house," Joe said. "And they didn't want us assuming it was all right for Ron to be in their house." He remembered the strained visit George had made to the police station, and how hard it had been for him to ask the police to keep his son from crashing in the Faroli house. George had been both ashamed and angry at what he felt he'd had to do, and Joe could imagine some of that ambivalence spilling over into his conversations with his son.

"So death made him a better person," Steve said, thinking it over. Tiny swung his head in his friend's direction, frowning at him. "Haven't you ever heard that? Death's supposed to make you a better person."

"It makes you a dead person," Tiny said.

"I meant the surviving relations, Tiny." Steve smiled at him. Tiny frowned.

"Miles wasn't the nicest guy in the world, from what I hear," Joe said. "He must have upset people over the years, maybe more so recently. He just got out of rehab, didn't he?"

Steve nodded, his expression unchanged, but Tiny was catching on. His eyes had narrowed and he squinted at Joe, like an animal sighting prey, unsure if it was safe to pounce on this creature.

"You had an idea about this, didn't you, Tiny?"

Tiny nodded, looking around to see if the area was still safe. He ducked his head and his chin almost disappeared beneath his soft flannel shirt collar. He was getting that look of a cornered animal. Miles's death had had an unusual effect on people. Along with the rampant gossip that usually accompanied the death of someone who had been in and out of trouble, Miles's friends and acquaintances seemed to withdraw, to seek quiet, obscure places to hide out. They didn't want to talk about this death—it made them uneasy. Joe hadn't heard any of the usual comments—he was doing something he ought not to be doing; he couldn't quit using; he knew it was coming and couldn't stop.

"You had a chance to take over Miles's place or get another room there, at Cleary's, but you said no. Isn't that right?" Joe said. "Felt too unsafe, didn't it?"

"Yeah. Not a good place to be. The Clearys are okay, but it's not a good place to be."

"Because of what happened to Miles?"

"Yeah."

"Who else?"

"Huh?"

"Who else, Tiny? Who else shouldn't move into Cleary's?"

"Why shouldn't someone move into the Cleary's?" Steve asked, his face a mask of confusion. Like a lot of suspicious people, he could see the sinister look, but not the long-term plan behind the bland exterior. "I don't get it."

"Who's in the crowd?" Joe said. "The night when Ron died—who was there? Someone took him to the emergency room—we know that. Most people assume it was Miles, but I think others were with them before Ron crashed. Who was there?"

"Ron Faroli was. Miles. Me. Bernard." Tiny started to turn his head toward Steve, but stopped. "Missi," he whispered.

"Really?" Steve said, looking like he was leaning over a precipice.

"What happened?" Joe asked.

"Ron and Miles were out at Ron's place. I see the pizza truck, so I'm thinking I'll stop by, you know. Bernard was there. I had some and left."

"So you left and it was just Bernard and Ron and Miles," Joe repeated.

"Missi saw my car and stopped in. She needed a ride for the next day, and then she left. She wasn't there long," Tiny said. "Yes, I was with those two guys that night, but when Miles pulled out the pills I left." Tiny's hands clenched and unclenched. "I can't go back there, Chief. I can't do it again. I know where they'll put me and I can't do it again. I won't come out."

"It's okay, Tiny. I'm not looking to charge anyone here."

Tiny visibly relaxed, taking a deep breath and letting his shoulders sag.

"So Miles had the pills," Joe said, half to himself.

"He didn't say what they were," Tiny said.

"What about the other stuff that Miles claimed was legal," Joe said. "You don't know about what he was using that he claimed was legal?"

Tiny shook his head. "I never saw it, but he was selling it. Said he got it off the Internet."

Joe felt his stomach seize; this was getting worse and worse. "Okay, let's take another look here," Joe said. "Miles jumped or fell from a window. Did he ever tell anyone, even as a joke, that he might kill himself? Did he ever talk about suicide?"

"Miles? Never." Tiny was adamant.

"Can you think of anyone, Tiny, anyone who had a reason to want to kill Miles? Anyone who threatened him at any time that you heard about?" Tiny shook his head. "All right, Tiny, now listen to me. Can you think of anyone who could be a threat to Miles and you and Bernard and Missi?" Joe's voice was steady but his hand had tightened over his belt, the prong digging into his palm.

Tiny shook his head again, slowly and laboriously. "I'm scared," he said. "We don't make enemies, not like that. We're not worth it. We're bums. No one cares about us."

Steve opened his mouth but just let his chin sag down. There was nothing he could say to sugarcoat that.

Faroli's Provisions was the kind of place Joe knew growing up—the corner store where his mother got credit between her husband's pay checks; where neighborhood kids got summer jobs as long as they didn't steal candy or produce; where the owners sold up and moved out after one zoning battle too many, driven out by the new supermarket chains on the main road half a mile away. They were a dying breed—places like Faroli's—and this one would go too now for sure. George Faroli had no one to take over for him, no one to carry on the family business—at least that would be the excuse. When he got tired of running the store, he could sell up or close up. He wouldn't have to keep the place going until he could talk his son into taking over; train him to manage the business he had never been interested in; watch him muddle the books, lose customers and alienate suppliers. George and Paula would never have to face their son's outright refusal to shackle himself to the family business.

Joe nodded to the two women working the cash registers and passed down the outside aisle. The butcher was rummaging for something in the meat case for a customer, a young woman in hip jeans that all but fell down to her crotch as she bent over to follow the butcher's probing hand. "Cleavage" had taken on a new meaning for older men.

George Faroli's office door was open, but Joe knocked on it anyway.

"In here," a voice called out. The office was cluttered with boxes on top of file cabinets squashed between desk and wall; crates stacked on the floor, high shelves overflowing with records. Joe moved to an adjoining room opening into a stairwell—going up and down—and found George Faroli checking off inventory with a young man in a long apron, once white but now streaked with a multitude of earth colors. The room smelled musty; thick with the odors of fresh picked lettuce and cabbage packed into crates; of flimsy wood and damp straw in wire crates piled up and waiting to be taken away; of mulch leaked from bags long sold to summer gardeners and a thousand other smells long ago sunk into rough-cut floor boards. George Faroli emerged from all this in khakis and pink shirt with his sleeves rolled up, a narrow blue tie spotted with sawdust and tucked into his shirt beneath an equally dirty white apron.

"Hey, Joe," George said when he saw Joe Silva in the doorway. "You understand it now?" George said to the young man, who nodded his head and looked vaguely at the clipboard in George's hand and the stack of crates.

"Yeah," he said.

"Okay." George sighed and handed over the clipboard. He turned to Joe, not quite rolling his eyes but his face set in resignation. "Come on in, Joe. We can talk in here." He motioned Joe back into the office and closed the door behind him. With a single motion, he pulled a chair away from the main door and closed that too.

"You don't do much meeting in here, do you?" Joe said.

"We don't have much need for luxury. Most of the guys I work with would just as soon sit on a wooden crate in the cellar." George swept a pile of papers off another chair and both men sat down. "Good thing, too. Fancy digs cost money."

"How'd you get Paula to stay on so long?" Joe said. George laughed and leaned over to prop open a window. The fresh air fell in, assaulting them with its clean sharpness.

"I forget what it's like in here I've been working here so long. I don't even notice the transition any more—that first step out the back door at the end of the day. Too long in the same place, I guess."

"I know the feeling," Joe said.

"So what is it?" George crossed his arms over his chest and dropped his voice.

"Do you mind my coming by so soon?" They had been friends for years, one of the men Joe had come to know early on and had come to respect too; George worked hard and never complained about the younger generation, or those who had it easier. He seemed to accept that this was how his life would be, and Joe admired that. He didn't like listening to whiners who couldn't understand why everything didn't go their way. George—like Joe—just accepted that life was going to be hard sometimes, and it was pure luck that it wasn't hard all the time. Over the last few days, listening to Edna Stine talk about George had put his back up. He had tried to be objective, reminding himself that maybe, this time, he should step aside and leave it to Ken or someone else. But then, Edna was Edna.

George took a deep breath, looked down at his arms folded across his chest. "There have to be questions—two deaths—friends." George's voice caught in his throat and he took a quick, short breath and pushed the window open another inch.

"It made me wonder—that and a few other things," Joe said.

"What other things?"

"They were part of a rehab group, right?"

"Ron was just out of rehab, yes, but he and Miles knew each other before."

"Who else was in that group?"

"Don't really know," George said, frowning. "Ron stopped talking to us years ago. He was just starting to come back. Just getting back to us." He dropped his hands to the chair arms and gripped hard.

"Who'd he talk about? Mention just in passing?"

"Why?"

"Humor me, George. It's my job."

"This is what makes you a good poker player. You're so unrevealing, at least you make us think you are."

"You going tonight?" Joe asked.

"Dunno."

"Don't blame you."

"I don't want to leave Paula alone just yet. She's pretty edgy. I always thought women were the ones who'd cry all the time but she's just frozen. She has me worried."

"Take her to see someone, George. Make the appointment and just take her."

"She'd kill me, Joe."

"Just do it. She'll get over it."

"Maybe you're right." He rose to fuss with the windows, then spun the chair around and sat down in it, swiveling from side to side, staring at the floor, beads of sweat breaking out over his upper lip. Joe had grown comfortable over the years always being on the outside of so much of life, and he considered it an asset most of the time. Today he was grateful—he didn't want to know how much pain this father was in over the loss of his only child. Just watching George in his anguish and fearing there was nothing the police could do was bad enough. "That guy named Tiny," George said.

"What about him?"

"That's somebody he mentioned."

"Good. Anyone else?"

"He, ah, seemed to think they were all pals, these guys in rehab."

"I don't think Tiny was in rehab with him."

"Well, in AA or whatever. It's all the same. They were friends. They all understood each other—he could talk to them. That's what he said." George paused, rubbed his hands along the soft polished wood of the chair. "He said that to Paula—must've sliced right through her."

"You didn't like his friends," Joe said.

"Miles Stine? Are you kidding? That—" He shook his

head, driving away the thoughts. "Look, I need to be honest about this. Ron's death is eating me up. You know it, everyone knows it. I was raised a Catholic—you know what that means. I've had thoughts that scare me. I figured I could do something about it, about hating him so much. I didn't like Miles, but I can't blame him for Ron's death. In my heart I do, but I know it isn't right." He took a deep breath, exhaled and seemed to come to a decision. "I told myself this would kill me if I didn't forgive him and move on. So I did."

"How exactly?" Joe asked.

"I went over to Miles's place and told him I didn't hold any grudge. I offered to shake hands." George stared down at the ground, as though he were ashamed of this.

"How did Miles take it?"

George started to laugh. "Like I was a cougar waiting for a chance to pounce. I had to say it twice, and you know, it almost made me change my mind. But I wasn't doing it for him, I was doing it for me." They stood in silence for a moment.

"Took guts, George."

"Yeah." He studied the old plank flooring at his feet.

"How about the others who were friends with Ron? Did you try to talk to them?"

"No, no one else."

"You didn't feel that strongly about anyone else, then? What about Steve Dolanetti?"

George drew his lips together, shook his head again. "Not that one. Can't say I ever heard that name before."

"Missi Lofko?"

"That's a name?" George laughed. "I may have heard it but it doesn't mean anything special to me. Ron wasn't sweet on anyone." He clenched and unclenched his fists as he spoke.

"I'm sorry I have to put you through this, George," Joe said.

"It's okay," he said. "You expect your parents to die. You figure out how you're going to deal with it and you do. No matter how long it takes, you know where you're going to end. They do too. It's not easy but it's predictable, and anyone who doesn't face it is a fool. And then you live without that safe place, that automatic thought that you have someone somewhere who cares about you, who knows where you come from. And you think I'm going to give that to my kid, my child. I'm going to be here for my kid, no matter what. He's going to know that he can count on me, no matter what. I'm going to be that safe place, that one place in the world where he can always come and be safe and know that someone loves him. You believe that, you live for it. And you might even make it happen.

"You face everything—the first time you have to take the kid to the emergency room because he's red and blue from coughing and he can't stop. The first time he falls off a stone wall and doesn't get up and you can't believe what you're seeing. You get him through school and college and you get him into a job—or at least you try to. You fight him and love him and keep trying to teach him things, how to be safe and smart in the world. And he gets mad at you and you think you can live through that too because life is long and there is time to get back on track.

"But you don't expect your child to die. No matter how bad things get, you never imagine that, you never go that far. You imagine pain, danger, accidents, trouble, sorrow, but not death." He took a deep breath, a rackety uneven noise. "I've always lived my life for someone else. I wanted it that way. It made sense to me. Maybe it's all I know how to do. I don't know. It's what seemed right for me."

A sheet of paper rose and trembled in the breeze, then settled itself onto the pile. George looked around his office, as though it were unfamiliar territory, like his heart, a large cluttered space that held secrets from years past, long forgotten but still taking up space, lots of space. Joe waited for his friend to compose himself.

"Maybe it was too soon," Joe said. It was always too soon to talk to a grieving parent. George Faroli would never be ready: he would be less composed or more composed, accepting, cooperative, but never ready. Parents never were. "I'll come back another time."

"Thanks. Yeah. I'm sorry, Joe. I'm not much help, am I?"

"It's okay, George. We can do this another time."

"Sure. Oh, yeah, that Bernard kid. He's young, isn't he? Ron knew him. I don't know how well he knew any of these guys. You get thrown into a drunk tank and you're liable to come out thinking all the others who don't try to kill you are your best buddies. Who knows what he was thinking? The truth, Joe?" George looked at him, his shoulders hunched over, his arms gripping the chair. "He was a stranger to me. He hurt his mother so many times I was ready to write him off. He came out of rehab clean, told us he was a changed man. Paula believed him. She was so happy she cried for days. I don't know why we believed him, but we did. When I first heard he tried that oxy stuff, I thought I'd—"

"Yes?"

"They never come back, do they? Not really."

"You believe that?"

"I guess I have to. It's the only way I can accept that what happened was for the best." George shifted in his chair, as if gearing up for more of a struggle. "Maybe I should take her on another trip."

"She loved that last one. Where was it?"

"The Seychelles. Ever been there?"

"Can't say I know much about it."

"It's an island off the coast of Africa, in the Indian Ocean. I never heard of it either until she came home with this brochure she got from some friend in her garden club. They were onto exotic plants, and so Paula wanted to go there."

"Maybe that's what you should do now, find an island and take a nice long trip," Joe said. "Just get away. Leave all this behind you and spend as much time as you need just being together and enjoying life."

"I don't know, Joe. Last time she had the doctor put so many holes in me. 'Nothing's going to spoil my vacation. You go get that shot, George.' So I got shot, Joe. Jees, and then the pills. Quinine this, and iodine that. I'll tell you, I couldn't live in a place where I couldn't drink the water. Not me."

"Don't know how lucky you are until you travel. Is that it?"

"In spades, Joe, in spades." George stood up and extended his hand. "Thanks. I'll be better help next time, I promise."

Chapter 7

Thursday Evening

The students milling around the Community Center were all ages and all sorts—the young twelve-year-olds who dreamed of being the next Britney Spears; the boys in their classes who jostled each other shoulder to shoulder, trying to figure out why they agreed to do this; the younger ones whose mothers thought a role in this year's Christmas play would be a treasured memory as the years rolled by; the teenagers who were ordered to perform a community service, opted for a tech role in the community production and were waiting to find out what they had agreed to; and the few classmates who worked hard in school to have some leverage with their parents when it came time to getting permission to sign up for acting as an extra-curricular activity. Chandra Stine was one of these.

Ann Rose had no trouble spotting Chandra's curly head of hair across the room—she was a good six inches taller than the others standing around with her and, unlike many of her peers, she never slouched. Instead, she used her height to keep an eye on just about everyone, peering over the heads of those standing next to her to watch the door, keeping tabs on who was here and who was late. She had a script rolled up in her hand and was alternately slapping it in short hard bursts against her thigh and swinging it behind her, where she grasped it with both hands. She was far more nervous than Ann had expected and almost as nervous as Ann was. Ann caught her eye and weaved her way across the room.

"I'm so glad you made it, Mrs. Rose." Chandra loomed over her so steeply that Ann took an involuntary step back.

"Well, it's quite a crowd," Ann said, looking around. She wasn't sure what you wore to a theater audition, so she had settled on neatly pressed, white corduroy slacks, a purple sweater, and a black jacket. She glanced around to see if she had chosen well.

"It won't seem so bad once we get into the gym. Really. You'll see."

"I'm sure."

"We just can't get in there until the smaller kids finish their recital this week. Next week, Mr. Alter will move us over there."

"Mr. Alter is our director?" Ann asked, looking around for the head of the high school drama department. Every year the department staged a Christmas play for the community, and the young actors were picked first. Mr. Alter was the originator of the idea that each child bring an adult, usually a parent, who would agree to be in the play. Ann had no trouble understanding Edna Stine's withdrawal from her commitment to participate, but she didn't quite understand her own weakness that let her be persuaded to stand in for Edna. But here they were—a teenage girl on the cusp of adulthood, fighting for her own identity distinct from the tattered reputations of her family, and Ann Rose, an educated woman of privilege who, if poked and prodded and pushed, would admit to an underlying prejudice against people of the theater. And beneath that was a fey curiosity about what really went on in the world of the theater.

"Did you have a chance to look at the script?" Chandra asked. "It's good, isn't it?"

"Well, it's Dickens." Ann plunged a hand into her black

leather tote bag. Part of her rationalization was that the play was, after all, by a major writer and she could consider this part of her effort to improve the level of culture among the young. If Joe Silva had even hinted at the possibility of Chandra being near the edge of impropriety, Ann would have felt she could back off without a twinge of guilt. After all, she was not qualified to deal with serious problems. But Chandra was Chandra: a remarkable island of sanity and decency in a family gone nuts, totally out there, as the kids might put it. Ann pulled out her script, which by now was unexpectedly tattered. Chandra blinked at the sight of it, but hurried on with her reassurances.

"I told you you wouldn't have any lines. It's really easy. You just come in with me and go out with me."

"I saw that, Chandra. I saw your lines too."

"I wish there were more."

Ann groaned inaudibly. She had spent a good ten hours going over the script Chandra had dropped off at her home—getting a sense of where she and Chandra entered in the play, how much time they had to spend onstage—what was she supposed to do with herself while they were all standing there? Did she have a prop? She must at least have a prop. You couldn't just leave someone standing on the stage with nothing to do for half an hour—well, maybe five minutes, but it certainly had to feel like half an hour. She couldn't just stand there like some statue, a dork, a nerd, with her arms hanging down. She'd be chewing her nails and picking her nose and god knows what else. The director would have to give her a purpose, a sense of mission for her part.

"Mr. Alter said if I did a really good job and they had trouble getting enough students, he might collapse some of the characters and give me more lines."

"Oh. Well, that's very nice of him, I'm sure, but what about the other students?"

"Most of them don't want lines, at least not as much as I do, and I have worked so hard for this. Mr. Alter knows how I feel and how hard I've worked."

My God, Ann thought, the girl is a spigot of ambition. "It's just that you should share the experience, let others have a chance. It's a community effort, after all."

"I'm really hoping I'll get more lines."

Ann groaned again. She really hoped Chandra didn't get more lines.

Ann, in order to calm her nerves, had memorized Chandra's short speech, just so she'd be able to prompt the girl in case she got lost or forgot her lines. But then, in order to know when to prompt Chandra to speak her first line, Ann had to memorize the "cue," as she knew it was called. But then to know when to be alert to the cue, she had to memorize—and so it went through the evening until Ann realized she was memorizing the play backwards. And that would never do. It was absurd. So she had capitulated and started over—from the beginning. It had taken her almost the entire night to master the play; she had no idea how unusual this was, nor would she have believed it if someone had told her. She was, in fact, the perfect match for Chandra—a woman who had an innate talent for theater and was a quick study, a very quick study, but had no desire to hog—or even to enter—the limelight. Ann was ready to stand on the sidelines and help in any way she could, and leave all the glory to the younger one. But she knew none of that. Instead, she was bone weary and her head ached and she thought if she got the slightest whiff of any grease paint, she'd toss her cookies for sure.

"Why would anyone want to go into the theater?" she

mumbled, her sense of propriety for the moment trumping her secret avidity for that inside look she was sure was coming. She had certainly heard all the reasons actors said the life was terrible—constant rejection, irregular work hours, paltry pay for some, a lifelong uncertainty for most— and yet there had to be something more to hold so many in thrall. "Why would anyone go into this life?" she said again, perhaps to remind herself of who she was.

"What?" Chandra, startled, swung around to look at her.

"Oh, butterflies. I'm incredibly nervous. Pay no attention to me."

"You wait until we get going," Chandra said, leaning over and whispering to her. "You'll fall in love with all of it. It's wonderful. It doesn't matter what's happening around you, or in school or anything. You become another person in another life." Chandra stood up and craned her neck to see over the crowd. She threw her hand into the air and waved at Philip McDuffy, who was hovering on the edge of the crowd on the other side of the room.

"I guess so." Ann began to feel out of step with the crowd around her: the young teens showing off their jeans or necklaces or other new item; their parents or other relatives chatting aimlessly to pass the time. It felt odd to suddenly be intimate with a world she couldn't see or touch, and yet Chandra's world seemed to have enveloped her.

"Listen up, everyone!" A voice boomed out across the chattering students and adults, breaking into Ann's and Chandra's quiet conversation, dampening the laughter and high spirits of the overanxious. "We're going to begin with a walk-through by scenes, so I'm going to break you down into small groups."

Oh, Lord, thought Ann. It goes from bad to worse.

★ ★ ★ ★ ★

The holiday season began early for the police, with special requests for police details for dinner parties, concerns about school events and parties, and all the background work that made things run smoothly. On Joe's desk now sat a dozen requests that had to be drawn up formally, examined, arranged, scheduled, and filed. And they were the last thing he wanted to deal with.

"Don't you have a game tonight?" Ken Dupoulis poked his head into the doorway. He was still in uniform but probably out the door himself. It was almost six o'clock.

"I was just going over the prelim from the lab," Joe said. "Did you look at it?"

Ken nodded. "Interesting, isn't it? I never heard of it before. How are we supposed to keep up with this stuff?"

"Salvia divinorum. It's scary. The same effects as LSD, and all legal." Joe rested his hand on the sheet of paper with his notes scribbled at the top. "That must be what Miles meant when he kept saying he wasn't going to do anything illegal. He found something that was perfectly legal—at least so far—and he imported it and he didn't have to worry about it."

"No one here has ever heard about it and we're supposed to know what's going on," Ken said, shaking his head and starting to laugh. "It's pathetic." He looked at Joe. "There's something else, isn't there?"

"Ron Faroli. Miles Stine. Tiny Morley." Joe rattled off the names. "Missi Lofko. Bernard Whitson." Ken didn't blink.

"Okay."

"A pattern?"

"You seem to think so," Ken said.

"Would anyone other than your astute self have noticed?"

"Only the relatives maybe."

"None of their friends then."

"The word in the alley?"

"On the beach, in the garage, anywhere."

"I've heard a few jokes like, 'So who do you think is next? Wanna bet on who's next?' That sort of thing."

"They're scared. They know something's wrong."

"You're not buying the accident?" Ken moved into the office and took the chair against the wall. "If salvia can be as strong as LSD, it's possible he had a bad trip and jumped."

"There was something else in that plastic bag," Joe said.

"Have they identified it yet?"

Joe shook his head.

"OxyC?"

"I don't think so." Joe swiveled around to face him. During the day, the misty sea air brought a cold damp that darkened the day, but in the evening it trapped the light and a golden haze shimmered in the harbor just outside Joe's window. It was a tradeoff he found he could still live with—a cramped office for a view of the inner harbor and the ever-changing kaleidoscope of the sea. "That was the obvious guess, and they checked that right away. But nothing. They're still looking."

"Edna, his mother, insisted he was clean. Just out of the Discover program and clean," Ken said. "He probably told her that and she was glad to believe him. She's the worst sort of mother—on her kids constantly to be better than they are, and going on and on about them but not really helping. She's got a bit of a problem herself, if you ask me." Ken often jumped into the local history he assumed—usually rightly—that Joe didn't know.

"Tiny let out that he was with Miles and Ron the night Ron OD'ed." Joe hunched his shoulders and leaned over, thinking.

"What's this business about Miles being angry about something?" Ken asked.

"It comes up a lot, doesn't it?" Joe reached for his notebook. "You know, as many people as say he was angry, no one has a reason why. No one even tried to explain it."

"Something must have happened." Ken paused. "A delayed reaction to Ron's death?"

"You think so, Ken?" Joe glanced at him, and Ken shook his head.

"Okay." Ken sighed, pushed himself up in his chair, as though he were coming to attention sitting down. "Okay. So what're we looking at?" Ken spread open his palm and began enumerating on his outstretched fingers. Out in the hall, the large wall clock that had hung facing the main door for the last fifty years began to chime the half hour.

"Ron dies on a Saturday from OxyC," Joe said. "His friend and cohort, Miles, is dead on Tuesday night, after the funeral."

"I would have said he was pushed if Edna hadn't just been there with him," Ken said. "She didn't pass anyone in the hall, on the way up the stairs, as she came down. She didn't hear anyone open a door and go up behind her. None of the other tenants has any connection with Miles or Edna. Everything says he was alone and just fell out the window."

"Or jumped."

"So what made him jump? Ordinary suicide attempt?"

"No sign of that," Joe said. "He jumped because of whatever he was on."

"And what he was on was legal," Ken pointed out.

"Some of it, anyway."

"Tiny has no idea what it might have been?" Ken asked.

"He really is trying to stay clean, and he's been trying to stay away from all this, as far as I can tell."

"He's been pretty successful, it seems. I don't see him around as much."

"He's around, and whoever wants him will find him."

"You're pretty sure of that."

"I'm very sure of it."

"So what'd you suggest?"

"I want a car near Tiny all night. He's the most vulnerable," Joe said, telling Ken where Tiny was parking for the time being.

"What about Steve?"

"He caught on before I did—he was out looking for Tiny, trying to find him and reassure himself he was all right, I suppose. I don't know what he was going to do after that—maybe try to get him into someplace safe. Which would be a shelter, most likely. Anyway, Steve was not part of Ron's crowd, and he has a better sense of the danger the others are in—he's out here to avoid a violent ex-lover," Joe added by way of explanation.

"I was wondering what brought him to town," Ken said. "He didn't seem to know anyone when he arrived."

"I think he knows what kind of danger Tiny is in and that he's safe himself. But just to be sure, he'll keep his head down—his doors locked and bolted and barricaded too probably."

"Missi?"

"Steve told her he was worried but I think she's peripheral. Still, I want to know where she is, where she goes. Let's keep an eye on her."

"Bernard?"

"I'll talk to him tonight. He's got family around here, and I want him to go stay with them for a while if he can," Joe said. "I don't want any of them out alone for the next few nights."

★ ★ ★ ★ ★

Bernard Whitson slouched in his chair, his dirty sleeves resting on the padded arms, his fingers splayed. His face was splotchy from lack of sleep and newspaper ink; he had a habit of picking at little spots on his face whenever he was nervous. He kept an eye on the television on the other side of the room, but he wasn't watching it. Denny Clark was in his walk-through before closing up the Community Center for the night. The last meeting had broken up, and the few souls still lingering would have to leave soon—he was already behind the regular schedule. He nodded to Joe Silva crossing the large room.

In the opposite corner, Steve Dolanetti was turning the pages of a book as Philip McDuffy leaned over to study each one. Every now and then Steve pointed to something and commented on it, and Philip nodded before jotting down notes. The two drew back and fell into an intense exchange for a moment, then returned to the book. Philip seemed re-laxed and curious, animated in his comments, attentive to Steve's, a far cry from his demeanor during Joe's and Gwen's talk with him the night before. Regardless of the trouble Philip was falling into, Joe couldn't see him as the ordinary troubled teen; there was something about him, something that said this one was different. Joe studied the boy on the other side of the room, and all of a sudden he felt a huge burden lifted from his shoulders. He hoped Gwen would feel this way too. A burst of laughter from the television drew Joe back to his original mission.

Bernard watched Joe approach out of the corner of his eye and squirmed upright in his chair.

"Good show?" Joe said, nodding to the television.

"Okay. Something wrong, Chief?" Bernard said.

"I'm just checking on a few things," Joe said as he pulled

up a folding chair and sat down. "Where're you staying these days?"

"Around."

"Okay." Joe turned to watch half a scene of a sitcom before turning back to the boy. "I'm kind of worried about you right now."

"I'm just sitting here watching TV."

"That's not what I'm talking about." Joe waited, but Bernard wasn't going to ease up. "You have family south of here, isn't that right?"

"So?"

"I want you to go stay with them."

"I don't have to do that. I haven't broken any laws."

"This is about your own safety."

"You think there's bad drugs out there and we're getting some here in town."

"I want you out of Mellingham for your own safety," Joe said, leaning toward him. "I can't order you out, but I'm telling you to leave, Bernard. This isn't the best place for you to be right now."

"At least I have a place to sleep here," the young man said.

"You can stay with your family for a couple of nights," Joe said. Bernard plucked at the chair arms, one broken fingernail snagging on the fabric.

"You're making me leave."

"It's all for your own good." Joe pulled out his radio and called for a car to pick up Bernard Whitson, then sent him outside to wait. The boy was right, Joe thought, I don't have the right to send him out of town, but he can't stay here.

The 7:04 pulled into the Mellingham train station just as Joe Silva hung his jacket on a peg in the kitchen at the back of the Whimsy Gallery. He heard it coming along the track and watched it pull into the station from a narrow kitchen window. A sliver of the train passed between two buildings and then stretched out along the track toward the cross street. He imagined the bars lowering and stopping traffic, and felt an enormous relief; he hadn't realized how worried he was about Bernard and the others until he saw the train and knew people were boarding, Bernard among them. All of a sudden, the evening of poker with Mike Rabkin became something he could enjoy, and he became just another guy spending the evening with friends. He was in a very good mood as he turned away from the window.

Located in a stately Victorian house, presiding like a grand old lady over downtown Mellingham, the Whimsy Gallery survived the vagaries of the economy because of the enthusiasm and aspirations of the students at the Massasoit College of Art. The gallery-cum-artists'-supply-store closed at five o'clock on Thursday evenings, to accommodate a weekly poker game. A devoted fan of any device that brought his pals together, Mike Rabkin set up a large round table in the center of the gallery every Thursday night at five-thirty. Customers who lingered sensed they would be moved on in a hurry.

"You know where the beer is," Mike said to Joe as he entered from the kitchen. Joe waved and turned to the refrigerator, tucked away in a closet transformed into a tiny pantry. He pulled out a Sam Adams and rummaged in a drawer for a bottle opener. He had changed out of his uniform and felt relieved of any number of worries—the hovering danger to Bernard and Tiny, the belt that was getting a little too tight, his growing concern over Philip. Years past he had wondered what it might be like if he worked at a job that didn't require a uniform; he had even thought about applying for detective in a city department, but there was something about his uniform. By then it had become part of his identity, and he was ambivalent about giving it up. Now he wasn't sure he could. He never wore it when he was off duty, but he couldn't imagine going to work, or going anywhere to do anything important, and not being in uniform.

"Okay, Joe. Hope you brought a lot of money. I'm planning a trip to Florida this winter." Gordon Davies, recently retired town clerk, set down an unopened beer bottle and pulled out a chair. He reached for the deck of cards. A meticulous man who always wore a thin sweater tucked into his pants over whatever kind of shirt he was wearing, even in the summer heat, he was usually the first to arrive and was always the first ready to play. He went straight to the table and set up the game. "Hurry up, you guys. I snuck out of the house early to pick up an extra pack of cards. Our old set were getting grimy."

"Sneaked, Gordon, sneaked. Snuck is not a real word," Mike said.

"You spend too much time around those college kids."

"Where're you planning on staying down there?" Joe asked. "A swamp shack?"

"You watch your tongue, Joe." Gordon began to shuffle the cards.

"Maybe George will make you rich," Joe said.

"Yeah, he's got money," Gordon said. "He was buying some nice booze just now."

"George isn't coming," Mike said. "He called earlier."

"Hmm." Gordon shuffled the cards. "So where's Henry?"

"On his way." Mike put two bowls of pretzels on the table and walked across the room to make sure the front door was locked. The back door opened and closed and Henry Muir, a sculptor with rock-hard hands and thick black eyebrows, shuffled into the room. He grunted hello.

"Gregory isn't coming till much later—if he can do that," Henry said.

The game had evolved out of a casual encounter of the men during a construction project on Gregory Stewart's property. He was extending his greenhouses, adding a new water distribution system, and in general sprucing up the old place. They all seemed to be there at once on Saturday morning some years back, and no one could quite remember whose idea it had been, but there they all were, sitting around a table at Mike Rabkin's the next Thursday evening, and there they had continued to appear—even when Mike was away.

"How's Marian?" Henry asked. Joe smiled. Henry had probably made a detour to say hello to Marian on his way over here—it was a short walk for both men. Henry and Marian had known each other growing up and shared a certain crustiness.

"Fine, fine, fine," Gordon said. "What're you so chatty for?"

"Sounds like a jealous man," Henry said.

"Was that you with the jackhammer the other morning?" Joe asked.

"Trying to drive us out. Well, I'm going to Florida, Henry," Gordon said.

"Not enough of us to get you to Florida, Gordon." That from Mike.

"Florida? You?"

"Yes, Henry, me. What's so strange about that?"

"It's hot down there, Gordon."

"That's the whole idea, Henry. Haven't you heard of sun?"

"You got something to drink, Henry?" Mike leaned in between the two men.

"We're missing Reg," Joe said as he pulled out a chair. The chairs were an odd assortment of office chairs, folding metal seats, dining chairs. No one seemed to mind except Reginald Campbell, owner of the Agawam Inn, who complained that this mix—all the rage now in new coffee shops and cafes—was an assault on the senses.

"I'm here, I'm here." Reg tossed his jacket over a kitchen chair and strode into the room.

"D'jou bring any money?" Henry asked, his lip curling.

"Why?"

"Gordon here wants us to send him to Florida," Henry said.

"What for? You going to be a snowbird? You?" Reg shook his head and collapsed into an office chair, which rolled backward under his weight; he walked it back to the table without getting up. "Jees, I never thought I'd see the day. Gordon, of all people." Reg shook his head. " 'Course, some of my best clients spend the winter months down there and a month or two up here. You selling your place?"

Gordon dealt the first hand.

"You have to do it legally," Mike said. "You can't cheat your way to Florida. There."

"Yeah." Henry glared at the cards in his hand.

"Marian would never let me sell. You know that."

"Someone has to have some sense in a family," Henry said.

"Two," Reg said. "Good thing Gregory isn't here. He'd want you to go up to those islands. What're they called?"

"Hebrides," Joe said. He had a love of islands and island cultures. He'd had no trouble understanding Paula Faroli's insistence on heading out to the Seychelles, regardless of George's resistance.

"Maybe George'll—"

"Forget George," Henry said.

"He hasn't been here in weeks," Reg said.

"Months," Mike said.

"Why is that? Two," Joe said.

Reg shook his head with the same expression on his face he got when people asked him how the hotel business was. It was never good. The choices were usually between 'I'll get through this week' to 'Nothing can be this bad.' The bottom was usually, 'Why did I ever think this was a good idea?'

"Good thing he's not here regularly," Reg said. Cards flicked against each other.

"It's tough," Gordon said.

"He was pretty sour before Ron died," Reg said.

"You think so?" Joe asked. "He sounded like it was a pose most of the time. You know, the crusty New Englander who hides his feelings and keeps on trucking no matter how tough life is. You know, the Yankee pose. Sort of like Henry."

"Pose!" Henry gaped at Joe, who smiled. Henry frowned, Joe knew, the better to plot his revenge.

"Sour," Reg said. "You know, Joe, he saw the flaw in everything. Never thought of it as a pose."

"I heard he was suing someone, one of his suppliers, for shorting him. He asked me if I'd ever had that kind of trouble with any of the suppliers for the Whimsy Gallery."

"We get that trouble in the hotel business all the time. The Agawam could be lifted stick by stick if I didn't watch everyone who came through the door." Reg reached for his beer. "And then the guests."

"I thought you didn't have any," Mike said.

"Well, when I do, they're as bad as the suppliers. That honeymoon couple that didn't come out of their room for three days. I thought they were—"

"We know what you thought," Mike said.

"Well, when I went in, the place smelled like a bar. And they weren't smoking cigarettes."

"You know," Mike said, "it's ironical that Ron Faroli might still be alive if he'd stuck to the usual illegal stuff—marijuana and heroin and cocaine."

"It's not that benign, Mike," Joe said. "But I know what you mean. We're sure upping the ante with every generation."

"I wouldn't have known where to get that stuff when I was a kid," Gordon said.

"Gordon, do you expect us to believe that?" Reg said, leaning toward him. "You just get on the train and go down the line."

"How'd you know that?" Gordon said, peering at him.

"The same way you did before you got senile."

"Gordon, go back to what you said about George and the trouble he was having with his suppliers," Joe said. "Was he in money trouble?"

"He was suing the trucking company," Gordon said.

"You would know," Henry said. "Nothing to do but gossip all day."

"Come on, guys," Mike said.

"How's that work?" Joe asked. "Suing the company that delivers. What happened there?"

"Well," Gordon said, warming to the topic. "George claims that the truck bumped into the building, damaging the foundation, and nicked some cars, pulled out a phone line. Said it disrupted his business."

"That's tight, that parking lot," Mike said.

"Said he couldn't check on his orders at night unless he used a cell phone," Reg said.

"He's just getting greedy," Henry said, banging down his hand. "What kind of hand is this, Gordon?"

"That's my Florida hand."

"I don't know George as well as I thought I did," Joe said. "I haven't noticed the change." Joe watched the faces around the table, trying to gauge just how carefully thought out their comments were.

"No change," Reg said. "He's always been like that."

"Come on, Reg. That's a little strong," Mike said.

"Nope. That's who he is," Reg said.

"Lately he is," Henry said, folding his hand in front of him. "You know, guys, we're talking about him as though he weren't one of us anymore." Gordon studied him over his hand fanned out in front of his nose.

"He went real quiet when Ron died," Gordon said. "Not like most people who are grieving. Something different."

"Yeah, you're right," Reg said. "Like there was something he just couldn't bring himself to say."

"Like what?" Joe asked.

Reg shook his head, then turned to Henry. He too frowned, but in the end just shook his head too. Joe looked around the table at the men, one by one, the men who had become his friends over the years, the ones he turned to when he needed information about the town, or someone to have lunch with. Henry was right: they were talking about George as though he had moved away, left town and left their circle. The silence lengthened, but no one seemed uncomfortable. The men frowned over their cards, and a desultory conversation began between Gordon and Reg.

"You know, Gordon, you could join the Chamber and do something about getting some tourism right here. There must be a way you could sell this town for tourists," Reg said.

"Business bad?" Gordon said.

"When is it ever good?" Reg said. "Where are the leaf-peepers? Not at my place, that's for sure."

"The season's pretty much gone, Reg. And it's not too long anyway," Mike said.

"And wait until that dredging picks up again," Henry said. "How much does that affect you?"

"Depends on where it is—inner harbor, wherever," Reg said. "If it doesn't spoil the view no one even notices it." They went on to discuss the dredging that would begin in March—an annual rite that annoyed some boaters and worried the locals near the coast.

Ignoring the other conversation, Gordon leaned over to Joe, and said, "So'd we help you?" Joe gave him a smile and a nod, and returned to his cards.

Mike scowled at his hand. "You know, Gordon, maybe I should look at that new deck."

Joe waved as Henry walked past him and turned up the sidewalk; he lived only a few streets away. Joe punched in the numbers on his cell phone and waited. Gwen answered.

"I'm just leaving," he said. "Want anything?" He pulled away from the Whimsy Gallery, coasted through downtown Mellingham, its shop windows and sidewalks lit by bright street lamps, and turned down Trask Street.

He tapped the brake, slowed, and saw a light glimmering on the second floor front—Gwen's living room. He swung the Jeep into the driveway, parked, and a moment later was climbing the stairs to Gwen's apartment.

"In here." He called out a greeting in response and dropped his coat on a kitchen chair. He could hear her moving around in the living room.

The refrigerator was full of an array of foods designed to satisfy the appetites of two teenagers. Gwen still shopped on Thursday evenings, a habit held over from her childhood, she once explained. He clattered around making himself something to eat while Gwen finished folding laundry. He pulled out a beer, looked at it, and realized it was his third of the evening. Actually, that wasn't what he was thinking about; it was one of those distracting thoughts that kept him from thinking about the other things that pricked at him throughout the day, about how old he was getting and how he worried that he was shortchanging Gwen, particularly now, when she needed someone to help her with Philip. He laid a chicken salad sandwich on a plate and turned to see Gwen.

"You're awful quiet in here," she said. "How was the game?"

"We're pathetic, except Gordon, so we accuse him of cheating."

"Does he? Cheat, I mean?"

"No, not Gordon. He has too much self-respect. Now that he's retired, he spends a lot of his time reading about great poker games, like some people read about bridge games."

Joe followed Gwen into the living room and sat down on the sofa. He kicked off his shoes and put his feet up on a newspaper on the coffee table. He didn't approve of people who put their feet up on the furniture—seats on a train, or subway, or coffee tables or chairs—so he looked for an old newspaper, even at home. It was a fussiness in him he had never thought much about but he had begun to wonder what it meant. Probably that he was becoming like his father. Joe could not recall ever having seen his father take his feet from the floor. He was a proper fellow—never slovenly. Joe had attributed this to ordinary self-preservation: with seven children his father hadn't dared relax around them. But as Joe grew older, he was no longer so sure.

Gwen let her eyes drift up to the ceiling, where she inspected the thin cracks created over the years by the heavy trucks lumbering past, the occasional shock wave from a distant earthquake, the natural drying and shrinking of plaster over the years. He watched her gaze upward, lost in her own thoughts, her interest in aging plaster. She liked to be able to sit quietly—it was for her the one sign of companionship she could not forgo—and he never called her back precipitously. Their relationship was comfortable, easy, safe, but also a screen. He had been an emotional coward, he concluded, hiding behind his work and his badge from a deeper commitment, a deeper life. He reached for the sandwich, wondering why he was being so hard on himself this evening.

She rested her head on the sofa back and turned to him. "Long day?"

Hiding was easy in this part of the world. Not much broke through the money and complacency to challenge anyone's thinking. And hadn't he come here in part to hide himself? Hadn't he tired of big-city problems, urban nightmares? Well, hadn't he?

But you are who you are, wherever you go.

That was his father talking. "It won't be different, you know," he said to Joe after learning that he was moving to Mellingham. "If you got a problem, you take it with you."

"You think I have a problem, Pa?"

His father had shaken his head and then, because a young cousin was getting married at the same time, his father had said, "The problems you have before you get married are the problems you have after you get married."

"Peter doesn't have any problems."

"Hmm." His father never elaborated.

But Joe was the only one of his father's children not married.

Joe took his feet from the coffee table and leaned over the plate on his lap. A car drove by too fast—Joe noted and estimated the speed—and the wheels on the pavement sounded like they were running on a wet surface. No rain, so the road must be sweating. He looked to see Gwen staring at him, her head resting on the back of the sofa.

"How's Philip tonight?" he asked.

"Better, I guess. He came in after school and we chatted a bit. He was polite and seemed okay," she said. "Then he went out for a while."

"He was at the Community Center this afternoon," Joe said. He watched Gwen, but she didn't ask him anything about it. "He's helping on that play the school is doing."

"Philip is in a play?" Gwen turned to study him.

"Not as an actor, I don't think. I think he's in the lighting or tech side," Joe said.

"Hmm." Gwen leaned back, getting comfortable again. "Interesting. Well, he got in about six-thirty. He was fine. Well, a little edgy maybe. Like he's uncomfortable with me." The last came out in a whisper and Joe was afraid she was going to cry, but then she laughed, managed a smile, and said, "I guess that's what being a teenager is all about—make those parents feel like fools. Revenge."

Joe reached over and squeezed her leg.

"You're not so worried about him tonight, are you?" Gwen said.

"He's a good kid, underneath this rebellion business. I think he'll be okay." He finished his sandwich and took his plate into the kitchen. He didn't want her to see his face, not yet when he wasn't sure what to tell her. He came back into the living room and sat down on the sofa.

"So what's bothering you," she asked. She was dressed in a loose cowl-necked sweater in her favorite shade of brown, something like chocolate ice cream; the collar brushed against her chin, and her earring looked like it might get caught on a loose thread. "Is it work?"

He shook his head and reached for the beer sitting on the table. He wasn't much of a drinker, but given a lazy afternoon and evening with a couple of good games on television, he could make it through a six-pack.

"It's those guys who died, isn't it?"

"Gwen, you're a good mother."

She sat up and looked at him. "Now what?" Her face paled.

"No, the kids are fine. They're not into any trouble. I didn't mean anything like that." She relaxed and her face became flushed.

"You scared me."

"That's the last thing I wanted to do." He couldn't seem to get where he wanted to be.

"Okay. So what was the first thing?"

"I don't want to drift anymore." The bottle was cool in his hands, the label wrinkled along the edges; he began to rub it off with his right thumb. She sat up a few inches, startled by his seemingly off-hand remark.

"Oh." She frowned and crossed her arms over her chest. "You think we're drifting? I thought we were happy as we are."

Her feet were a few inches from him and he reached out and grasped her white-stockinged toes. She never wore slippers in the house—just thick, white winter socks. When they wore out, she threw them away and got another pair. It was her one indulgence, she told him, and she refused to feel guilty about the waste. He studied her face, waiting for a real response.

"I thought you were caught up in those drug deaths."

"I am."

"So you think someone had a hand in it?"

"I'm not so sure about Ron, but Miles? Yes, definitely," he

said. She wiggled her toes. "Ron's story is the typical sad one of someone who experiments too much and it catches up with him, but Miles's death has too many odd details. Things don't add up for him. Plus the doctors were all over Ron when he was taken into the ER."

"And what are you going to do about it?"

"What do you think?" He squeezed her toes and leaned back against the sofa.

"I ran away, didn't I?"

"Yeah."

"Guess my first reaction to anything is to feel skittish and get ready to bolt." Gwen paused. "That's not very honest either." She took a deep breath and let her arms relax. "I feel safe, Joe, and every time we talk I'm afraid we'll upset things. Everything is going so well for me, for us, and I know it's selfish but I can't stand the thought of changing anything because I'm afraid it'll fall apart without our meaning it to." She leaned toward him. "Sometimes I can't believe how happy I am."

Joe leaned forward and kissed her lightly on the lips. "Yes," he said. "I know what you mean." He ran his hand over her cheek. Her skin was smooth and soft, and he loved the feel of it. "But I know what I want in this life, and I'm not sure I'm willing to walk away from it." He watched her eyelashes flutter.

"I can't face anything less than what life can be, not after what I've been through."

"I meant to take you out to dinner and do it the way people tell me you're supposed to."

Gwen leaned forward. "That's sweet." She half-closed her eyes, as though trying to remember something. "I don't think I've thought about that kind of real life since I was a kid." She looked up at him. "Life gets away from you, and when something wonderful happens you feel so lucky and you just want to hang on to it. But to think of reviving all those dreams you put away because they seemed so childish—"

"I've waited too long for something that means so much to me." He tried to study her face the way he would someone he was interrogating, to figure out if he was making a mistake, misjudging her feelings, her desires for the rest of her life, but he couldn't see anything but the woman he loved, the woman who made him think about his job second after her.

"You know, I don't think I was starting to take us for granted. I think I was afraid to look closely for fear the whole thing would fall apart," she said.

"It's not too late," he said when he began to relax, no longer afraid he was on the verge of destroying the one part of his life he could no longer live without. "I thought we could go out to dinner, celebrate our engagement, and then set a date." She drew closer to him and, without a word, slipped her arms around him, and he knew she understood how much it had cost him to admit aloud how much he wanted her.

Chapter 8

Friday Morning

Thanksgiving was next week. Less than a week—six days. The thought struck Joe like an epiphany. He hadn't noticed Thanksgiving creeping up on him, hadn't even thought about the holidays moving closer. And now they fell into his consciousness like a whiff of perfume from a passing stranger. He felt like he had almost missed it, and this year his holidays were going to have real meaning for him.

Joe hummed to himself while he unplugged the electric kettle and poured himself another cup of hot water. His mother had never made a cup of instant coffee in her life but when she came across the kettle in K-Mart she had been fascinated by the odd perspective on life it gave her. The only person she knew who didn't have someone making real coffee for him was Joe, so she had given it to him, but Joe was never convinced that she believed he used it for instant coffee. Along with this gift came her regular offering of freshly ground beans. He poured the water into the tall glass and watched it bubble among the ground coffee. It was 6:15 a.m.

For a fleeting moment he wondered how his parents, in their very late years, would react to his new future. He wondered how he would react. By remaining single well into his fifties, while his brothers and sisters married, raised children, showed off grandchildren, he had taken on a certain role as outsider. His parents had gone on into their eighties, stumbling into old age like a foreign land, refusing to be old when it didn't suit them, insisting they were old, old, old when it did, which wasn't often. Both had kept their sense of humor, and he was especially glad of it now. Joe was marrying well outside the culture, but he was pretty sure his family would embrace Gwen.

He couldn't lose that sense that things were changing for him—his life was moving onto another plane. He was ready for it, eager. Why had he taken so long? Gwen had surprised him with the ease with which she let her thinking change, looking around the apartment as she wondered where they would live. He had left her an hour earlier as she roused Jennie and Philip for school and began getting ready for work herself. Life would be easier when they had one home—he wouldn't have to worry about living in two homes, and wondering where he left important papers or badges or whatever. His condo began to look different to him also, a place too small for a family with two teenagers.

He stared through the glass door facing the inner harbor, which lay just beyond the trees. Wisps of fog drifted erratically in the early light, as though uncertain of their role in the coming day. In late November the leaves were gone, the ground was bare, and Joe could look through the woods up and down the coast as though a curtain had been lifted. This was the time for a walk, a hike along trails little used because people along this part of the coast flew to Montana or Peru or Switzerland to hike. There was nothing here, or so they thought. Here, on a quiet fall day, Joe felt he could see past all the secrets and concealments with which people surrounded themselves and their homes, past the dips and twists in the path. He could see all the way into their hearts—or so it felt.

Joe found his thoughts drifting into the future, imagining the moment of truth when he presented Gwen to his family.

The Silva homestead, a tidy Queen Ann on a side street, with nothing to recommend it except its good repair, had remained a main stop on his siblings' journeys throughout the week. No one made it through the week without stopping in to show off baby photos, pass on the news of a child in college or changes in another neighborhood or just to say hello. Any reason would do, or no reason at all. The visit was the thing. And the largest number of visitors showed up on Thursday evenings and Sunday afternoons.

The steam from Joe's coffee cup left little kisses of moisture on the glass door near his fingers. The misty shapes puffed and shrank and rose and fell like a flame. Joe drew the cup to his lips and drank; the cloud evaporated. He waited for the knock on the door, which came a little after 7:30. He opened it without surprise to Philip McDuffy, Gwen's son.

"She doesn't know I'm here," Philip said as he entered. He sized up the living room before walking into the center of it, as though he had to be reassured that no one suspicious was lurking in the corners. When he reached the center, he stuffed his hands in his pockets and turned to face Joe. "What'dya want from me?" He looked around at the furniture, his eyes bouncing from one item to the next, his shoulders rising and falling as though he were doing shoulder rolls for exercise.

"You had breakfast?"

"Yeah, sure."

"Come on." Joe put his arm around the boy's shoulders and led him into the kitchen. Joe opened the refrigerator, pulled out a carton of eggs, and began to make scrambled eggs for both of them. He toasted bread, made more coffee, poured juice, and nodded to the table in the next room. "I know you ate, but try this too." The boy wolfed it down, barely looking at Joe in the process.

"So you're going to marry her?" Philip said when he was finished. He still hadn't looked at Joe, but Joe was patient.

"We're talking about it. How do you feel about that? Would it bother you?"

Philip began to squirm in his chair while trying to shake his head no.

"You don't mind having a cop for a stepfather?"

Again, the shoulders lifted and sank and rolled, and the head shook back and forth. "She likes you okay."

"I hope so." Joe pushed his plate away and poured himself another cup of coffee. "So, tell me, Philip, why are you trying so hard to be like that group of kids?"

Philip glanced up at Joe and stared at him before dropping his eyes to his lap. "I don't try to be like anyone else."

"No?"

"No."

"You can do things in your own time, but make sure what you do is what you want to do. Not what you think you have to do to get through high school." Joe leaned back in his chair and waited. He had gambled on Philip being a decent kid, someone who would own up to his problems given the right environment. When Philip hadn't protested in a bitter retort that Gwen wasn't really his mother during their confrontation earlier in the week, Joe knew they could work it out.

"What does that mean?" He gave his plate a surly look.

"I mean, when you're ready. Your mother loves you—no matter what, she loves you. She'd cut off her arm for you."

"Yeah?" His look was defiant and cynical. "That's what they all say."

"Who's they? Steve Dolanetti?" Joe said. Philip's mouth dropped open. "Is that what happened to him?"

"What?"

"He told his parents he was gay and they threw him out?"

"Are you going to tell her?"

"Hell, no, Philip. It's your life. It's up to you. You have to make the decision, whatever it is." Joe leaned forward, wondering how Gwen would react if she learned about this meeting. She would either love him for it or hate him for it. "You have to be who you are, Philip. No matter how hard it seems at first."

"How do you know?" Philip asked, growing less surly.

"That's not important. Maybe I'll tell you some time, but right now it's only about you."

The message was waiting on Joe's desk when he got there before eight o'clock. One of the investigators at the state lab had called to make sure Joe knew what was in the plastic bag taken from Miles's room. The combination seemed so odd and so potentially lethal to him that he wanted to be sure Joe knew about it. That was his message, but, unfortunately, he wasn't available when Joe arrived in the office, and Joe was left wondering what was so dangerous about mixing salvia divinorum and anti-malarial medication. The fax from the state lab had the usual matter-of-fact statements and nothing to indicate why the investigator was alarmed or wanted to follow up.

"Who has that travel clinic?" Joe asked Maxwell as soon as he had reread the message.

"That's the clinic down on Main."

"Good. Then I can kill two birds with one stone," Joe said.

"Don't let Ken hear you say that," Maxwell said.

"I think I'll just finish this up and then I'll head over there," Joe said with a laugh.

Joe left the station and crossed the village green. He could see the clinic from his office window, and knew the practitioners were there even if it wasn't officially open. A large sign in the front window announced that OxyContin was not available in the clinic, a warning that had become necessary in recent years to ward off those who had become desperately addicted. A white-haired man peered through the window at the sound of Joe's shoes on the stairs; a nurse in a maroon blouse over brightly patterned cotton pants opened the door to his knock. Joe made his business known and Dr. Baldwin invited him into his office in the back.

The Mellingham Clinic was a small business with three doctors, four nurses, office staff, and a series of tiny offices and exam rooms. It survived in this era of high-tech medicine because a good number of Mellites hated to leave town for any reason, including life-or-death medical care. When that changed, Dr. Baldwin would go out of business, but by then he'd probably be retired, Joe thought.

"This must be about Miles Stine's death," Dr. Baldwin said. He was a large man with fine white hair that drifted down over his forehead in a deep wave, and a barrel chest and short legs. If he had a dog, it most certainly would be a bulldog—friendly, but a bulldog nonetheless. He moved with unexpected grace and quickness.

"I have some information that doesn't make much sense to me, and I was wondering if you could help me with it."

"I suppose," the doctor said. He looked like someone who not only didn't suffer fools gladly but also didn't suffer anyone else either; gruff, brusque, and efficient, he probably intimidated his patients into getting well regardless of their illness.

"I want to know about something called mefloquine," Joe said, checking his notes.

"Why?"

"It's not necessary for me to impart that, Dr. Baldwin," Joe said.

"All right. Mefloquine is a new anti-malarial drug that's considered quite effective. It has side effects that are hard for some people to tolerate, but otherwise is a good drug for its purpose."

"And what are those side effects?" Joe asked.

"They vary," Dr. Baldwin said, changing position in his chair. "Dizziness, unsteadiness or imbalance when walking, headaches, muscular aches in the neck, motion sickness, fatigue, loss of stamina, an inability to concentrate, that sort of thing."

"Anything else?"

"Such as?"

"You tell me." Joe watched the man change position again and wondered that they didn't teach body language in medical school. "Other side effects could be worse?"

Dr. Baldwin grew still and studied Joe, as though checking out his appearance for signs of illness. "Well, there have been some studies indicating irritability, loss of self-esteem and depression, and vertigo leading to complete disability."

"That doesn't sound deadly but it could work out pretty bad for someone," Joe said, trying to feel his way through this morass of information.

"It could."

"So exactly how might this play out?"

"Someone who is pretty quiet and upbeat could become moody and depressed," Baldwin said. "Something like that."

"Or someone who has always been pretty mild can suddenly turn nasty? Is that possible?"

"Yes, something like that."

"And he could start turning on his friends?"

"He'd be irritable, possibly, and they might take it like that."

"What about the vertigo?"

"Someone not expecting it might find himself on a bridge and suddenly feel like he's losing his balance and falling. Vertigo can differ in people."

Joe waited, thinking. "So someone taking this could get angry, lose their balance, and maybe fall to their death?"

"Possible." Dr. Baldwin studied Joe carefully. "Are you making a connection to that death earlier this week?"

Joe ignored the question. "What about mixing it with something hallucinatory?"

This question finally hit home. Baldwin whistled softly. "Bad. Just hypothetically? Someone on a hallucinatory drug isn't seeing reality clearly, and with a medication with psychotic side effects, he'd be very vulnerable to poor judgment. Anything could happen."

"That makes this mefloquine pretty dangerous," Joe said. "How is it sold?"

"It's generally prescribed for travel to areas where malaria is common."

"Brand names?"

"I've only prescribed one, Lariam."

"How commonly available is this?"

"Travelers like to be safe," the doctor said. "No one wants their trip interrupted with a serious illness. Malaria is serious."

"It sounds like the medication alone could ruin a trip," Joe said.

"Yes, some people have had psychotic reactions to the medication and have had to be hospitalized until it wears off," he said.

"Have you prescribed this for anyone recently?"

"Recently? No."

"Maybe we should get our terms straight. How about in the last year?"

"I'd have to check," he said, steepling his fingers.

"I'll wait."

Startled by Joe's response, the doctor looked him over, then picked up his telephone and gave an order to the person on the other end of the line. When he put the telephone down, Joe let the silence lengthen.

"I think Edna Stine works here, doesn't she?" Joe asked when the doctor began to rearrange the files on his desk.

"Office manager, sort of," the doctor said.

"How long has she been here?"

"Years. I'd have to check but probably near to ten years."

"How's she taking her son's death?"

Dr. Baldwin's eyes flickered and Joe wondered if he was censoring himself from giving something away. "She's confused right now. We've given her some time off, of course."

"Her son wasn't one of your patients, was he?"

"Miles? No, I don't ever remember seeing his name here," the doctor said. "He's not an official patient of ours, but last week he was in trying to get a flu shot. Is there some connection between his death and Ron Faroli's?"

"Not that we know of," Joe said, putting him off.

Baldwin glanced out the window at the large oak tree growing at the edge of the sidewalk. Though it was tall, it was a midget compared to the giant Dutch elm that had marked that spot for years, living long past most of the other elms cut down by Dutch elm disease in the 1950s and 1960s. It had finally succumbed, and only the old-timers remembered it with longing. A woman pushing a baby carriage passed along the sidewalk. "Hard to believe the things that can happen in this town—it's beautiful and clean and full of decent people just living out their lives. But whatever the poison is somewhere else, it seeps in here too."

"It's too bad these miracle drugs are turning out to be such a mixed blessing," Joe said. "We had that case of someone overdosing on OxyC last week, and that was supposed to be such a great breakthrough for pain treatment." The doctor nodded and seemed to relax with the change in the direction of the conversation.

"Some of the new medications are so potent that doctors outside of the research laboratory are a little afraid of them," he said.

"I noticed your sign on the door out there," Joe said. "Just in case? Or did you have some trouble that persuaded you to not carry it."

"We thought it would be safer to get it out there right away," he said. "About a month ago we had a patient who called and only wanted pain medication. You know who is having trouble among your clients and we just didn't want to give it to him. If that's all the patient wants and won't follow other medical advice, we face the decision of dropping them from our practice. We can't operate on the receiving end of what is basically harassment from a patient seeking safe access to an addictive drug. That's when we decided it would be better not to carry it at all. If we really need to get it or something like it, we can. It's only a matter of a day."

"Did you have many patients for whom you prescribed the drug?"

"Two or three," Dr. Baldwin said, pausing. "We've had our doubts about it too."

"Can you give me a list of the patients?" Joe asked, confident now he knew at least one name on the list. The doctor winced and started to lean forward, but Joe wouldn't add to his comment. The silence deepened.

"You're looking for one name in particular, aren't you?"

"Mrs. Stine," Joe said.

"Yes, she had a prescription." The doctor looked like he

might be sick; he began to breathe heavily, as though his ashen face meant loss of oxygen.

"You weren't worried about her and the other patients? You just quit carrying it?"

"We have other resources," he said. "So we'll just send it back."

"You will send it back?" Joe repeated.

"Yeah."

"You mean you haven't yet?"

"No. Not yet."

"It's just sitting here?"

The doctor studied him, trying to figure out the point of Joe's comment. "I wouldn't put it that way. It's locked up in the store room."

"Your clinic got a call after Ron Faroli's death about whether or not you had any OxyContin," Joe said. "You were away on vacation last week, but the answer my officer got from your partner was no, there was nothing here."

"I don't know who took the call," Dr. Baldwin said.

"Your colleague."

"Well, he may have had to consult someone else. Anyway, the person who answered the question may have misunderstood it," Baldwin said, looking concerned. "We tell anyone who calls we don't have it, unless, of course, it's another doctor."

"So you do have it here?" Joe said.

"Yes and no. We carried it and decided not to after that difficulty," he said. "And we arranged for the supply we had, small supply, I should add, to be sent back. And it should have been sent back by then. Everyone in the clinic probably thought it was already gone, since that was the declared plan. We made it clear to the whole staff that it was no longer going to be available and what we had was going back. Whoever took the call may have thought it had already gone back to the supplier."

"Why the delay?" Joe asked.

"Our regular courier was out sick and, with something this important, we didn't want to take a chance on someone we didn't know, so we put it aside until we could get our regular guy."

"Fair enough," Joe said.

"It didn't seem a big deal to us."

"One of the things we couldn't figure out was where Ron Faroli and his friends got the OxyC that killed him. The drugstores don't carry it and we couldn't track down anyone who had lost a number of pills or anyone who had filled a suspicious prescription." Joe paused, wandering if Dr. Baldwin was interested enough to follow this to its logical end.

"What're you getting at?" he asked.

"I'd like you to inventory the OxyC," Joe said.

Dr. Baldwin looked worried but he nodded. When the telephone rang, he picked it up and listened, then hung up. "We prescribed Lariam to four people in the last nine months." He recited the names; the last one was Paula Faroli.

Before Joe pulled out of the clinic parking lot he called in instructions to the station and waited a few minutes for a reply. The answer came just as a battered black Honda drove past him.

"I see it now," Joe said. "Probably heading for the Community Center." He pulled out of the parking lot and followed the car, parking along the sidewalk as the other car pulled up in front of the Community Center. Chandra Stine climbed out, unfolding herself with the gangly awkwardness that promised future graceful beauty. She ran up the steps to the Center just as Joe approached the car. Edna Stine emerged from the other side of the car and hailed him. She turned to the sidewalk leaving her car door ajar.

"Have you talked to the funeral home?" she asked without preamble.

"I'd like to talk to you, Mrs. Stine," Joe began.

"What about the funeral home?" she said. "I talked to them yesterday about planning the funeral and they were very helpful—I suppose they're always helpful; it's their job, isn't it? But when I called them about the date they said they couldn't quite settle it just yet. 'Couldn't quite settle it.' That's what he said. He said," she continued on, beginning to sound breathless, "that he hasn't got a release or the information for a certificate or something. How can you not have the information for a death certificate?" She glared at him.

He watched her shift her weight, one hip pushed out. She gave no sign that she sensed in Joe a less than engaged listener, someone without sympathy or even much interest in what she was saying.

"My son's body is just sort of hanging around waiting. I want to know what you're going to do about it."

"We're just waiting for some information before we go ahead. That's all." Joe smiled at her waiting to see if she would accept the delay, but that's not what happened. She repositioned her feet on the ground and stiffened her neck.

"What's going on here?" she said. "You're not telling me something."

"Why don't you tell me something," he said. His demand caught her off guard and she blinked once, as though to make certain he was really there talking to her.

"What?"

"Ron and Miles got together last week when they got hold of some OxyContin pills," he said. "There were several of them hanging out together, but only two of them shared

208

the pills. Ron and Miles sent the others away. When it got out of hand, Miles took Ron to the hospital and left him there. We know all that, Mrs. Stine. We know what they took together."

"He took—" She stared at him, unable to finish the sentence.

"We want to know how he got it, Mrs. Stine." Joe waited. Edna looked dazed, as though she couldn't fathom what Joe was saying.

"He had a bad back," she said. "He hurt his back."

"And you told him you had something better than aspirin," he said. "What did he tell you?"

"Well, I don't know. Nothing special. I mean, he's a boy, my son. What do people talk about?"

"About his bad back?"

"Sure. He hurt it."

"How?"

"I don't know. He didn't tell me. I . . ."

At the sound of a car driving up she turned with a hopeful expression on her face as though someone might be passing who would rescue her. She had begun to rub her shoe along the ground, not quite a shuffling of the feet but an edginess in her limbs she couldn't control, and was probably not even aware of.

"How many pills did you give him from your prescription?"

"Me?"

"Yes. You had a prescription and you shared it with him. How many?" He leaned over her, his face within six inches of hers. Her face twitched as she tried to figure out what he was saying and the implications.

"You can't ask me that." There was no conviction in her words, but she seemed to gain confidence or stubbornness as she continued. "I know my rights. I watch those television shows. You're talking out of turn, Mister Chief Joe Silva."

"We can do this down at the station."

"You can't talk to me like this."

He waited long enough for her to absorb this. "Shall we go to the station?"

She shook her head.

"How many pills?" he said.

"One."

Joe sighed and pulled back. "One," he said.

"He had a bad back and he was hurting. You can't imagine what it was like for him to have to spend a night in jail in Boston or wherever. That's why he drank and did—" Now that she was free to tell all, she did—every excuse, every rationalization, every grand theory tumbled forth. She had clutched each one, refined and stored it, brought each one out at its appointed time, but now all of them were hurled at him like so many medieval weapons. Joe wasn't really listening; he was waiting until she ran out of steam—or illusions.

"How many do you have left?"

She shook her head and the tears welled in her eyes. "None." Barely a whisper.

"When did you find that out?"

"The day we found Miles. I—" She pulled out a tattered tissue and dabbed at her eyes. "I was upset. I went home and I found the bottle but . . . nothing."

"How many were in the bottle before Miles asked?"

"I got the prescription about six months ago, when I had a fall. I never took more than one a week. And I had about six left. I just kept the rest, you know, in case I needed something."

"Only six. Do you remember taking any yourself?"

She looked up ready to speak, opened her mouth, and stood there, a look of confused awe on her face. "I think I should stop talking to you."

"You'd better come along to the station," Joe said. He glanced down the street to see another police car pulling up. He'd get her down there with Maxwell. "We need a statement."

She blanched. "He was facing a tough week, that's all," she said, unable to stop herself from defending her dead son. "He had a meeting with a probation officer on Tuesday and a job interview on Wednesday and a meeting with a counselor on Thursday. It was a rough week. There isn't any law against giving your son—"

"Did he know you got your prescription through the clinic?"

"Probably."

"You didn't tell him?"

"It's a clinic, isn't it? I work there and I get my health care there too. He did too sometimes."

"When?"

"He went there for a flu shot. Had to wait forever. They said he wasn't on the list and they had to be sure they had enough before they gave him a shot—they kept telling him to go to the Health Department, but the Health Department didn't have enough serum. What kind of service is that? I worked there—"

"So he was sitting there in the offices for quite some time."

Joe imagined Miles camped out in the waiting room while Edna tried to get on with her work. Was he studying the habits of the employees and the location of their resources? Was he figuring out where the drugs were kept? And when his mother tried to reassure him he'd get his flu shot, was he laying the groundwork for something else? Was he planting ideas in Edna's imagination, setting her up to help him? If he'd already taken her pills and was asking for more, would she inadvertently glance toward the room where medicine was stored, telling him where to look when no one was around? Was she a victim of his manipulative addiction, or was she just as alienated, willing to steal from her employer for her only surviving son?

Joe returned to his original problem.

Three, maybe four, good friends who regularly got together after getting out of detox.

Ron Faroli. Miles Stine. Tiny Morley. Bernard Foster.

Two down and two to go.

Joe watched Edna Stine climb into the back seat of the other squad car. He drew his hand down his tie, making sure it was in place. A callus on his index finger snagged on a fiber and he felt it pull.

Denny Clark was crossing the large room when Joe caught sight of him. When Denny turned at the sound of Joe's footsteps, their eyes met and Denny at once changed direction and headed to his office. Joe followed and closed the door behind them.

"What can you tell me about Bernard Whitson?" Joe said. Denny shook his head and leaned against his desk.

"Haven't seen him today and can't really remember yesterday. The days start to blur—"

"How commonly known was it that he hung around with Ron and Miles?" The easy confidence and businesslike air seemed to turn stale like cooking odors late at night.

"Lots of people knew," Denny said. "They spent a lot of time in detox together. Sometimes people make real friends in a program. Most don't but it happens sometimes."

"And it happened this time," Joe said. Denny nodded. "And it was common knowledge."

"Yeah. It was." Denny looked uncertain how to continue. "They hung around together. People saw them together. But people saw Bernard with a lot of people, and, well, the other two had grown up here so no one was surprised to see one or the other of them talking to someone else. Bernard was new; he didn't know many people."

"Outside of their closed world, who else knew these guys were close?"

"I dunno."

"You knew."

"Well, sure, but—"

"But what?"

"Nothing, I mean—"

Joe took a step toward him. "Denny, you're pretty good at hiding things, starting over as though nothing had happened. But you know what's going on here."

"What's that supposed to mean?"

"You knew enough about Miles not staying clean, almost right out of detox, to warn his sister to stay away from him—"

"I just told her—"

"To stay away from her brother and his friends. Yes, I know all about it."

"It was just a bit of advice, that's all."

"Like you gave that boy in Connecticut?"

Denny blanched. "You—"

"I know all about your year off for medical reasons—six months in, six months probation. Easy time, for almost killing someone for just talking to your daughter."

Denny's fists were clenched, his breathing grew shorter and noisy, like a pair of old bellows that wouldn't quite work—the leather stiff and old and tired. His lids fell halfway down over his eyes, and then he took a deep breath and let it out, just as Joe was beginning to wonder if the man was going to have a heart attack right in front of him. Back among the living. At least he remembered that much from his anger management class, Joe thought.

"Yes, I did time. But no, I had nothing to do with Ron and Miles's deaths. Nothing whatsoever." No word of sympathy, no soothing words, just a denial. Joe was pressing the smoothness out of him like oil from an olive.

"You warned Chandra as though the threat were now, right now."

"It was. She's young. Miles—" He stopped abruptly. In that moment his posture changed and he looked at Joe squarely. "That's how it happens. It's the older brother or sister who introduces the younger one to drugs. She's a nice girl. Someone has to look out for her."

"You think Miles was pushing drugs on his sister?"

"Joe, I think—" Denny took a deep breath and started again. "I think he was selling to the younger kids, to make a few bucks."

"Are you sure of that?"

"I saw him every now and then talking to someone in high school, one of the kids that seemed on the edge, alienated from his parents, living at a friend's house, that sort of thing."

Joe paused, thought about it.

"There's a crowd of them. Joe, Gwen's son is in it."

Joe stepped back. "Where were you Wednesday night from ten o'clock on?" he said. Denny looked befuddled, but then his face cleared. Ah, thought Joe, as Denny's mind caught hold of a forgotten reality: like the hand discovering an extra ten dollars forgotten in a coat pocket, like discovering the train is late too and so you haven't missed it.

"I was on the phone with my ex-wife and my computer

most of the night, planning my trip." Denny said, "And I was on a chat line with friends who know me. We travel together sometimes."

"Where're you going?" Joe asked, still waiting for the crack in the blue sky.

"I can see my daughter once a year," Denny said. "I wouldn't miss it for anything." He wasn't pleading. Joe believed him. He spoke without tension, without fear he would not be believed. And he spoke from the safety of distance—he had found he could love his daughter without fear if he loved her from afar. By letting go, it had all come to him.

"I'll send an officer around to take a statement from you," Joe said. "I'll need your ex-wife's name and address."

"No problem, Joe."

"Who else did you warn?" Joe said, turning to the hope Denny knew something useful.

"What'd you mean?"

"Who else did you warn? Did you tell Edna Stine her son should stay away from Ron and Bernard? Did you tell Bernard he'd be safer elsewhere? Did you tell George or Paula Faroli to keep Ron away from Miles and Bernard? Did you tell Tiny and Steve, or maybe Missi to stay away from Ron and his friends? Who else did you talk to? Who did you warn?"

"I didn't warn anyone." Denny looked surprised, as though Joe's suggestions had never occurred to him.

Joe shook his head. Rumors of who was doing what spread across the town like the random movements of flies, but the rumors weren't random and who knew what wasn't true.

"You know," Denny said, looking thoughtful, shaken, perhaps relieved that someone now knew his secret. "I tried to tell Paula once about how worried I was about the secret drug problem here in Mellingham, but I think she already knew. This is a wonderful town for the small family that wants to just raise a family and work nearby and live a simple, old-fashioned life—the kind that everyone thinks is safe and healthy. No one talks about the stock broker who takes to using coke because he can't stand the stress of the market going up and down like a yoyo, and then mostly down. Or the lawyer who gets into a drug problem and uses up his clients' trust funds. There's a lot of stuff hidden in nice homes that gets ignored while the rest of us worry about the ones who are out in the open and seek treatment or go to jail. We jump on the obvious."

"That's not what we're dealing with here, Denny." Joe could feel it all coming together and he didn't like it at all. "So you shared your concerns about drugs with Paula."

"I don't think any of it was news to her."

"What gave you that impression?"

"She didn't seem surprised or upset, the way some women in town are when they learn that Mellingham isn't perfect. She listened to me and then started going on about the people Ron knew and how hard it was for him going in and out of detox. He had a pretty bad record with those places, you know."

"Yeah, I know," Joe said. "It can take a few tries before the whole thing sticks."

A low-level buzz filled the Mellingham Community Center and greeted Joe as he stepped out of Denny Clark's office. He felt like he had stumbled into a doll's house with little snatches of innocuous conversation wreathing the rafters overhead. Not a soul in the room was unfamiliar with tragedy or pain or sorrow but they didn't show any of that; they chose instead the face of optimism and good cheer. The roles we choose are for ourselves and no one else, Joe thought.

"Chief Silva!" Ann Rose caught him as he was reaching for the front-door knob. Joe turned at the sound of her voice.

"I'm in a hurry, Mrs. Rose," Joe said.

"I won't take a lot of your time. I really owe you an apology," she began and Joe reluctantly turned away from the door. "I know I must have sounded just awful about Chandra yesterday, all that worrying that she might be using. I'm not sure what came over me—it was all anxiety and worry talking, no common sense at all."

"Don't worry about it," Joe said. "It's a normal concern these days."

"Well, I do worry about it. I know I'm overreacting. I tend to do that—I suppose that's where I get a lot of my energy—I see something and I react and it sends me off like a rock in a catapult. I'm off and running, so to speak." She stopped to take a breath. "But I was worried about Chandra. She's such a sweet kid, and really, life should be good to her. It's hard not to worry about her with all that's going on in her life."

"She seems fine, though she might want to talk to someone about her brother's death. I can pass along a few names, if you think that would help." But it wasn't going to be that easy, he realized; he wasn't going to slip away on the promise of a few names for referral.

"It's just that everyone seems so fraught these days, if you know what I mean," she said.

He allowed as he did and moved toward the door. "I appreciate that, Mrs. Rose," he said, reaching for the doorknob.

"Well, I thought if nothing else, we should take a leaf out of Paula's book," she continued, oblivious to Joe's drift toward the door. "I have such admiration for her. I don't know if I could do the same thing in her place. She's been through hell and yet she's still generous hearted and forgiving and it's amazing to me."

Joe nodded. "That's good," he said, moving away.

"It seemed that we could help her by coming together as a community. You know, holding a healing service and talking about the strengths of the community and remembering Ron in a more positive light and how people can help each other. I don't quite know where this is going, but I was hoping you'd be willing to help out. Well, be part of a program or something like that."

"I'd be glad to, Mrs. Rose. Just let the office know what you have in mind when you get farther along with your planning."

"Well, that's just it," she said, moving closer to him. They were inching their way to the door. "Paula is so full of compassion and forgiveness and I think we need to do something now before it's too late for her to appreciate it. Or need it. Lord knows, the whole town could use some healing after all this. Two deaths in a week. That's shocking."

"I agree with you there."

"I could not do what she did," Ann said, shaking her head. "Honestly, I could not."

Joe could only nod.

"Granted I don't have children. But if someone killed my husband, I could no more go to that person's house with a family treasure and say, 'Here, you were once his friend and I know you meant well.' If someone drove him down with a car or knocked him into a tree while skiing, I could not feel any kinder toward the killer than I do toward an ordinary murderer." Ann Rose looked up to see Joe staring at her.

"What family treasure are you talking about, Mrs. Rose?"

"That box that Ron made in high school. Paula said Ron had made it when he was a teenager, and it was something that he had kept for himself over the years. She and George had decided to forgive Miles, and this was how they were showing it. Sort of a symbol of their forgiveness." Ann stopped and pulled out a Kleenex and wiped her eyes. "It makes me so emotional every time I think about it. I can't imagine being that altruistic."

"Nor can I," Joe said. "Who told you this?"

"Paula. I saw her going into the Cleary place carrying this large canvas bag. I didn't think anything of it, but when I saw her later downtown I asked her if there was more trouble at the Cleary's and she said no, she'd just gone over to tell Miles that she had forgiven him. She didn't mention the box but I could see it in the bag when I drove past. It was sitting on the sidewalk while she was getting something else out of the car. I asked her about it, and I think it embarrassed her when I mentioned it. She is modest about what she does in town as a volunteer and that sort of thing."

"She told you Ron made it and she was giving it to Miles?"

"Isn't that amazing?" Ann said. "I don't know where people get the courage. I'm not sure I could have done that."

"Did she ask you to keep this quiet?"

"Well, yes, she did, but she's always like that—she's very modest. She doesn't like a lot of fuss, you know, and I don't blame her. I know she would be touched if we did something for her. She and George deserve some support for all they've been through. And Edna too," she added as an afterthought.

"How did Paula feel about that?"

"Oh, I didn't mention that part to her. It's a little early for that, don't you think?"

"It's a fine idea, Mrs. Rose, but I think for now I'd keep it very low key. Don't start planning anything until you talk to me. Agreed?"

"Well, I suppose so." She gazed at him with a certain skepticism. She had wanted his involvement, but not quite to this extent. "If you say so. But we'll talk soon about this, won't we? I don't think I should let it go too long."

"We'll talk soon, for sure," Joe promised. "For sure."

Chapter 9

Friday Afternoon

The parking lot of Faroli Provisions was almost full, as it usually was on a Friday afternoon, with families shopping for the weekend, gathering up those last few items—rosemary vinegar, freshly ground mace, cilantro, a certain kind of polenta—crucial to a new recipe but overlooked nonetheless during the previous shopping trip. Joe drove down back and parked by the delivery door. The parking lot was clean, recently swept according to the striations in the sand along the edge. The occasional cigarette butt along the stone revetment had little impact on the overall effect of tidiness.

Joe moved past the two checkout lines to the office in the back. A small store with only four narrow aisles, deliveries sometimes spilled out of the back room. The accountant's office was on the top floor, in the converted—and cramped—attic. A tall man in a long white apron hailed Joe.

"I'm looking for George. Is he here?" Joe said.

The clerk shook his head. "Hasn't come in today." He pulled a crate into line atop four others and turned back to Joe. Marley had a ruddy, lined face as though he worked outside in all seasons throughout the day—and had done so for most of his life. His hands shifted, lifted, moved, carried crates and boxes all day long with an ease that belied his thin, wiry frame, with never a pause for an extra breath. Shrewd and quick, he had managed the business with George for probably thirty years or more, but considered himself just another employee.

"Is that unusual?" Joe asked.

"Right now, his life is unusual, isn't it?" He reached for a clipboard and dropped it onto another stack of crates. "He's been up and down since Ron died."

Joe prodded and Marley drew them into the back office—dark and cramped, something out of Dickens with its old wooden desks piled high with papers and a thin film of dirt interleaving the stacks.

"At first he took it really hard," Marley said. "George came in—what, last week—doesn't seem possible. Anyway, he was like a robot, just working but not really working. The guy was drowning. Then after the funeral he seemed to buck up."

"Buck up? How do you mean? Did he say anything?"

"No, just buck up. He seemed to be back in the world." Marley paused and crossed his arms across his chest. "He kept saying it was an accident, that just as Ron was turning a corner, there was this accident." He shrugged and spread out his arms in a futile embrace of empty air.

"Did he say anything more?"

"Just that he said a few days ago that Ron didn't know who anyone really was, but more like he meant we don't know people well even if they're our friends. That's an odd comment from George."

A bit of something damp fell into the office from the top sash where it had dropped down and gotten stuck over the years as the building shifted.

"George isn't the philosophical type," Joe said.

"Too right. Too right."

"How did you take it?"

"I just thought he meant that he realized he didn't know his son very well and regretted it," Marley said.

"Where is he today?"

"Don't know. Haven't seen him since last night."

"Here?"

Marley nodded. "We're open till seven on Thursdays and I had just locked up and was out the back when I saw George's car pull into the parking lot. He came in to pick something up, I guess."

"You didn't talk to him?"

"Nope. I was done for the day, and I figured if George wanted to talk to me he would've called before seven."

"He didn't see you?"

Marley shook his head and scratched under his chin. "I walked home along the canal and came out on Trask Street up a ways. He probably didn't even know I was there."

"So you don't know what he wanted at that hour." Marley shook his head. "Was he alone? Was Mrs. Faroli with him?"

"Not Mrs. Faroli. That Bernard kid. One of the people Ron hung around with."

"Bernard Whitson? You're sure? You know who he is?"

"Oh yeah. He and Tiny and Ron used to come in here to pick up a sandwich from the deli counter; sometimes Ron ran up a pretty big bill—steaks, deli items—everything but liquor. I thought maybe that's what George was doing here—getting food for Bernard—but there was nothing missing this morning. No notes about what he took, nothing like that."

"No sandwiches."

"Nope."

"Nothing else disturbed? Nothing?"

"No prep food but I didn't check anything else. As for in here—" He looked around as if to say, no one would know if anything had been taken or moved around anyway. He looked at Joe with renewed interest. "I missed something, didn't I?"

"Did you see them drive away? Up Trask? Main?"

Marley shook his head slowly, his long solid fingers pulling on his arms as he tried to remember. He was a man without suspicion; he would listen and answer questions without making a judgment about anyone or later eagerly telling his wife about what he'd talked to the chief of police about.

"Look, I don't know if this is any help," Marley said. "But last week, out of the blue, George said to me—he was sorting through some papers in here and I thought he saw something out of the window that got him talking. He said, not really to me, maybe he didn't even know I was in the room, but he said, 'Ron.' Then he said, 'Tiny, Bernie, Miles. All those friends.' " Marley ran his hand across his mouth. "He wasn't talking to me, I guess."

"Had he ever mentioned Ron and his friends before?"

"Oh, sure. Once Ron came in with Tiny and went up and down the aisles pulling things off the shelf and then charged them to his dad. George was furious when he found out, but he didn't say anything to anyone here. Tiny never came in with Ron again."

"Anyone else?"

"Ron did that kind of thing with everyone. Buying friends, that's what I call it. Druggies don't know what real friendship is, or how to make friends—you know, loyalty, trust, honesty—those things we take for granted—so they get people to hang around by spending if they have it, or sharing drugs they do have. Buying friends."

"Who else knew about this?"

"Everyone. The girls who work up front don't have all that much loyalty to the store—they haven't been here that long, I guess. They love George and Paula, but Ron was just a problem. Everyone in town knew about him. It was no secret George and Paula were really struggling with Ron."

"Did he ever talk to you about his feelings about what happened to Ron?"

"You mean other than telling me the world had gone to shit?"

"That's it?"

"Well, now that you mention it, he did say a couple of days ago that his one fear was that this would eat at him for the rest of his life."

"What exactly?"

"We were talking about the deli assistant—she obsesses something fierce about her boyfriend's mother. It's sort of a joke around here. How was your weekend, Sally? You will not believe what Bobby's mother did, and on and on. George didn't want to be like that."

"George's spent his entire life here, hasn't he?"

"Every blessed year except for two years in the army—he was sent to Fort Knox, I think. It was during the Vietnam era, right at the end, but he never served overseas. This is his life, this town."

"And someone poisoned it for him," Joe said.

"I wouldn't know about that, but I guess I'd have to assume, yes. What he's going through is tough."

Joe pulled onto Main Street, nodding to Sergeant Dupoulis as he drove past, on his way to the Farolis' house. Joe had called the station as soon as he got back to his car to have Ken check out the Faroli place, but Joe didn't expect Ken to find George there. It was time to question Paula about George's whereabouts, but without spooking her. At this point, Joe couldn't decide what Paula's role had been, nor could he calculate confidently the role she would adopt if she tumbled to what he was thinking. She might be the virtuous, self-sacrificing helpmate, or the innocent and wronged grieving mother, or something else. The possibilities were endless, limited only by her imagination. Joe had decided to send Ken with the idea that he might seem less threatening than Joe. If the sergeant went instead of the chief, how big a deal could it be?

The police car cruised along Main Street while Joe considered one route after another. Not since his older brother had been sent home from Vietnam in the early 1960s, before it was a war to protest and argue about, before it was Vietnam, a name that resonated all over North America and beyond, not in almost forty years had Joe felt such shocks all over his skin, as though every hair on his body was a needle and each one electrified. He had watched his brother emerge on a stretcher from the back of an airplane, remarkably, surprisingly still alive, with no one expecting him to live—but he had.

Joe was finishing high school, feeling that tug which said the world is larger than you think—and all of it just waiting for you. And then here came Paulo, his older brother, the one he truly respected—not idolized—that was for dreamers. Joe trusted Paulo, believed in him, understood the choices he had made—or so Joe felt. To see Paulo on a stretcher, so vulnerable, looking broken, his big chest staved in like the side of a ship, was to see his own mortality. Joe didn't even know he was crying until he felt the wet tears dribbling along his chin.

In subsequent years no other family tragedy had affected him as much—he had learned the philosophy that unless the end result is death, it isn't worth the hysteria. And if the end result is death, hysteria was the least useful reaction anyone could come up with.

As he drove down a tree-lined street Joe recalled Paulo's

figure on the stretcher, his face so pale only his black hair told you he was there. But it wasn't Paulo's face he saw; it was Philip's, a mere boy, a kid starting out. A boy, a child. So Paulo had seemed when they brought him home. Joe turned left and cruised past the Community Center—no sign of Tiny. The fall leaves were no longer fragments of gold floating through the air. At the end of the street he turned right and drove on toward the shore.

Joe turned into the beach parking lot; at the opposite end sat Tiny's beat-up station wagon. Joe pulled up alongside, got out, and peered into the back at a sleeping bag and various piles of possessions. But no Tiny.

The dark green benches, bolted in place on concrete platforms, looked uninviting; protected by straw-like beach grass bending under the weight of the coming winter. Joe set off down the path in search of Tiny or anyone else who might help. Two other cars in the lot meant that most likely someone else was around. He could see two people walking dogs near the rocks at the far end, but neither one looked like Tiny. And Tiny wouldn't be walking a dog, his or anyone else's.

"What're you looking for, Chief?"

Joe swung around at the sound of a voice, tried to get a bearing on it, and pushed his way through the thick undergrowth. He emerged into a small clearing to see Tiny and Mack, a zealous DPW employee and defender of all qualities of beach life, wrapped in blankets and sitting on beach chairs.

"Tiny, you're a hard man to find. Hello, Mack."

"I am?" Tiny said. Mack nodded, and settled a little deeper into his blanket.

"I'm looking for Bernard, and I think we need to find him fast."

A glazed look came over Tiny's eyes. Tiny was going to be barely able to hold himself together through this, but there was no other way to reach him, Joe thought.

"I don't know where he is."

"He was supposed to leave town yesterday but he never got on the train. Someone saw him with George Faroli last night."

Tiny and Mack glanced at each other, their faces blank. "George Faroli? Him and Bernie ain't friends." Tiny shook his head as he spoke.

"Did he stay with you last night?" Joe asked.

"Me?" Tiny shook his head again.

"Where would he go if he wanted to hide out? Who're his friends?"

"Me and Ron and Miles. That's all I know about."

"How about Steve Dolanetti?"

Tiny shook his head. No doubt there.

"He had to go someplace last night. Think, Tiny. Where would he go?" Joe crouched down and looked Tiny in the eye. "If George says let's go talk somewhere, where would they go?"

Tiny continued to shake his head, looking more and more confused and desperate; the kind of desperation that grew out of the soil of badgering. Joe took a deep breath, reminding himself that he was really talking to a small child hiding inside the huge body.

"You have lots of places where you can go to talk, to hang out, to be safe from people coming along and bothering you."

"Oh, yeah, Chief. You gotta—especially in this town. No offense, Chief."

"None taken."

"Mack here. He gets it. Don't you?"

Mack nodded, too enthralled to interrupt with so much as a grunt of assent.

"I know some of those spots," Joe said. "The beach walk here. This is a nice one."

Tiny smiled broadly. "Yeah. It's really nice in the summer."

"And the one near Black Beach. That clump of trees."

"Yeah, that's good in spring. The sun is good."

"And how about your camp site off Spring Street."

"Yeah. That's good too. Cold this time of year."

"So you guys wouldn't think of going there first."

"No, too cold." Tiny shook his head.

"So he might go up there," Joe said aloud to himself.

Tiny wrinkled his nose, a large fleshy thing, as though it itched and he didn't want to pull his hand out from beneath the blanket into the cold to scratch it.

"What is it, Tiny? He wouldn't go up there? Did you camp up there last night? Did you see something?"

"I didn't camp up there. No, no."

"Why not?"

"I couldn't. I mean, maybe I could."

"What happened, Tiny?"

"Nothing happened."

"Something must have happened. You went up there to camp out and changed your mind. Did you run into someone? Did you see something?"

"Yeah."

"Yeah? Which one? You saw something?"

"I saw a car—the back of a car—heading up the track."

"So that's why you didn't camp up there?"

"I figured I shouldn't go up there—someone was on the lookout for campers. I figured I'd let them think there weren't no one up there and leave it alone for a few days." Tiny tugged on the blanket, pulling his hands together. "They forget about you after a while." Tiny looked to Mack for confirmation.

Joe took a deep breath and stood up. Tiny had the instincts of an endangered animal. He could smell fear; sense danger even if it might not be coming straight at him. And he could get skittish and flee without thinking about what he was running away from or toward. Joe paused, reminding himself to be careful, very careful of Tiny. "Okay. Look, Tiny. I want you to do me a favor. I want you to come into town with me and stay at the police station."

"Huh? Me? I ain't done nothin'."

"I know. Tiny, take it easy. I just want you to help me out. Mack, you have any water?"

"I ain't done—"

"No, you haven't, Tiny. It's okay. You're not under arrest. You can stay right here if you want. There's nothing to worry about." Joe backed off as Tiny grew more agitated.

Tiny nodded vigorously, rocking his large body forward and back. Joe held out the water bottle, but Tiny ignored it.

"Tiny, I want you to promise me something. Are you listening to me, Tiny? Okay? Listen to me. I want you to stay away from" —from whom? Tiny stayed away from almost everyone anyway as it was— "stay away from anyone you don't know well. Stay with Mack."

"Mack, I want you to stay glued to Tiny until you hear from me. Got that? And I mean glued to him. Not nearby, or within shouting distance. I mean glued to him. Tie your shoelaces together if you have to."

Mack's mouth fell open and he bobbed his head up and down.

"Tiny, the two of you should just hang out together. Don't go off with anyone else for any reason. And tonight. Park your car in the town lot back of the station. It's okay, Tiny, you have my word. No one will bother you, but I want you where I can see you."

Mack turned to stare at his friend, a look of alarm stealing into his eyes.

Joe cruised down Trask Street, his mind on the expression in Tiny's eyes: a look of dismay and effort to understand that he, Tiny, could have made any kind of impression on anyone, let alone one that might lead to danger. But then Joe swung the wheel, straightened out, and was passing Gwen's place, and Tiny's pain was gone. It made sense then—everything he was doing, everything he had to face, it all made sense. Thinking about Gwen got him out of that small world of one person causing pain to another. He wasn't smiling as he came to the intersection for Spring Street, but what he was doing— what he knew he had to face—became easier, and when it was over he knew where he would go to talk it out and be free of the worst of it.

As he headed down Spring Street, the noise of traffic on Trask all but disappeared into the afternoon quiet of any neighborhood whose residents leave early for work and return late in the evening. Farther down, toward Pickering Street, he could hear a radio playing *NSYNC, punctuated by hammering—workmen on a roof somewhere, he guessed. He swung right onto Old Town Lane, the dust not rising more than a few inches off the ground—the damp air pressed down on the town like the bad mood of a dinner guest.

As the road ascended toward the woods, Joe turned left onto the dirt track and followed it into the trees. The clearing seemed unchanged from yesterday but Joe parked close along the edge, trying to pull up where he had parked the day before. He left his car and walked along the perimeter looking for signs that another car had used the clearing since yesterday. A set of tracks across the grass opposite his patrol car seemed new, but there was nothing more to indicate it was what Joe was looking for. He turned to the woods.

The woods surrounding Mellingham had once been clear fields and hills, and not very long ago, but unlike other parts of New England, the area had not been crisscrossed with stone walls. A few straggled on into the trees but farms had stayed on level ground in Mellingham. Old fire roads ran through some parts of the area but here there was nothing, just neglected woods not yet slated for development.

Along the perimeter of the clearing Joe noticed a number of broken branches on the wild mountain laurel bush, leaves disturbed, a small tree branch overturned, the rotting underside up. Joe moved carefully, parallel to the trail that revealed itself foot by foot. After half an hour, he found himself near a fragment of stone wall, its lichen-encrusted boulders and rocks scattered across an opening. One section only still stood defiant against the winter storms, summer rains, hurricanes, and time—the harshest enemy of all. He circled the pile of stones and tried to understand what he was seeing. Joe was not the typical New Englander, at least not the kind people in other parts of the country imagined when they thought about this region. He was not the New Englander who rushed off on weekends to go hiking or skiing or sailing. When he first encountered a cairn in the woods years ago, he thought it nothing more than a child's play at sculpture. The only paths he had ever followed were those made by the neighborhood dogs through parks and vacant lots and across fields, and he'd rather drive than walk any day. He liked the life of small cities, felt comfortable with the walls of buildings delimiting space and behavior.

Confronted with a hiking trail, Joe was more likely to go looking for a highway or a sidewalk.

The wall fragment curved inward, away from the coast. As Joe moved around it he could see signs of recent disturbance—leaves brushed into piles at one end, and spread smoothly, evenly, at the other; branches and twigs scattered about in a manner that didn't seem natural to Joe, and perhaps only appeared so because of his suspicions. But mostly, it was the boulder sitting on the ground just beneath a spot on the wall where stone was unweathered, and grubs were still looking for paths away from the light. He knew enough about the natural world to know that these changes had not occurred weeks ago. They were recent.

Joe pushed away the leaves and felt the loose earth—a dark, rich brown—moist, not yet dried out by sun and air. He brushed his hand across the soil. If no one knew what to expect, the shallow grave would be absorbed into the forest like anything else left there, and in a month the ground would lose any telltale signs of disturbance discernible by the unsuspecting visitor.

Joe rose and turned back to his patrol car.

Joe pulled into the dirt driveway of the Faroli house and parked behind Ken's patrol car. Joe had waited in the woods until the slim young body had been pulled from the shallow grave; the dirt dusted from his face; his skull with blood-caked soil wrapped in plastic.

"Do we know who this is?" the ME asked. Joe couldn't leave until the boy was safely wrapped and taken away, as though his caring could make any difference now. It would matter only to the boy's family.

Paula Faroli answered the door with a look of curiosity but not concern. There was an air of lethargy about her, as though she had been on a binge and just crashed. She had gathered all her energy and flung it into the sky, like a starburst. Now she had only what was left—ashes fallen to earth. She led him into the living room and motioned him toward a chair. She wasn't interested in his apologies for bothering her with more questions. She was long past that.

"I worry about George," she said. "He's trying to keep up the usual front, but he's falling apart inside. No, I don't know exactly why I think that. I just do. I told Ken all that."

"George told me he was able to forgive Miles for what happened," Joe said.

She fixed her gaze on him and draped one arm over the back of the sofa. "Yes, he talked to me about that. Forgiveness."

"Ann Rose told me you felt the same way," Joe said.

"Really?"

"Yes, really."

"Would you like something to drink? No? Would it be terrible if I had something? Of course not. The bereaved parent understandably indulges herself and everyone understands." She meandered to a built-in bar and poured a glass of wine. The first time Joe had been invited to the Farolis' house, he had been impressed with how well they lived. It didn't look like the home of a man who ran a small grocery store, but someone later pointed out to him that he ran the only grocery store in town, didn't have to buy it or set it up himself, and marketed to the high end of buyers.

Joe waved away her second offer of a drink. The living room was all in white with color coming from accent pieces—silk cushions, oriental rugs, a blue and orange wall hanging. The color scheme made the house feel more opulent than it really was.

Paula drank down half a glass of wine and topped up her

glass. "People are terribly understanding at a time like this. No one's going to say, Oh, my, look at Paula. She's really putting it away these days." She put the glass to her lips and again poured half into her mouth. "I like the taste, the way it fills my mouth, the bite. The buzz is good too but mostly I like the way it fills my mouth."

"Tell me how you felt about George's idea of forgiveness?"

"It's a good thing. Isn't that what all the churches preach?"

"He told you he was going to forgive Miles, is that right?"

"Forgiveness. As though it could cure something."

"So you disagreed?" Joe said, watching her. She had sat on the arm of a chair, with her wine glass resting against her cheek.

"No, I didn't," she said in a whisper. "I wanted more than anything else to be free of everything I was feeling. You can't imagine the nightmare. I couldn't stifle anything I was feeling—no matter how frightening or painful it was. Forgiveness. It sounded like a good idea. I heard the word and I felt like a drowning woman thrown a life preserver." She took a deep breath.

"But?" Joe said.

"But then when I thought about Miles, well, it didn't feel quite the same. Still . . ."

"So you took Miles something," Joe said, wondering if Paula was, in fact, sane.

"Yes." She looked at him then, as though he'd been speaking a foreign language and she wasn't sure she had caught it all. She moved to sit in the chair and said, "So what? It was a stupid, maudlin, Pollyanna thing to do, but I did it."

"You took a home-made box over to Miles's place?"

235

"Yeah, and then I came home and had a bottle of wine for lunch."

"Tell me about the box, Paula."

"You don't approve of drinking, do you?"

"Tell me about the box."

"Ron made it in high school. It was lovely, from a mother's point of view, that is. It was a box. Not perfect, just a box. But Ron was so proud of it. It's something he actually kept. And didn't sell. Can you imagine that? He didn't sell it, and he might have gotten a couple of dollars for it and who knows how many pills—"

"Paula, stop it." Joe thought she might break into tears but instead she raised her glass of wine.

"What else did you do?"

"Nothing."

"You just thought, I'll do what George suggests. I'll forgive Miles. I'll give him this box."

"The box was George's idea. I thought the whole thing was stupid. I told him, what am I supposed to do? Walk up to Miles on the street and say, 'Guess what? I forgive you for killing my son.' "

"What did George say?"

"He said I should take Miles a gift. He suggested the box. You don't want it, Paula, and I don't want it. So why don't we give it to Miles?"

"Did George do anything to the box? Did he fix it up at all?"

"No, he just cleaned it up and that was that." She sank deeper into her chair. "Forgiveness. I don't think I was ready, Joe. I just don't feel it, and I don't want to look at what I do feel."

"What about George? Do you think he feels it genuinely?"
She shook her head.
"Why?"

"Just little things, I guess. Like his phone calls."

He repeated the phrase. She offered him a half smile.

"What telephone calls?"

"You're very single-minded, aren't you?"

"Paula."

"George makes calls. They're harmless. He thinks I don't know but I do. Nine hundred numbers," she said. "You know what they are. Those 900 numbers? 'Course you do. It's his way of, I don't know, having a reckless life without leaving his wife, without actually being reckless. Just flirting with danger."

Paula stood up and returned to the bar. "It's terrible when a good friend has to see you at your worst. And you can't even sympathize, can you?"

"About George, Paula. You have to talk to me about George."

"George. Ah, yes. Back to the telephone calls. He's been doing this for years. It's harmless, like I said. Usually at eleven, eleven-thirty. When I'm supposed to be asleep in bed he gets on the phone and does his thing. Or, I guess, the woman on the other end does the thing, whatever it is. You know, it could be nothing more than erotic poetry. Men are funny that way. They think about sex all the time, talk about it all the time, but get them near a bed and all of a sudden that's not what they really want. They want the fringes of sex. And they can't admit it. They're ashamed of the strangest things. Are you like that, Joe?"

"Is that what your vacation was all about?"

"That's right," Paula said, giving him a quizzical look. "We had a great time. I should have known—" She began to work her mouth. "You know how whenever something incredibly wonderful happens, you have to pay for it later." She began to stretch her neck from side to side. "He said to me after Ron's death that he thought I was still the woman he married."

"That's very nice," Joe said.

"No, it's not. We were kids, Joe, just kids. We took that exotic tour because I wanted him to see me differently. It cost a fortune. Us! Going to the Seychelles, of all places. And nothing, absolutely nothing. It made no difference at all."

"You wanted to put an end to the telephone calls."

"Yes." She sighed. "It didn't work, I guess."

"What about the night of Ron's funeral?"

"I couldn't find him. I picked up the telephone to call my sister, and realized he'd probably be on the line, but he wasn't."

"Did you go looking for him?"

"No. We've been married a long time. You may not know how that is but after twenty years you don't feel you have to be in each other's pockets all the time. We don't spend all evening together."

"All right, go on."

Paula held her glass of wine up to the light, and apparently found the color or quantity satisfactory. "After I talked to my sister, I got worried and I did go looking for him."

"Where was he? Was he in the house?" Joe asked.

She shook her head. "He was out near the garage."

"What was he doing?"

"He was carrying some things in from the car, some of Ron's things we'd picked up from his place and left in the trunk. He's asked me to go for a walk earlier and I'd said no. I didn't realize how much he had wanted to go out. I said no, I just couldn't do it. I should have. I should have gone with him. He looked so tired."

"Did you talk to him when he came in?"

"No, no." She glanced at the chief and gave a rueful smile. "George is the strong, silent type. He doesn't have weaknesses. He's always trying to comfort me, but he never needs comforting himself. If he wants to talk, that's fine. If he wants me to talk, fine. But if I want him to talk, not fine. He doesn't talk." She put the wine glass down on the table, bumping the stem and foot against the edge.

"Tell me about the trip you took. How was it?"

"Pretty good," she said politely. "We met some nice people—it was a tour, you know." Paula began to list the countries she and George had visited.

"I suppose you have to get a lot of shots for that."

"Some."

"And take pills for water and what else?"

"Not any more. We got anti-malarial pills but we didn't take them."

"Why not?"

"I told someone I was getting things together for my trip and that I'd gotten these pills for malaria and she told me her daughter took them in the Peace Corps in Africa and had to be hospitalized for a month. So I looked them up on the Internet and found out that they had terrible side effects. I told George I wasn't taking them after that."

"Do you still have the prescription?"

"Sure, I guess so." Paula stared at him, her hands draped loosely over the chair arms. "Why, do you want them, Joe? Why do you want them?"

"Why don't you just get them for me, Paula?" He waited for her to stand up, and after she managed to get to her feet, he followed her from the room. She led him down a long hall to a bathroom with a storage closet. On the middle shelf, in the back, behind an array of shampoos and conditioners and shrink-wrapped containers of creams and conditioners, sat a box of miscellaneous bottles. She pulled out the box and rummaged through it.

"This is it," she said, handing him a small plastic bottle. Joe took it and read the label; he wrote out a receipt. He placed it in Paula's hand and it fluttered to the floor.

"Why didn't you throw them away?"

"They were expensive," she said, staring at the little bottle. He slipped the bottle into his shirt pocket and buttoned the flap. "You've been his good friend for years, Joe. What's going on? You're not making sense."

Joe closed his notebook and slipped it into his pocket. "We've played a lot of poker together, haven't we?"

"He loves that game. All his friends. Friendship means a lot to him, you know," she said. Her eyes were beginning to lose their focus. "He kept saying Ron needed better friends. If he just had better friends. He kept telling Ron that, too—you need better friends."

Joe led her back to the living room. He knew by the way she was walking and muttering that she would not remember everything later in the evening, and she wouldn't put two and two together until tomorrow unless someone told her how things added up. "Where is George now?"

"At work, I suppose." She shrugged. "George read somewhere that marriages often fall apart after an only child dies a violent death. He keeps telling me we have to be careful, watch out for fate, or something like that. Fate's going to do us in because our son died the way he did. Do you think that's true?"

"I don't know, Paula."

"Nothing has to be true. Just some things are, that's all." She reached out and grasped his hand. "I've been thinking about that a lot, wondering what's going to happen to me and George. If I just knew that, I think I could figure out how to live."

★ ★ ★ ★ ★

Whenever anyone asked Joe Silva about the advantages of living and working in Mellingham, he said simply, 'It's a small town.' And whenever anyone asked him about the disadvantages, he said, just as simply, 'It's a small town.' Never was that truer than now, as Joe let the cruiser drift toward Main Street; listening as Ken Dupoulis reported a sighting of George Faroli driving down Trask.

"He's in no hurry, Joe," Ken said, before turning onto a side street. Maxwell sighted George seconds later turning into the store parking lot.

"Looks like business as usual," Maxwell said.

It was getting on toward six o'clock. The store would be closing up; downtown Mellingham disappearing behind an eerie façade of nicely kept shops along the clean streets of a wealthy small town. It happened quickly, as though someone pulled out an eraser and cleaned off a backdrop sketch. Joe pulled into the parking lot just as a small red Saab lurched onto Trask Street, swinging wide and swerving into the opposite lane. Joe passed on its description to Ken and drew into a space at the back of the lot, near George Faroli's car.

In a few minutes Marley would appear, locking up the front door on his way out; leaving George to pull the shades and turn out the lights after preparing a night deposit. George never liked handing over the final duties to anyone else, not even Marley, and had often grumbled about how hard it was to take a vacation because of this. Most of his fellow poker players offered him no sympathy; they had grown up with Marley too, and knew it was all just George being George.

Just George being George.

Joe had no illusions about any of the people he knew—he never took their failings personally, as a betrayal, the petty needs that sometimes come over someone: the request to fix a ticket, to look the other way when a relative got into trouble. After all, Joe hadn't been perfect either. But over the last few hours, Joe had struggled mightily with keeping a fair distance from his feelings about the man he believed had murdered two young men. And that was the problem—he couldn't see George as a suspect, only as the one-time guilty party, the perp, no reservations whatsoever. Joe knew he had to get a grip on himself or he wouldn't get through the next few hours.

The sound of his own car door slamming behind him startled him back into the present. The evening mist was soaking up the yellow light from the front windows. Joe knocked on the glass door. George emerged from the back office, ready to wave off the would-be customer, but lowered his arm when he saw who it was.

Later Joe would wonder if George made a decision at that moment; if the blue uniform and silver badge merged into an image of Ron in his casket, in his blue suit and blue and silver tie. A shiver went through Joe when George faced him, the glass door propped open with his right hand.

George Faroli led the way to the back office with the usual patter about it being Friday evening, hard to close on time, but his voice was curiously flat and the words without feeling.

"I almost didn't let you in," George said. He leaned against a desk with his hand resting on a shelf covered in papers, an old pencil box perched among the piles.

"You sound kind of angry, George." Joe heard the words but couldn't figure out why he'd said them.

"It's hard going on like nothing's changed, like life is not so different from what it was two weeks ago. 'Course I'm angry. You would be too if—" He stopped and reached out to slap a sheaf of papers beginning to slide off the desk. He didn't have to finish his sentence. Joe knew what he was going to say: *"If you had a son."*

The sheaf of papers began to slide again and George gathered it up and looked around the room for a place to lodge it safely. The room seemed to be made of papers all propped precariously on other papers; none of it important, it seemed, just old and curling and yellowing. George's words reverberated though he treated them as nothing more meaningful than a comment on the weather.

The words rattled through Joe's brain. The distance between Joe and his feelings began to close. "We found a body up in the woods this afternoon. Bernard Whitson." In another few years, it could have been Philip, Joe heard himself thinking. That was what was driving him—it could have been Philip, and that meant Gwen could have been hurt beyond Joe's reach.

George grunted. He was staring past Joe, his eyes on a memory.

"I'm going to caution you, George."

The other man shook his head slowly, from side to side to side, as though he could wipe away the words; turn them into mist and blow them away. He kept his eyes from Joe while he recited the warning.

"I didn't think you'd get to me so fast," George said.

"Let's go." Joe was beginning to feel sick. He had no stomach right now for explanations, excuses, pleas for sympathy. He hated the sort that blew off responsibilities and then wailed excuses, when confronted. He was pleading silently that George wasn't that sort; that he wouldn't abase himself with pleas for understanding; that he wouldn't soil their friendship, or what was left of it.

"I thought I'd have time to clean up, get it all sorted out."

"We have it all sorted out. You were seen picking up Bernard and driving here. We'll find—"

"You shouldn't have told him to leave, Joe. It really pissed him off," George said. Joe's fingers clenched around George's arm, squeezed.

"Let's go."

"He only wanted to hang out. You could see it in his eyes. He was a kid who wanted someone to notice him. Well, I noticed him. I thanked him for coming to Ron's funeral and he was so grateful, pathetically grateful that I noticed him. It was an invitation, Joe." He looked pleased with himself, pleased with his insight into another human being.

"Careful what you say, George. You've been cautioned."

"He was gonna skip the train and find Tiny and camp out with him." George shook his head. "An open invitation. So I offered to get him some provisions, for him and Tiny, seeing as how they'd been—my son's friends—they came to the funeral and all." He didn't seem to notice Joe's hand on his arm. "It was so easy. I told him to stay low in the car—in case the police saw him—I wasn't thinking of you; he just said the police told him to get on the train."

"He was going down to stay with his family" —words he wished he hadn't said then or now.

"Who was gonna care?" George said.

"Let's go."

"Just one second. I need to finish something up for Paula."

Joe's grip tightened. George looked down at the hand shackling him.

"Have a heart, Joe. There's no reason Paula should pay for this. At least it'd give me a chance to do something right in the end."

"You should have thought of that when you got her involved with Miles's death," Joe said. "All that talk about for-giveness."

"She didn't know what I was doing, Joe," George said, starting to breathe in quick, short gasps.

"What exactly were you doing, George?"

"I thought you had it all figured out," George said.

"I want to hear you tell it."

"You cautioned me, Joe. Did you forget that?"

"I have all the pieces, George. It doesn't matter what you tell me."

"The mefloquine was a stroke of luck," George said.

"Did you buy the salvia over the Internet or use Ron's supply?"

"It was in that box," George said. "That's probably where he kept his stuff anyway. I'm telling him not to crash at home while we're away and he's storing his drugs there. Jeez."

"So you just added the mefloquine and waited for Miles to destroy himself."

"I put a few of the pills in and mixed it in with the stuff Ron was smoking. I knew Miles would try whatever he found there. He was a junkie."

"You didn't think about what might happen if someone else came across the bag?"

"I thought he'd smoke it and get himself killed in a car ac-cident or get into a big fight and get beat up or get arrested," George said with a half smile. "I didn't think he'd just fall out a window and kill himself. It was so easy—" He glanced at Joe and grew anxious. "Paula had no idea what I was doing. It was all my idea."

"You sold her on the idea of forgiveness," Joe said. "It might have been a good thing if you'd been sincere."

"I got her to go over there with the box because she's so concerned with doing the right thing. It took some doing to talk her into it, but in the end she went." George looked down at Joe's hand. "I'm not going anywhere. Give me a break for a minute."

Joe shrugged and relaxed his grip; George reached for a tattered wooden pencil box, a beige oval label advertising Royal Pencils with Fine Erasers from South America. "She's a saint, she really is." All the air seemed to turn to lead. "She deserved someone better than me. She never complained but I look back and I guess I know I'm not much. She never said one word, but I could always feel I wasn't quite good enough."

"Let's go, George."

"Okay. You know, that's the one thing you can't get past. No matter what, you can't really have a marriage if somewhere inside your wife thinks she's better than you. And she is. She's better than me. I never really belonged to her."

"George." Joe began to move him toward the door. George held the pencil box in front of him. "Funny, I thought it'd be Miles that tripped me up, not Bernard."

"You're talking too much, George." Joe clenched his teeth; he would do this right. No one would accuse him of taking advantage of a friend. "Be careful of what you say. I've warned you twice now."

"Me? You're telling me to be careful? Do you know how much I kept to myself? How much I had to swallow? Do you?"

"I've warned you, George."

"They turned my son into a junkie—Miles and his friends. It was safe in this town. I grew up here. It was a decent place. You could have your life without someone screwing you." His voice caught in his throat.

Joe reached for his arm.

"I thought if Ron could just get away from those others—" He held the box against his chest.

"Let's go, George. Marley can do whatever needs to be done. I'll give him a call."

"He can't do this." Tenderly, George lifted the thin cardboard top while Joe kept his eyes on George's face. It was a second or two before he realized what George had in his hands. The long thin blade flashed as the box of cutting implements fell to the floor, just before George turned the stiletto toward his own chest.

Chapter 10

Friday Evening

The second Joe saw the stiletto in George Faroli's hand, two thoughts flashed into his mind, coming to him instantly, and yet it seemed as though they rose from the twilight like a banner streaming behind a plane. He saw the words waving in the breeze of a shudder: you wouldn't be in this situation if you had treated this crime, Miles Stine's death, like any other and called for backup, and stayed in touch with your men. But you didn't, Joe, a voice said to him. You let it get personal. Now you're in trouble and you didn't even see it coming.

At once, he felt the instinct that drove him as a policeman: the need to keep another from making a stupid mistake, no matter how determined that person might be. Joe saw that blade and George turning it inward, toward his own chest, and thought, *George Faroli, you are not getting away with that. You are not cheating me, the state, and Bernard's family, Chandra. You are not getting away with it.* He might even have said it aloud, so close were his thoughts and actions.

Joe raised his right hand and grabbed George's wrist, his long strong fingers tightening like iron coils. His touch seemed to alarm George, awaken and frighten him at the same time.

"Let go, Joe. It's only a matter of time." His teeth were clenched and he hissed. George pulled back, throwing Joe off balance, and fell onto the desk. Joe grabbed George's forearm with his left hand and pulled it to the side. George's arm went limp but Joe held tight.

"You don't get it, Joe."

"I can't let you, George. I can't."

George nodded, his arm swinging out. Joe released his grip on the man's forearm and began to pull George's arm away. George snapped his wrist forward; Joe's grip slipped and George turned the blade toward his own neck. Joe kicked his foot behind George's knees and the other man collapsed, his hand swinging wildly as he stabbed once in the air, then buried the knife between them. Both men fell to the ground, Joe crushing George beneath him. Joe pulled away and jumped up; standing astride his old friend, Joe brought his foot down on George's hand. Bones and cartilage crunched under Joe's right foot and the blade rolled away from George's open hand. With his left hand, Joe pulled out his handkerchief and wrapped it around the end of the blade, lifting it onto the desk.

"Joe." George stared up at him, breathing heavily, his mouth open and his face mottled red and white. "Joe."

Joe kept his eyes on George's hands as he called for backup.

"It's over, George. That's what you want, really."

"I was only going after Miles," George said. "That's all I wanted. I had to."

"But you didn't stop there, did you?" Joe said.

"I was a coward, you know. I did it sneaky like. Putting temptation in his path, and knowing what would happen."

"And what about Bernard?"

"It's easier the second time. You think about it differently. I knew what I was doing was right then. I knew it. You would have done the same. I know you would have. You know what family means, you know what it's like. You'd do anything to protect Philip—I've seen you with him. He's a good kid. He's Gwen's boy. You know how I feel. They were getting to him, Joe. He was going down the wrong road. You might have done it yourself—"

"Don't waste your breath, George."

"You know what I'm talking about. Bernard—I'm sorry about him. But he was just standing there, like he was waiting for me. A gift. I had to. I owed Ron that, owed it to him. I'm his father. A father has a debt to his son. I did Gwen a favor, and Philip too." Outside an icy wind was moving in, bringing the change in the air that said fall was gone, winter was here. A window sash rattled.

Joe listened to the radio, answered, and waited.

"I'm just an ordinary man, Joe. You know what that means. You can't stand by, you can't ask me to just live with what he did to my son. He's my boy. I owed him. What was I supposed to do?"

"You were supposed to let me handle it, George." Joe looked down at him, flat on the ground, chest pushing up from the hard wood floor littered with papers and boxes. He hated to see a man looking so weak, so beaten, so he moved his eyes to George's hands, the plaid flannel shirt that was frayed at the neck, was missing a button, and had a slight tear in the pocket.

George went on whispering the same thing over and over. He lay beneath Joe's foot, not struggling to be free, but to be known, understood. And Joe couldn't tell him—didn't dare admit—how well he understood every word, every distorted, hateful word.

The suitcase was barely half full. Edna Stine poked the top navy blue sweater, patting it down, and wondered if she should put in a raincoat. She had a pair of boots ready to go in and, of course, her makeup case. Even then, there would still be room. And time. She had plenty of time—an hour before the airport limo came to pick her up.

Her sister in Ohio had not been pleased to hear from her, but Edna had glossed over that and managed to invite herself for the weekend. She had mumbled some reason for her abrupt call, but she had wangled an invitation, that was the main thing. She wasn't going to have to stay in Mellingham right now. She needed a break, and her sister's was the best place for it; just for a while until she figured out what she wanted to do and how she was going to handle matters. She'd come back, of course, after she'd had a rest, a real one. She was emotionally exhausted after the last few days, and who could deny she was justified in feeling wrung out? Her son had just died and the police were investigating. No mother should have to go through that.

She felt a surge of anger rush through her. She hated this little town, with its too-perfect sidewalks and little shops, and its just so sweet town fairs and its just wonderful scenery. She hated it, hated it for what it concealed and revealed, for what it offered with one hand only to take away with the next. She was going to live the rest of her life here, and now this. This hypocrisy and meanness and self-righteousness, and just when she really needed a friend and some support.

It amazed her how little her loyalty counted for. She had worked at the small clinic on Main Street in Mellingham for years—years, she couldn't remember how long. And when she had gone in this afternoon to talk about suspicions about the pain medication, the lead doctor—Dr. Baldwin—had listened without so much as a murmur of sympathy, a note of gratitude for her loyalty and concern. Not so much as a smile of friendship for the years of working shoulder to shoulder with him and all the rest of them.

"We're inventorying right now, Edna," he said leaning forward, his hands clasped in front of him on his desk. He paused, then leaned back and drew open a lower drawer and pulled out a manila folder. He put the folder on his desk and opened it, as though he had all the time in the world. "You've been a pretty steady employee, Edna. You worked out your problems with the other staff members, and you're prompt." He began to leaf through the papers in the file folder.

The man was a tight little bastard, she thought. Always had been. Hadn't even wanted to give her a vacation the first five months she was there, even though it was July and hot, and everyone, but everyone, in the office was talking about where they were going and what they were going to do. Edna was the only one not going somewhere and all she wanted was a few days off to stay home and get caught up on her sleep. But no chance of that. Not with Mister Doctor Everett Baldwin. No sirree.

"We know how many are missing," he said. "Eleven."

She opened her mouth to speak, like a puppet whose jaw falls open, but no voice came forth. Eleven? Surely not. Miles couldn't have; he wouldn't have. She cast around in her memory for some recollection of what she had actually said to him about the clinic pharmacy. To Dr. Baldwin, she babbled on about her loyalty and integrity in coming in to him today, but he just kept looking at her, never blinking, just looking. It meant there was something wrong with him—she was sure of that; people were supposed to blink. But he didn't blink; he just stared at her. Then he started asking her about the day Miles came in for a flu shot, but she was working that day. How could she remember what he did? She didn't give flu shots. Why wasn't he asking the nurse? He was looking at her as though she had taken them. And there wasn't even proof that Miles had taken them. He just wanted a flu shot. He wouldn't listen to her either, so she had to sit there with her legs crossed around each other so tightly she was afraid she'd never get them apart when she had to stand up to leave.

There wasn't much in the refrigerator but she had stopped for groceries on the way home—cans of tuna, Stouffers and Lean Cuisine dinners, a jar of peanut butter, chips and salsa. Chandra didn't care much about food but she'd need something in the house to eat. She could always hang out with her friends or eat downtown. Chandra was old enough to take care of herself—and sensible. Wasn't she always asking about more freedom, more responsibility? She was definitely at that age when she didn't want a mother hovering around her. When she looked back on the past few months, Edna realized that she sometimes went for days without seeing Chandra. That girl was busy—she was either studying or in school or doing some extracurricular thing. She was so incredibly responsible. Edna didn't need to worry about her at all—just let her go and do what she did. She was so good at taking care of herself—she was a model teenager, absolutely a model teenager.

Edna pulled a cookie box out of the cupboard and opened it to an assortment of bills—one hundred dollars give or take a few ones—the household money. Edna hadn't put much into it over the last few weeks—too busy with worrying about Miles, and now with the funeral delayed and Joe Silva coming over all self-righteous, there wasn't much reason to keep building up this little nest egg. Edna counted out all but twenty-five dollars and pushed the box back into the cupboard. She had maxed out her credit cards with that last purchase of a plane ticket, but she remembered another offer coming in the mail. She stuffed the money into her purse and went in search of the wastebasket.

It occurred to Edna that she had no idea where Chandra was, but she was a big girl; practically on her own this whole last year. The girl had been demanding more and more freedom—to show how reliable she was—and this would be a good test. And why not? Chandra was sixteen and old enough to be on her own. Hell, Edna had been working full time and living in that terrible trailer with whatsisname when she was Chandra's age. This would be a good time for Chandra to learn more about freedom and responsibility, and it wasn't like it was forever. This was just a transitional period until Edna got herself set up somewhere else and then Chandra would have a nice place to move to. The future began to take shape in Edna's imagination.

She found a pad of paper and a pen and composed a note to her daughter, giving her sister's name and address in Akron, and promising to call over the weekend. She anchored the note to the kitchen table with a jar of strawberry jam— Chandra's favorite, Edna thought, pleased with the satisfying feeling that she'd thought of just about everything.

A car horn sounded, and she hurried to the window. She waved to the driver and he came up the porch steps to claim her suitcase sitting just inside the front door. She locked the front door and followed him down the steps. All the way into Logan Airport she went over what she'd say to her sister and what she wouldn't say; she refused to think about Joe Silva and she could barely keep herself from spitting when she thought of Everett Mr. Big Man Baldwin.

"So that just leaves sending someone out to tell Mrs. Faroli. Everything else's covered." Ken Dupoulis checked off a number of items in his notebook. "And Monday morning, maybe, for the arraignment." He looked up at Joe Silva, arms akimbo, nodding and looking at the floor.

"I'd better get over there, before someone calls her," Joe said. He was hot and tired—it was nearing eight o'clock—but he couldn't let himself think about that. George Faroli had been carried off—his last words echoing in everyone's ears. "You would have done the same, Joe. A son wiped out? You would have done the same. I know you would have. You're a good man. You understand family."

"If there's nothing else . . ." Ken began.

Joe shook his head. The lapels of his jacket hung open, unzipped, the cuffs loose around his wrists. He was keyed up still, still running on adrenaline.

"What's that?" Ken pointed to Joe's shirt. Joe pulled away the lapel and tried to get a look at his shirt. It was torn and stained. "Is that what it looks like?"

"I dunno." Joe pulled off his jacket and dropped it on the chair, then pulled his shirttails out and unbuttoned his shirt, pulling it off and dropping it over his jacket. His T-shirt was stained red—just a tiny patch. He pulled the T-shirt over his head and balled it up in his hands. Both men stared at the tiny patch of blood between his shoulder and collarbone.

"Jesus, Joe," Ken whispered. "It looks small, but that could be deep."

"I didn't even feel it," was all Joe could say.

"Doesn't matter. It could still be deep. What was it?"

"He has a pencil box for all his little box cutters—every kind imaginable. It was one of those—sort of like a stiletto." It was a tiny spot, not even the size of a dime, but the tear in the fabric of his shirt and T-shirt spoke of the violence with which George Faroli had met Joe's challenge. "I guess I'd better do something," Joe said.

Ken left Joe to finish dressing.

Joe's fingers fumbled over the buttons and he stopped once or twice to warm his hands, flex his fingers, trying to get himself back on track. He had planned to go over to Gwen's as soon as he'd spoken with Paula Faroli and made sure she was all right. He wanted to spend some time with Gwen before Philip tried what Joe suspected would be a number of forays into breaking the news to her that he was gay. He looked down at his chest and knew Ken was right. He'd better let Ken make the visit to Paula while he went on to the hospital.

"Hey, it's me." Joe cradled the phone on his shoulder while he buttoned his shirt.

"Something happened," Gwen said matter-of-factly.

"You hear the sirens?"

"Uhhuh." She paused. "I don't really want to know because I know it's going to hurt. Tell me."

"We arrested George Faroli tonight for the murder of Bernard Whitson."

"Oh. I thought it would have been for Miles Stine."

"It would have except we have better evidence for Bernard's death. We may go for both if we can pull it all together."

"That doesn't sound like you," she said.

"I guess I'm a little tired. How about you?"

"Confused on this end."

"Why?"

"Philip and I had a talk this evening. He wants to be in the Christmas play—as a technician," she said. "I never knew he was interested in the theater. Joe, I'm worried. Last week it was—what's that stuff? Rap? And those cat stories?—and this week it's Dickens. What's happening to him?"

"He's just growing up. A technician, huh?"

"He said Chandra talked him into it. Do you know what he told me?"

"What?"

"That she's his best friend. Joe, she's three years older than he is, and in high school that's a big deal. Three years is a huge difference. I don't want him dating girls that old—it's a terrible idea. I'm very concerned. Joe, why're you laughing? It's not funny."

"It will be when you hear the rest of it."

"What do you know that I don't know?"

"Not much. But I need a ride over to the hospital. Wanna drive me?"

"Oh, Joe, what happened?"

"Not much, but I have to get it checked out."

"What checked out?"

"A little stick." He heard her gasp, then nothing. In the silence he felt himself falling, falling, falling into a darkness no light could penetrate.

"Oh, Joe, if anything happens to you—" He heard a ragged breath. "You won't keep anything from me. Promise me. I'll be right there." She hung up the telephone without waiting for him to answer. He let the receiver slide down his shoulder into his hand, caught it, and slipped it onto the cradle.

Ann Rose shivered as her gaze passed over the bottle of milk, package of hot dogs, and containers of yogurt staring back at her from the wide-open refrigerator. She settled on a plastic container of left-over chicken curry, and rice. But just as she reached for it, she paused, thinking, Can you serve a guest leftovers? Well, maybe she's not really a guest, not the usual kind, any way.

"What's that one?" Chandra's voice broke into her thoughts.

"Chicken curry and rice."

"Ooh. I love curry."

That settled that. Ann pulled out the container and slammed the refrigerator door shut. "Why don't you just sit there and keep me company while I assemble your dinner." Ann began to reach for plates and cutlery on her way to the microwave. "Do you want me to put that away?" She nodded to the plastic sandwich bag in Chandra's hand and then wished she hadn't. Chandra's fingers closed around the bag and she drew it closer to her; peanut butter and jelly oozed out and smeared the inside of the bag.

"Yeah, take it." All of a sudden Chandra shoved the bag toward Ann and looked away from it. The decision was made. The icon of comfort was banished.

"Okay." Ann gingerly lifted it and carried it to the refrigerator, placing it on a shelf as though it were a live creature. "It's right there if you want it." She gave it a gentle pat before closing the door again. "Now. Dinner."

Ann could turn opening a can of soup into an event, and tonight she felt the need to draw on all her resources just to get through the pick-up meal. Chandra was settled on a stool watching every move, her eyes apparently unable to disengage from the meal being heated up. Since she had rapped on Ann's front door an hour ago, with an incomprehensible tale about her mother and the airport—much of it mumbled in asides that only Chandra understood—Ann had been alternately stunned and confused. She'd done her best to get Chandra to relax, speak calmly, but even when the girl had managed to do so, the story remained bizarre.

Edna Stine had flown the coop—headed to Logan Airport and taken off for well-known parts—her sister's home.

"We've done that before," Chandra explained. "But I'm pretty much an adult so I'm staying here."

Ann had a lot of trouble grasping this and gently probed for a deeper meaning but Chandra stuck to her story until she blurted out the totally unexpected and truly bizarre.

"You could adopt me."

This was when the refrigerator became surprisingly attractive.

Chandra's vacant look vanished as she watched Ann's preparations, and the meal took all her attention for a good hour—the cooking, the eating, the cleaning up. It gave Ann time to think—particularly the eating part, when Chandra hunched over her plate nibbling food from her fork—but as much as she tried, Ann couldn't get past the sheer bizarreness of the situation. Edna Stine had run off and left her daughter behind. Simply left her. Left her in the house with peanut butter and jelly for sandwiches and a few dollars for groceries and a promise to return soon. Soon. What did that mean? How in hell did a mother go off and leave her daughter? What had gotten into the woman?

Ann had heard of such things—a friend of a friend of a friend had blah, blah, blah—but to be presented with the reality in her own kitchen was too unbelievable for words. She could pass the gossip off as exaggeration, but when it showed up in her own home, well, that was a different story. These things were stories, outrageous tales passed around at the grocery store or over lunch to make the women feel they were good mothers—we would never do that, we would never run off and leave the kids. But hell's bells, Edna did. And here was the proof, sitting right here at Ann's kitchen counter, eating Ann's leftovers.

"Do you have any—other—kids?" Chandra asked.

Startled, Ann turned from putting the dishes into the dishwasher and tried to catch onto where the conversation had gone. Other kids? Did she have other kids? She didn't have any. The entire world of childrearing had eluded her and her husband—except, of course, for the usual passel of nephews and nieces.

"Ah, no," Ann said, trying to figure out why that didn't seem like quite the right answer. The interchange trickled uneasily down into her consciousness. She began to feel the need for a distraction while she got a grip on the situation, if anyone could get a grip on the insane, the irrational, the bizarre. "Would you like some ice cream?"

Philip leaned forward in his chair, wringing his hands and glancing at Joe every now and then. Joe leaned back, flexing his right hand so it didn't get stiff, and watching Gwen with an amused expression.

"She's crying, Tio," Philip said.

"I know, but she's not crying out of misery."

"But—" Philip was plainly confused.

"It's all right, Philip. Some day maybe she'll explain it all."

Gwen threw herself back against the sofa and rubbed her hands over her face. Her eyes were red and her cheeks blotchy and her hair flattened where she had brushed it against her head. "I don't know how I'm supposed to feel. But I'm so relieved partly and partly I'm just scared and partly I'm so totally confused." Philip turned to Joe for guidance.

"She's fine," Joe said. Gwen rose and crossed the room to where Philip was sitting.

"When you were little, maybe five or six, I bought a book at a yard sale with all these photographs of costumes from the nineteenth century. You wanted to look at it and I used to let you have it for an afternoon sometimes. One day I came home and you had cut out all the soldiers and torn up all the pictures of women. I thought it meant you wanted to be a soldier when you grew up."

"Mom, you're weird."

"Mothers are, honey. It's part of the job description."

"But what about what I said? Do you understand?"

"Yes, I understand. I do. And I want you to understand, honey, that I love you no matter what. I just want you to be happy."

Philip stared at her as though he wasn't sure she was speaking English. After a moment, he said, "So are we going to be in the Christmas play?"

"Well, I guess so if you want."

"Thanks, Mom." He kissed her on the cheek and hurried off to his room; a moment later Gwen could hear him speaking softly on the telephone.

Gwen turned to Joe with a blank look on her face. "Did I do all right?"

"You were great, Gwen, just great." He leaned over and kissed her gently on the lips.

Gwen took a deep breath and settled again beside Joe on the sofa. "Every day I wake up frightened about what could happen to him and Jennie. The thought of drugs—it's a never ending nightmare."

"I don't think you'll have to worry about Philip and drugs anymore. I don't think he's much of a candidate for that world."

"God, I hope you're right. I sure hope he grows up fast. I have no idea what I'm doing." She sank back against his arm, then turned to him. "What am I going to do?"

"Well, first of all, you're going to join PFLAG," Joe said. "We all are."

"And second?"

About the Author

Susan Oleksiw is the author of the Mellingham series featuring Chief of Police Joe Silva, who was introduced in *Murder in Mellingham* (1993). *A Murderous Innocence* is the fifth title in the series and continues the story of Joe Silva and the people of Mellingham.

Oleksiw introduced a second series featuring, as an amateur sleuth, photographer and Hindu-American Anita Ray, in a series of short stories set in India, including "A Murder Made in India" (*Alfred Hitchcock Mystery Magazine*, 2003).

Also known for her nonfiction work, Oleksiw compiled *A Reader's Guide to the Classic British Mystery* (1988), and edited five more volumes in the Readers' Guide series. As consulting editor for *The Oxford Companion to Crime and Mystery Writing* (1999), she contributed several articles on crime fiction. She has written extensively on this genre and other topics, and is well known as a reviewer of crime fiction for *The Drood Review of Mystery*.

Trained as a Sanskritist at the University of Pennsylvania, where she received a PhD. in Asian studies, Oleksiw has lived and traveled extensively in India. Her academic articles, on law and literature, were widely published.

Oleksiw is a co-founder of Level Best Books, a cooperative venture that publishes anthologies of crime fiction by New

England writers, and publishes the winner of the Al Blanchard Crime Fiction Award in its annual anthology. She lives in Beverly, with her husband and their two cats and dog.